Bazoomerangs

Bazoomerangs

by
Ann Crawford

Stephanie Castle Publications

an imprint of
Perceptions Press
Victoria, BC
Canada

2024

Bazoomerangs

Copyright © Ann Crawford 2024

Published in paperback in 2024 by Stephanie Castle Publications

Cover Design: Margot Wilson (Midjourney)

ISBN: 978-1-998924-85-1 (paperback)
ISBN: 978-1-998924-86-8 (Kindle e-book)
ISBN: 978-1-998924-87-5 (Smashwords/Draft2Digital e-book)

Published in Canada by
Stephanie Castle Publications
www.stephaniecastle.ca

an imprint of
Perceptions Press
www.perceptionspress.ca
Victoria BC
Canada

Perceptions
Press

Contents

Dedication

To all the folks in my life
who inspired me to give life
to the characters of
Jaye, Alice, and Starr

Trigger Warnings

This book includes scenes dealing with:

Abortion
Physical Assault
Rape
Suicide / Death
Transphobia

Petaluma, California
2019

Prologue

No, no, no. Please, dear God, no. This can't be happening. This can't be real. But it is, because the smell of blood is about as real as it gets.

Chapter 1

Jaye—age 20

Life, yo, why'd you have to wait this long to be this good? Okay, yeah, it's not like I'm thirty or something, but still. Man, oh man. Wait—cancel that. Woman, as in WOAHman, oh woman.

But here it finally is. This life, this good, right here, right now.

And that includes shopping.

"Ooooooooooooooooh!" my two besties sing out as I spin this way and that in my beyond-fab frock in front of the department store's three-way mirror. And who else should appear in that mirror, coming out of a dressing room?

"Mom! What are you doing here?"

Not only is she photobombing my life, she's in the same dress! I wear it much better, though. On me, it gracefully cascades to my knees. On her, it lurches to the floor after bulging out in all the wrong places. My golden tresses drape over its loveliness while her matronly hair-do-not does not do anything for it. How can one dress look so different on two different people?

Her one word comes out in a gulp. "James."

"It's Jaye," I say to her for the millionth time. Maybe two millionth.

She scurries back into her dressing room. Still by the mirror, I turn some more—although now, it's that way and this—admiring my resplendent (if I say so myself) reflection. Mom, still pulling on her ever-present gray sweats, bolts out of the fitting-room door into the great beyond. Which to her, I think, must mean anywhere beyond where I am.

Oooouuuch!

Wait, no, cancel that ouch and the heart pang accompanying it. I'm so beyond ouches and aches from her.

WTF, anyway? She never goes shopping!

As my friends and I grab some grub, I attempt to explain the woman they just saw, since I usually try to keep her hidden away.

"Your mom drives a Buick?"

I put my hands over my eyes as if to erase the image. "And it has a Trump sticker on it—from 2016, mind you, not even for next year."

"Ewwwww!" my girls sing in unison.

"I can't believe she voted for that orange-
  whack job. How am I related to that person?

She's just a bit of a strange brew. And yet, somehow, *I'm* the insane one."

We giggle, but then I do that thing I do: snort. No matter how hard I try to be super femme, I still snort. Thanks, Dad—I get it from him. That and his height and his huge Adam's apple. My snorts combined with my food give me the hiccups, which makes us giggle all the more, which makes the snorts, well, even snortier.

Whhhhssssssss. That could be the air escaping from one of the tires but, no, it's the air escaping from me, decompressing as I climb into my car and shut the world out.

Mmmmm. It's quiet in the car if not in my head. Oh, that woman!

Well, it takes a lot of grit to be a woman. And I know because I am one. It's a lot easier to be a guy. And I know because I was one.

Maybe I'm pushing too hard in this being-a-woman thing, being way too out there now after being way too in there for way too long. Over the top after being under the bottom, hiding in the shadows. It's not like I'm trying to fake it around my peeps or anything. It's more like I've been finally let out of jail, and I'm so in the mood to let loose.

But Mom. Still. Hasn't. Gotten. It.

That fact hit me with the grace of a boulder. I came out to her two years ago yet she's still choosing to be clueless. Did she think it was some passing phase?

Well…Get. It. She. Will. If I have to hit her over the head. If it's the last thing I do.

I shudder, then shake like I'm ridding myself of a demon, and finally start driving home.

Yo, it's not like this trans thing came once upon a random Wednesday afternoon or something. "Hey—I know, I'll become a female! What a fine idea!"

No, not so much. The thought had always been bubbling away inside, as far back as I can remember.

I've always known I was different. I guess maybe we're all different. Of course, we have to be. There's no point in Life duplicating any of us. From an early age, though, I knew I was *really* different.

But Moms never understood me. Nada. Zip. Zilcherooni. I'm so way beyond dumbfounded that she never, ever figured out that I never, ever wanted to be a *son*.

I did try.

"Mommy, let's have a tea party," I'd say. Or, a few years later, "Mom, let's go see *The Nutcracker*." And then, there was, "Mom, let's watch *Princess Diaries*."

To each, along with a quadrillion others, came, "James! That's not what little boys do."

Oh, did I ever get worn out from being "corrected" every day. Somewhere along the line I must've figured I'd wait her out. But it's not like any of this was crystal clear all along to a kid who wanted to buck the status quo yet had no support in that whatsoever—either from Mom or Catholic school.

Back to the present imperfect, and I don't mean that in the grammatical sense. Nowadays, I have a lot of doubts and questions about a lot of things. About being a woman? That's not one of them.

Unfortunately, I wasn't lucky enough to be born in a woman's body. (Insert that oh-so-adorable wailing emoji here.) But at least I'm lucky enough to be born in a time where trans is a thing and becoming more and more of an acceptable thing at that…somewhat acceptable, anyway. At least in some places.

Not in this place, though. I pull into the circular drive and park behind the Buick. My grandmother's mini-RV sits by the garage, still gathering dust since her stroke a couple months back.

Mom does have such a pretty piece of real estate, I'll give her that: a Victorian, complete with a turret, where younger me would often pretend to be Rapunzel.

She sure loves her yellow, though. Looks like someone sandblasted the place with a pineapple-orange-juice cocktail. Inside, too. Even the massive garden is all dotted with yellow. Gag me. Paint it black, I say.

No sooner do I walk in the back door than Mom vamooses from the way-too-cheery kitchen, where the pineapple-orange-juice theme continues, without so much as a backward glance at my shopping bag and me. The slam of her bedroom door echoes through the house.

Ouch. Wait—maybe that was just half an ouch. Hey, progress.

Gram, nestled into her usual spot at the kitchen table, snickers and says, "Oh, not to worry. Your mom will come along for the ride. Eventually."

She's so cool. I mean really cool—like the coolest grandmother ever in the history of grandmothers. Gram *gets* things.

Supreme hipness obviously skips a generation, though. Speaking of Mom, she's ba-a-a-ack! This oh-so-not-lovely walking explosion of a woman walks back into the kitchen to, well, explode, Mom-style.

"Let Him into your heart."

Yes, Mom just loves to shower her Catholic Crazy shit all over us. Yes, she's just a lotta bit into her Bible and Jesus being her Lord and Savior and trying to convert everyone and that whole scene. I've heard that Catholics aren't all that into the Bible. This particular one is, though, mostly because she did a lot of exploring before deciding to be Catholic. So she's really into Jesus and Mary with a hodgepodge of the most annoying Bible verses thrown in.

None of this mombastic stuff would be much of an issue if I didn't have to live with her yet again. Thank you, tuberculosis—not! Who the hell gets TB in this day and age, anyway? Well, I did. (Insert that wailing emoji here again.) But as soon as I get all better and out on my own again, I'm going to show this woman how to really live a life.

I guess I'm starting to realize I'm mad at her. No, angry. No, livid. For denying me, *me*, all these years. Plus, I remember how much she loved James. I want that back. I know she can do it. I have faith in her. I mean, of course, she still loves me, underneath everything. But I want it back, overneath everything.

When she gets going on the sin of homosexuality, though, I put my hand on hers, and she stops jabbering. Is that all she thinks I am? That's so 1980s.

"Uh, Mom? Let's get one thing straight. I'm not."

She's stunned silent. That's been happening more and more lately, along with the deluge of door slams.

"And it's the *Bi*ble. Not the *straight*ble." I laugh at my joke, lame as it is.

She is, like, so not amused.

But I have to continue. "And just for the record, you do know King James was gay, don't you?"

Chapter 2

Alice—age 48

Oh, this life of mine! I just can't take it. I have to leave before I start wailing, flailing, or smashing things. Or all of the above. I race up the stairs to my room, my holy sanctum that serves as my best beast blockade.

Oh, dear Lord, as I live and breathe! Hail Mary, full of grace. That child of mine is going to be the death of me yet! King James, gay. Where does he come up with this stuff?

How could he—emphasis on *he*? In a *women's* dressing room? How could my beautiful son—oh! What did I do? Where did I go wrong? How can I fix him?

After I hear him slink into his room, I head back downstairs to gulp a glass of water. And then another. Isn't this far too hot for March?

"Hey, Sunshine, you're thumping around," Mother says from what seems to be her now-permanent (oh!) perch at the kitchen table.

"I have a lot to be thumpful for."

I collapse into a chair and glance over at her just sitting there, smiling at her laptop, not a care in the world. Probably because she's not of this world.

Argh! Why doesn't she have a husband and a 401(k) to rely on instead of me? A steady job in her past? Something stable ever? Mercy, no—too much of an albatross for her. So, that all means she's recently had to move in with me since her stroke a few months ago. Did I just mention an albatross?

She's almost as bad as he is. He. Him! He's a him, not a her. How could this happen? I've always been stable, solid, steady as she goes. I've done everything right.

"How could everything go so wrong?" Oops—I didn't mean to say that aloud.

Mother knows exactly what I'm whimpering about, as I haven't whimpered about much else lately, at least, when James is out of earshot. "Maybe it didn't. Maybe it went so right."

Oh, dear Lord, please give me strength. Hail Mary, full of grace.

○

"Oh!" I shriek out to my bedroom. But the blackness doesn't answer me. I hear a dull drumbeat from down the hall, so James probably didn't hear me over his music. And Mother is probably off visiting some distant star system in her dreams.

Still sitting up in bed, I try to calm my pounding heart. I reach for some tissues to dab at the rivulets of sweat streaming down my chest. A deep breath evades me. Third time this week this has happened—and it's only Tuesday. No, this has nothing to do with menopause and everything to do with…my son. My *son*! Oh, dear Lord. Please help me.

I hear James in his room, unpacking his dress with as much fanfare as he can muster—and that's a lot. Could he possibly crackle that shopping bag and tissue paper any louder?

Strange smells and sounds emanate from the guest room with its now-permanent (oh, again!) guest and snake under my door like the creepy crawly things that they are. My mother's a boomer's boomer. In the midst of her den of fairy lights and harem-tent bed canopy—that she did *not* ask if she could put up in there—Mother's doing…whatever it is she does in there. I'll never understand.

And that goes both ways. My mother never fathomed me. Ever. She reveled in the free-spirited counter-culture life and thought my longing for walls and structure was just some pesky quirk I'd outgrow. But *I* was not the one who had to grow up!

I always knew I was poles apart, at least from the people I found around me at a young age. My flaky, flippy, airy-fairy, flower-power mother has never gotten over the fact that the sixties ended. She's…well…*out there* is putting it mildly.

She still has her long hippie hair, though the blonde shifted to white, and lives in yoga pants. She looks like her closet exploded: a rainbow of scarves, clunky necklaces, dangly earrings, a multi-colored suitcase-sized purse. How could I have been born to such a woman? Yet, she's always looked at *me* with a "Where did I go wrong?" look.

Early on in our courtship, Dan, my ex, wondered what my mother thought of me. "She's never known what to make of me," was my answer.

"But isn't she a hippie living in a van?" he asked. "Twenty-plus years" (at the time of this conversation) "after Woodstock?"

"Right. She's more than just a little loony. But somehow *I'm* the odd one out." I waited a minute. "Um, about Woodstock…"

When I told him about being, uh, well, *created* there, he just laughed. And laughed. And laughed.

Cut. I have to be in the right mood to talk about Dan. Meanwhile…oh, that wild child of mine. I'm always in the mood to talk about him because he's right here, mocking me and all that I stand for.

Rolling over doesn't help. Nor does rolling the other way. Nor does lying on my back. Or stomach.

I didn't ask for the zaniest childhood ever, then ask for the zaniest child ever—a son who would one day up and decide to become a daughter. Who is this person I thought I knew but didn't know at all? What did I do to deserve this? Oh, why couldn't he just be gay? I mean, that's still really bad, if you ask me, but not as bad as…this!

Oh, dear Lord—please give me strength. And could I please get some sleep?

○

Then, along comes this kind of occurrence: "Ooooooohh, Alice! How are you? What's James up to these days? My Alan is off at Harvard. Pre-med, of course!"

Luckily Robin, my acquaintance from James' old junior high soccer days, doesn't even wait for a response. Does she actually say "Toodle-oo" as she dashes off? Please, by all means, toodle and dash, dear.

I walk into the nail salon—my one indulgence—Robin had just exited. I've never been so grateful for the language barrier between my manicurist and me, nor for the warm water she sets out for my aching feet.

Thank goodness my work at the hospital is one (twelve-hour) day on, one day off, with the on days being Tuesday, Thursday, and Saturday. That gives me four days to recover in between shifts. Or try to. The inundation of my family doesn't allow for much recovery.

Next stop. Okay, fine, massage is another indulgence. Forgive me, but I'm going through a time.

"Youch!"

My massage therapist jumps three feet. I didn't mean to yell that loudly.

"Alice, you're so tight, even more than usual. You very upset about something?"

"You could say that."

Okay, yes, I have even more than these two indulgences, as shown by the dreadful dressing-room scene the other day. I do enjoy some shopping here and there. Plus, while I don't attend many gala events, my church and the hospital where I work do host them from time to time, so I need to be prepared.

Oh! I cringe again, just like every time I think of it. James, in a women's dressing room, in a dress.

The umbilical cord is never fully cut. Ever. And what no one ever tells you—or no one ever told me, anyway—is that when you have a baby, your insides are ripped out of you. And then, *your* insides are traipsing around the world. I'd say it's like having my heart out there, but it's more than that, even. They (those crazy insides of yours) can be out there doing unconscionable things—like becoming a transgender Democratic Socialist—but you love them (those crazy insides of yours) anyway…darn it all.

Ah, all those stories about mothers and children being best friends. Lamentably, that's not what this story is about. I don't even wish for that. Somebody—me or the ones in either generation I'm sandwiched between—would have to be a completely different person.

Chapter 3

Starr—age 68

"What *are* you doing?"

"What are you *doing*?"

"What are *you* doing?"

The first comes from Alice to me as I walk in with Aurora, Amorah, and Arienne. That's a lot of As, come to think of it. The second comes from me to Alice, as she and her fellow church parishioners (I can tell by their frumpiness, bland colors, and automaton blank look) sit in the living room. The third comes from Alice to Jaye as the latter parades in with her group of gothies, or whatever you want to call them. I don't mean any disrespect—it's all good.

"Séance," Jaye answers as she leads her friends upstairs.

"The Age of Aquarius is coming," I tell them. "We're having a discussion about it." To their even more blank faces, I add, "We'll meet in the kitchen." My A-group and I head thataway.

Alice hovers in the hallway after her robotinous creatures leave, waiting for my galactic gang to depart.

"You're never home on Wednesday nights!" I say, hopefully pre-empting this A's initial blast to me. Her church circle never meets at her house these days. I wonder why?

"Everyone else had something going on at their place, so it had to be here."

Something thumps in Jaye's room, and we both look up the stairs.

"The specters must be restless. Ooooooh," I moan, imitating a ghost.

Alice looks like she wants to cry. But it's often much easier and less painful to be angry, at least for the moment, so she does that instead. "Ohhhhhhhh!" And off she stomps.

I put a bubble of light all around my energy field, which protects me, anyway. Unfortunately, I think her anger just bounces off and flies right back to her, making her even worse. Hmmm, I'll have to figure something else out.

Early the next morning, Alice storms into the kitchen and out the back door with her usual less-than-subtle thundering. My daughter is a Taurus through and through. Stubborn bull. But then, I'm a stubborn goat, Capricorn. Jaye's a Leo—a fiery lion, but of course.

Uh-oh, the bull is back. She must've forgotten something. Alice thunders up the stairs and the floorboards overhead shudder under her stomping.

Oh, Alice, Alice, Alice. This life of yours could all be so much easier than you're making it. Just let people be who they are. Is that so hard?

I chant to myself: *Om Namah Shivaya. Shiva Om Namah.*

"You have a trans grandchild?" a new acquaintance asks me as we settle into the comfy chairs in the café.

I find potential friends at every turn: the produce aisle, the farmer's market, Copperfield's Books on Kentucky Street, the library restroom.

"Cool," he says. Ah, a compatriot.

But then, after I share a little more family lore, "Your daughter did what?" he asks.

"She voted for him!" His mouth is a solid O. "I cried—for days…more over her vote than that disgusting orange predator who got elected only with help from the Russians."

I don't think this fellow will want to hang out with me again. His loss. But I can't be the only one around here with a Trump-supporting daughter, can I?

As I wait outside the café for the Uber driver to take me home, I spot a woman my age walking arm in arm with who appears to be her daughter.

Pang! That was my heart.

Although Alice's anger mostly bounces off me, thanks to my light bubble, I can still feel her pain. Ah, Alice. Whatever happened to make you like this? Did I do this to you? What am I going to do with you? I tried. Really, I did. I wasn't expecting such a…conformist. You should've been my mother's daughter. You both would've been much happier with each other than either of you were with me.

Alice, Alice, Alice. We've traveled across the space/time continuum to be together. All that space, all that time, and of all the people in the world we could be with, we're with each other. And yet, it doesn't always work out quite the way we expected. They (that wackadoo who's traveled lightyears to be with you) can be out there doing horrifying things sometimes—like turning to established religion and voting the Republican ticket—but you love them (that being from across the galaxies) anyway. Dagblammit! It's just what happens...no matter how much of a fiasco they make of their lives, and no matter how often they tell you that you're the cause for the fiasco they're making of their lives.

Could've been worse, I suppose.

Wait...give me a minute...I'm trying to think of how it could've been worse.

Of course I'm kidding there. Oh, well. It's her journey, her life. It's up to her.

Hmmmmmm. But what she's doing to Jaye, well, that's not up to her. I'm almost well enough to hit the road again, but I should stick around for Jaye's sake.

Maybe it's a block in Alice's second chakra. And her first...and her third...and....

◯

"Your grandson is trans?" asks another new acquaintance (they're everywhere!) as we, too, share our life summaries.

"Granddaughter. Yes."

"Cool."

That's a true friend, on my wavelength. Then, I tell her a bit about Alice, though.

"Your daughter does what?"

"Well, I don't know if she's actually protested at a clinic lately. But she's a maternity nurse and she donates to a home for teen mothers. Putting her work and money where her heart is."

"I suppose."

Well, she is, I want to say. Hmmmmmm. Sometimes, I still want to defend her—she's my daughter, my own flesh and blood, after all, even though I still need to vent about her.

I don't think I'll search out friendship with this woman. Funny how people around here handle the info on Jaye far better than that on Alice.

Speak of the angel.

"Mother, let the Lord into your heart."

Perhaps when the pain gets to be too much, another thing that helps is to turn the focus on to something, or someone, else—like the Lord.

"You talking about my soulmate Yeshua again? Oh, he's already there in my heart. Not to worry. I'm already saved. We all are."

Kibosh! No more soul conversion, at least for this moment in time. Ah, Alice. She just doesn't understand my version of things. And do I have quite the version of things.

Oh, how I wish my daughter and I could be best friends. I wish this story could be about that. Maybe in another time, another dimension…

Family just might be the most wackadoo configuration of all. There's that Ram Dass quote that goes something like this: "Think you're so enlightened? Try spending a week with your family."

Yeah, well, try twelve weeks. And counting. Doo-wacka-doo-wacka-doo-wackadoodle-doo!

Chapter 4

Jaye

Moooo!

Baah-GOK! Bok-bok-bok-baah-GOK! That's a chicken, in case that's not obvious.

Cluck! Cluck! Cluck! It really does sound like that when a hen lays an egg.

BLEERRRRuuuhhhhhhh! That last one is a tuba blaring. This shit's hard to spell.

Does our town ever know how to throw a party, or what? Make that a parade—the annual Butter and Eggs Day Parade, to be exact. No, it's nowhere near as dull as it might sound. It's the most colorful parade imaginable, second only to Pride in San Francisco. Pride is more colorful than anything, and I mean that both physically and metaphorically.

Picture a street lined with people cheering floats made up like a peacock, a garden, or a chick hatching (a kid popping out of a paper mâché egg). Petaluma Pete plunks out ragtime on his piano. Classic cars. Dancers. Biker dudes and dudettes. Clowns (fun ones, not creepy ones). Kids' faces in cutouts of giant chickens. Clo, the mascot for Clover Dairy, always makes a big appearance—emphasis on big, since she's such a cow. Ha!

There's the cutest chick contest and, hey, that's me this year. But they really do mean the little-fluffy-yellow-bird kind. But still, I'm dazzling—if, yet again, I say so myself. Just this once, I'm not in black. My short shorts hide under a flowy yellow shirt, topped off with my yellow feather boa scarf, all kind of chick-esque.

I have lots of company with that last accessory. In addition to feather boas, though, people also wear animal costumes, cowboy duds, anything with cow or chicken patterns, public service uniforms, farming gear, and sometimes very little attire at all. After all, yo, it's, like, crazy hot out.

Iiiiiii love me a great parade (I'm singing that kinda like the old song). I love Petaluma so much. She's the best hometown ever in the herstory of ever. Half the town—at least—comes out to celebrate everything egg and butter because for so many around here it's their...

well, bread and butter. They don't call us the egg basket of the world for nothing.

Half the town? Uh, that includes Mom. I didn't mind until I saw the look on her face: "How can I escape this person and this moment?" Big yikes.

Ou—no, fuck you, ouch. Go back to the nothingness you were a minute ago.

WTF—what the flock? ha!—is she doing here anyway? She absolutely despises anything to do with chickens.

I throw my arms around her before moving on with my hatch of ghoulish chicks. A glance back tells me she's still not vibin' well with me, this moment, this day, this existence of hers. At all. She looks like an old hen whose egg got stuck in the chute.

Oh, c'mon, Mom. You know that's just going to make me push it all the more, right? I have to get you unstuck. It's my mission. Just chillax. And love me.

○

"Hey, Dad."

"Hey, Jaye." At least, one of my parents is with the program.

Yeah, about Dad, though. When I was ten, he said, "I love you very much, but I can't live here anymore." Then, instagone! But I saw him about once a week, and he was sooooooo much happier. Plus, he's a banker dude who still loves to deposit some of his green stuff into my account. Making up for leaving? Whatever. I'll take it. And I think his leaving might've made all my realizations easier.

"How are you?" I ask him.

"Good. You?"

"Good."

Okay, so we don't have the deepest conversations two people ever had. But better than the momster.

○

How's this for a major f'rinstance about that mother of mine? Here's how telling her, like, the biggest news of my entire life went down. "Mom?"

"What?"

"I'm a woman."

She laughed. Laughed! The woman *laughed* at me. She quickly stopped when she saw I was serious, though. I'm way glad she wasn't sitting in a swarm of gnats just then, because she would've sucked them all into her lungs with that gasp she took.

Something outside the window attracted her attention, but then, she slowly drew those giant, rounded eyes back into the room and tried to focus on me.

"I didn't do this to you, did I?"

"Oh, Mom," I wanted to groan.

I'd started seeing a counselor to start my change, who told me that all her counselor peeps tell all us trans peeps that parents might take this choice personally, even though it's not about them or their parenting so much. It just is.

But tears were filling Mom's eyes, so it wasn't the time to light into her. Wait, this was supposed to be my moment, though. Thanks, Mom— not! Then, her tears were replaced by something else. Dread? Horror?

It's not like she didn't have warning. Seriously, my suggesting tea parties and *The Nutcracker* must've given her some idea of what could be coming down the highway.

Oh, Mom, I wailed inside. Is it your religion? Is it your politics? What prevents you from saying, "Darling, how wonderful. Whatever you want to be is fine with me. It's your life to experience however you want to."

Instead of these words, though, she seemed to find a sudden intent interest in her…foot. Her fucking foot. Anything but me—right, Mom?

This conversation and non-conversation took place about a month after high school graduation and two months before I was leaving for San Diego State.

"Mom? You okay?" She nodded and then jumped as my fist hit the table. "But, damn it all, this isn't about you. This is about *me* right now. I'm finally making a huge decision for something I've wanted my whole life, which isn't exactly easy."

She still didn't say anything.

"Can't you be happy for me?"

She swallowed but her voice still came out in a whisper. "Yes. Of course."

But her eyes said, "No. Not in a zillion years. And how can I get out of this life with this person without making a scene?"

Hey, go for it: make me full-on psycho, why don't you? Deny me *me*—my me-ness—for eighteen years. And then still deny me at that most important moment of my life with you.

But I dropped it for the time being and figured I'd just do the formal switcheroo to outwardly expressing as a woman when I left for college. Too much hassle here on the home front. I did start female hormones that summer, though, with the help of my counselor.

"You're doing what?"

"Leaving school. I'll try this another time."

And then, I showed up on Mom's doorstep as what I'd always been in my heart, a member of the female persuasion. In a dress. And stockings and heels. And makeup and eyelash extensions. And... Maybe, I shouldn't have come to live with her after leaving school. What a joke.

"Hey, Mom."

SLAM! All I'd done was walk into the room. At least, she kept her total batshit crazies behind her slammed door. Usually.

"You're doing what?"

"Heading to SoCal," I said as I honked the horn of my borrowed van. "See ya, Mom."

And off I went to Southern California, Venice Beach to be exact. Somehow, though...

"You're doing what?"

"Coming home," I said to Mom over the phone. "Have TB."

By then, Dad had a new wife and a baby on the way, so I couldn't exactly take my TB-ridden self there. Since Mom hadn't undone my old room yet, I just fell into my old bed.

Where I got the TB from, I have no idea. Apparently, you have to be around someone who has it for quite a while before you get it, and, since I was mostly living in the van and all, I wasn't really around anyone that long.

Actually, maybe, I got it from my then boyfriend, who probably got it from his previous girlfriend, who might've gotten it from her previous girlfriend, who...

"She has to do what?"

Mom had her phone on speaker, so I overheard the rehab nurse repeat her words. "Your mother needs a place to recover. Her stroke wasn't all that bad, but bad enough. Can she stay with you?"

Luckily, by then, I was over the TB. Mom's being a nurse does come in handy from time to time, despite that glare from hell about having to take care of us. I bet she was really regretting having those extra beds lying around so we could come lie in them.

And…here we all still are. Aren't we the lucky ones?

All right, all right. The woman did give birth to me and nurse me back to health from an oh-so-two-centuries-ago, weird-ass disease. Maybe I can work on my attitude…at least, when I'm around her. Naaaaah—don't want to.

I suppose I could hit the road again and be with my people until Mom catches up. Naaaaah—don't want to leave Gram alone with her.

Give out whiplash much? Yeah, I often have that effect on people. It's just how I am.

Hmmmmmmmm. While I'm here, what else can I do to drive her as crazy as she's driving me? She totally needs to lighten up. Like, the woman doesn't even own a vibrator—unless her hiding skills are better than my sleuthing skills, which would be quite a feat. That one addition of that one accessory to her life would certainly help everyone involved with her life.

The thing is…this me-ness I just talked about. She's denying me, *me*, even now, still. My me-ness…my her-ness. Her. Me. ME! HER! MEEEEEEEEE! HERRRRRRRRRRRR!

Teardrop. And another. Okay, here comes the flood. Sometimes, I want to scream, cry, smash something, all of the above for the time wasted…that's still being wasted.

Thudkapoomph! There it goes again—my way-too-heavy heart dropping to the pit of my stomach, as it does over and over and…so I physically ache from all those years of having to suppress my me, my her.

It's getting less and less, though, as she (my she) realizes more and more that she's here to stay. Maybe, that's why I'm such a wild thing now, going to the X Games of Life here. This is my life, my *her* life now. James has graciously stepped aside, and Jaye's the reigning woahman. Look out world!

So, it's not that I'm being a snarkelope just to be a snarkelope around her. There's a method to my snarketology, which is I'm just trying to make a point here. And if I had to think about exactly what point that is, oh, I suppose it'd be something like this….

"Out with it!" Mom shouts as we pass each other on the stairs after I've given her the silent treatment for like two days. "What are you trying to tell me without telling me? Without using words like any other normal human being would?"

My hand presses against my head…*à la* something my great-great-great-grandmother would've done because her corset was too tight. Then, I wave my hands in front of my eyes, fake drying fake tears.

A strange sound erupts from Mom's throat. "Oh, Lord help me because I can't help myself. I think you're taking this female thing too far. Are you trying to be a caricature, or something, of the most pathological woman you know?"

"Uh, first part, that'd be no. Second part, that'd be you."

"But the way you move, the way you talk…"

"I am whatever I want to be in any given moment, after a lifetime of not being what I wanted to be in any given moment. Ever."

"That's not true!"

"Stop denying me my reality!"

Another strange sound starts to emerge, but Mom clamps her hands to her face, all silent-scream like.

"What another adult does with her body is absolutely none of your business."

Her seething is as deafening to me as my recent silent treatment must've been to her.

"How about just loving me no matter what, like that Jesus guy you love so much tells you to? Just love me as I am. It'll be good for you."

Chapter 5

Alice

"I do love you no matter what," I say. "Regrettably," is the word I don't say. But somehow my offbeat offspring hears what I don't say more often than what I do. And it's not that I really mean "regrettably," it's just that everything he stands for is everything I don't.

Yet, he's my child. I can't say, "See ya! Have a nice life." I love him more than life itself. And he horrifies me. Our every interaction takes my stomach on a Tilt-a-Whirl ride.

Oh, this son of mine. Ack, I'm supposed to say daughter. Oh, dear Lord. Oh, the hell with it. He's not here. And, for the record, my son is another cuckoo bird, just like his grandmother.

I'm sure all those hip, happening, with-it moms take their son saying, "Mom, I'm a woman" and totally accept it. Bully for them. I'm not where they are. At least, I'm not right now. And probably won't be for the foreseeable future, such as the rest of my life.

Oh! Dear Lord—please give me strength. Hail Mary, full of grace.

Love the sinner, hate the sin. Love the sinner, hate the sin. At least, all of these prayers and devotions are helping me if not my mother and child. I can't imagine what a basket case I'd be without my prayer practices.

○

Yet again, I pass James on the stairs as I'm heading off to work and he's heading to bed. Sunrise comes in an hour, so I guess this still counts as night.

A tiny, furry face with beady red eyes pokes itself out from James' collar.

"What on God's green Earth is that?" I scream. There it still is, shaking its whiskers at me.

"This is Ratness." James pulls a shivering, white creature out from inside his shirt, which this former All-American athlete happens to be wearing over a bustier.

"That's a rat!"

"Yes, she is." He holds the creepy little critter with surprising tenderness in those big, masculine paws of his. James has huge hands. "But she's a she. She doesn't pee all over you and everything like a male would."

"I can't tell you how relieved I am." He's still holding that…that… that thing like it's the most precious creation ever, well, created. "Ratness?"

"As in Her Royal Ratness. She's a rescue." From what, the sewer? "Rats are excellent pets. You won't hear a peep out of her."

If I ever wanted to faint, this would be that moment. A rat! In my house! People pay good money to not have rats in their houses. But for half a second, I was very touched by this gentle giant (at least he's gentle when his mouth isn't motoring) with the little varmint.

Enough. I have to get to work. Maybe, I could move into a hospital room and stay there.

◯

"Surprise!" James and Mother call out to me.

Birthday streamers and balloons fill the kitchen, while the aroma of Chinese takeout—my favorite under normal circumstances, and these aren't those—wafts through the air.

"Oh, you didn't have to do this!" I really mean it, in part from still feeling stuffed from the treats my coworkers plied me with all day. Only in part, though.

"We knew you'd be too beat to go out after work," James grins.

"So, we brought the party here." Mother's grin matches his.

Oh, please. But I grin, too. It's what we do, right?

After dinner, Mother hands me a card with a coupon for a facial. I was just thinking about getting one the other day, but felt it'd be too extravagant, even more than mani-pedis and massages. I've never appreciated this ongoing mind-reading thing she has.

"Here." James hands me a painting.

What the Hell is that?

"Sorry, I couldn't wrap it. It's kind of big."

It's the ugliest thing I've ever… "Sweetheart, thank you. It's beautiful!"

We don't go to Hell for these kinds of lies, do we? The Lord is too merciful for that. He must understand we have to survive here as best we can.

Where can I hide this monstrosity? The painting, not James. Although, sometimes…

I'm such an awful person. I'm such a horrible mother. Lord, please forgive me.

Thankfully, James rushes off to one of his ever-important-and-quite-mysterious events. I don't even want to know. I'm grateful, though, as that means he won't want to hang the painting up right away. It seems to be just arbitrary shapes and colors dabbed here and there. At least, it has quite a bit of yellow in it. He does know things, sometimes.

I polish off the piece of birthday cake on my plate. So much for feeling full even before this dinner. Sometimes, I wish my appetite would disappear the way my son did, but if anything, it's growing. Like I seem to be.

Mother takes a tiny bite of cake and pushes the rest of her serving away. Why didn't I inherit that? Well, it's not like I inherited anything else from her and her too-tiny body, so why start there?

I drop my face into my hands. "Why him? Why me?"

"Because this being knew she'd need a safe place to land, and as annoying and tone deaf as you sometimes are…"

"You have to stop holding back so much. On my birthday, no less."

"…you're still a safe landing spot. So many of my kids had parents who tossed them out, disowned them entirely." Mother volunteered at a homeless shelter before her stroke.

"I didn't expect this," I howl. "He…"

"She."

"…told me years ago. I thought it'd just go away. What comes after shocked—gobsmacked? That's me—gobsmacked."

"You're just getting to expand your definition of love. You never stop loving your children… even if they commit murder. Or become a Republican," my lovely mother just has to say.

"Boom!" My lovely child just has to say as he just has to reappear in the doorway. And then, he just has to add, "By the way, I don't mean to drive you crazy. It just comes naturally."

◯

"Hail Mary, full of grace, the Lord is with thee. Blessed art thou among women, and blessed is the fruit of thy womb, Jesus. Holy Mary, Mother of God, pray for us sinners now and at the hour of our death. Amen." I even bow my head when I say "Jesus," like we're supposed to. Wow! Praying for all us sinners now and at the hour of our death must keep her immensely busy.

Mary lovingly looks back at me. I've positioned myself, as usual, in line with her gaze. The afternoon sunshine streaming through the stained-glass windows casts a violet glow over the two of us, human and statue.

Mother of God. Mother. Me. I put my face in my hands.

Oh, James, my darling! What did I do? What can I do? How can I reverse all this…this… *this*?

No, my words are not a bleeding-heart liberal discourse on the rights of trans people, much as I'm working on that. Mine is a heart-felt reaction, perhaps with some weeping and gnashing of teeth along the way. This is my child and no matter what he, *not* she (dear Lord!), says or does—even murder, like Mother said—that love will never die.

But it doesn't mean I'm devoid of emotions along the way. And I can't be made to instantly understand by just adding water.

I shouldn't think any of these things about transgender people. But that's where I am. I can't be someplace else until I get through where I am. My car dashboard and bed pillow have absorbed more than just a few screams of mine. That does help.

I'm just being completely honest here. Out there in the world, I have to have every hair in place, walk the talk with my church friends, be Mother Teresa at my job, toe the party line with my political people.

But here, all by myself, I'm messing up my hair. I'd probably fail a DUI walking test because I seem to be stumbling all over the place. At least, stumbling through my life.

This is sheer lunacy. Sure, there might be people who legitimately feel they were born in the wrong body. But a whole generation of 'em, all at once?

There's that saying, "We can't go home again"? I'm sure whoever said that meant a home we once lived in, not the home we currently live in. But I don't want to go home these days. Strange nuisance animals have taken up residence there. And I'm not talking about the rat. A rat! Dear Lord. So, I've been sitting under Mary's gaze more and more often.

Mother I can somewhat handle—on a good day. But James? Oh, James. Where did you go? When will you come back? Where'd my sweet, kind, adoring son go? Who's this hellion who's taken your place? Please come home. Then, I'd want to be home.

When he, I mean she—oh, Lord, just let me call him a he, that's what he is in my heart, and I can't switch my heart just like that—first told me, I was one, huge, silent scream.

But I had to smile and say, "Oh. Of course. Whatever you desire, sweetheart. Whatever your soul yearns for."

Thank Heavens, I was calling forth my mother right then, which was good because what I really wanted to say was, "You—and all you kids who are into this whole made-up gender-issue thing—are self-centered, overindulged, mollycoddled, narcissistic brats. Every single one of us is born with conditions we don't want. All around this planet—this very minute—are countless people in detestable situations: being sex trafficked, starving, you name it. They'd give their eyeteeth to be sitting in your warm home, with your full belly, experiencing your life as your original gender."

Of course, he doesn't remember "whatever your soul yearns for," just what I didn't say.

I admit, I'm not the most PC person anyone's ever met. I'll work on that as well as the accepting part of my brain. But not today. Right now, I want to vent. I wasn't made for this new-fashioned world. I just want to curl up in Mary's arms and swoosh away the demons with a flyswatter.

Before I leave the church, I light a couple of candles, one for Mother and one for James. I look at the candles lit by others for their loved ones and wonder what they're going through. Did someone die? Does that candle over there mean someone's sick? Do I have the right to be so upset when there's so much tragedy in the world? All the flames blur together as tears sting my eyes.

Jesus! And I mean that with all my heart. Jesus, please help me. This is a tragedy—to me. My life is...well, tragic.

As I approach the vestibule, I dip my hand in the holy water and make the sign of the cross. In the name of the Father (touch the forehead) and the Son (touch the heart) and the Holy (left shoulder) Spirit (right shoulder). Those motions always lift me up.

Mother's parents were strict Catholics, so that meant she had to raise me as some vague brand of nothing. Putting up a Christmas tree was the extent of her religion. I hated that lack, too. I couldn't wait to grow up, find my own way, work at a real job, go to a real church, have a real family, have a real home with a real garden, and…and…and…

Oh, those childhood dreams of ours. Some of the items in that list worked out very nicely. But about that family situation? Well, someone's not going to get out of that house alive. Probably me.

Oh, dear Mary—please give me strength.

Oh, dear Mary—please. Strength?

Oh, dear Mary—please.

Oh, dear Mary.

Oh, dear.

Oh!

My hands have never shaken this much before. I drop the phone a few times before I can finally punch in 911.

"Please help us," I tell the operator. "Please send someone right away."

Chapter 6

Starr

"Why does life have to be so hard?"

"Hard?" Alice's question yanks me down from being captivated by the clouds and the beautiful spring day as she drives me to another doctor's appointment. Here she goes again. I know what she means but I refuse to go there with her. "On Jaye? Because she signed up to break down barriers in this lifetime."

"'In this lifetime.' Oh, honestly. No, hard on me."

"Great galaxies above! You're making it so much harder than it has to be."

No response. Until, "I just hate it."

I follow her glance and notice two men holding hands as they stroll down the street.

"Oh, horse malarkey. Love is love. People can love whoever they want."

"I hate that they called straight people 'breeders.'"

"Oy. That was one guy, one time. *And* that was, what, thirty-five years ago already? Get over it!"

Back in the eighties I had a nanny gig near San Francisco's Castro District, where Alice received this "breeder" comment. What was she, all of sixteen? Hardly thinking of breeding anytime soon.

"There were others, too. But even that one would've been one too many!"

Once again I have to remind her, "After a lifetime of suppression and having to hide, that area was their special place, their world."

Was it living near the Castro that sent her reeling in this crazy direction of hers? Or was it living in the chicken coop? Okay, it was a renovated, converted chicken coop on a friend's farm. I loved it. She's never gotten over it.

She sure loves this boxed-up life she's created. My brother came home in a box from Viet Nam, though, so I wanted nothing to do with boxes. Not in a million million evers.

In addition to when she's thundering through the house, Alice is also a bull when she's tossing and turning and making her bed creak. Very loudly. So, here I am, tossing and turning, too.

I know she went to church again today because I could smell it on her. It does help her sometimes, but today's visit doesn't seem to have settled her soul to let her sleep.

Ah, life. Life, life, life. The times are still a-changin', Bob. They always will be—that's what times do. Is it me, though, or are times getting even wilder?

I roll over and hug my pillow like I'm hugging the past. Speaking of Bob Dylan, ah, the sixties. Now, that was a decade. It was wild, but with a purpose to the wildness. Now, it's just a wild to the purposeness. No, that's not supposed to make sense—just like life.

They say if you remember the sixties, you weren't there. But I was there, and I do remember everything, especially about Woodstock—the music, the rain, the mud, the vibe, and…something else.

I remember Janis's screeches electrifying every nerve in my body. Joe Cocker's raspy voice sang about getting by and getting high with a little help from his friends. Grace Slick belting out those final lines of "White Rabbit" gave me goosebumps on my blood! And the Grateful Dead…and…and…

It was just this teeming mass of happy-hippie humanity. My girlfriend and I had brought our sleeping bags along with a tent. By the time we got there, after walking five miles because the cars on the highway had come to a total standstill, the fences had come down and no one was taking tickets.

Now, about that "something else," the main thing that happened there—for me and my life ever after, anyway. The music was so…oh, how to say it…visionary. It made everything that happened seem so…transcendent. I felt every single note in each one of my cells. The singing and strains lifted me to realms I hadn't experienced before. My whole body seemed to be moving of its own accord, dancing as if to the music of the spheres.

What was that? Wow. Someone's hands were suddenly on my hips—not at all in what we'd think of today as perhaps a disturbing way. It was as if the music itself was calling this moment forth out of the ethers. I turned around, and there was the most beautiful young man I'd ever seen looking back at me. I still see those brown eyes, lit up by the lights from the stage, looking into mine. My head had to tilt back and up while his had to tilt forward and down, since he was so much taller, as we pressed our foreheads together. Quite the shaggy guy, his curly brown hair fell to his shoulders, and his beard and mustache would've made Mr. Garcia envious.

Our bodies merged as we rocked and swayed to the music. Barely cognizant of what I was doing, I stole away with him, leaving my girlfriend and the small circle of strangers who had suddenly become our best buds. He and I reached my tent near the edge of the crowd, and without saying a word, we slipped through the folds into the dark canvas burrow and into my sleeping bag.

The magic moment—my first—happened the next morning, while Jimi forever gifted us all with his rendition of the "Star Spangled Banner." Maybe, that's where Alice gets her patriotic groove.

I don't remember experiencing any pain, just...enthrallment. When we finally emerged from the tent, we noticed the crowd had thinned way down. I often wonder how many children were conceived that weekend, because we definitely weren't the only ones slipping off.

And then, he was gone.

If I'd known my encounter with this magical, mystery man was going to give us a daughter, I would've tried to get his phone number. Or at least his name.

◯

Alice has his eyes, but hers have such a sad cast to them, I think as I watch her putter around the yard the next morning. Did I do that to her, give her that sadness? That's the last thing I ever meant to do.

At least, she has gardening, where she's probably nurturing herself more than the earth she's tending. Work nurtures her, too, especially those beautiful beings she ushers into this microcosm. And she nurtures those babes right back. We're not all crazy all the time.

Hmmmmmmm. Maybe, if I smudge the house more often. Or put up more white lights. Or offer to give Alice a massage and sneak in some craniosacral therapy on her. Just looking at that furrow between her brows makes me wince.

As Jaye joins me in the kitchen—ah, must be after noon—I sing out, "Just look at this glorious day!"

Jaye growls as she shades her eyes. "It's very bright."

I laugh. "Having a stroke, even a small one, makes every single thing so much more precious."

"Don't you be taking off to any hereafters anytime soon." Jaye takes my hand and holds it to her face for a few seconds. I repeat the gesture with her hand to my face, and we smile at each other. Then, out of the clear nowhere, she asks, "Have you ever thought of being a model?"

"Are you kidding? Never! Not for one second have I thought of that."

"But you could be a model—no pun intended, or maybe it is—a role model for people getting older. Everyone could sparkle as much as you do."

"No one sparkles from the outside."

"Then, show them all how to sparkle from the inside."

She grabs her smoothie and leaves. As I watch her cross the yard, she and Alice give a short wave to each other. Lovely.

I stand and start folding up the yellow tablecloth to give it a shake and a wash. Alice sure has a yen for yellow, but she goes for a muted version. The rug under the table? Mustard. The sofas, pillows, and blankets in the living room? Honey. Looks like she plastered pots of melted butterscotch candies to the walls. I'd go for sunshine and lemon with accents of saffron or persimmon.

Alice definitely does "home" well, even if darker than I like. She certainly didn't get that from me. She even has a big Pooh Bear with a (fake) jar of honey sitting in the window seat off the living room.

I look out the window again and notice when Jaye's car turns onto the street, Alice slumps over. As does my heart.

I remind myself again and again there are no failures, really, in the cosmic scheme of things, but when it comes to Alice, those words don't help. What is it that happened? What did I do? However did I fail her?

Wow. Circles and boomerangs. Tonight, I overhear her ask her bathroom mirror, "However did I fail him?"

Chapter 7

Jaye

Oh, for fuck's sake! Did she think I wouldn't hear her? So, she thinks I'm a failure? Thank you too much for the vote of confidence, Mom. How warm and fuzzy and reassuring you so aren't!

"Just take me as I am," is all I want to say to her. "No matter what I'm wearing, saying, doing, being. No matter what body I'm in. No matter what. Is that so hard?"

A few days later, I wander into the kitchen at my predawn hour of 11 a.m. "What a shocker to find you two here!"

Gram smiles. Mom…well, Mom moms—does her mom bit. Her smile looks more like a grimace. Once my smoothie is smoothed, I join them at the table.

Mom looks me over, clearly finding me lacking.

"Can I help you?"

Mom shudders, then blurts, "Could you please tell me what is wrong with being a man? You were born male. What is wrong with that? What is this issue—or non-issue, really—all about?"

Wow, wow, wow. She doesn't usually travel down this particular unpretty path with me, usually preferring to detour at the slightest sign of roadwork. Why now? Where do I begin?

"Saying 'born male' is not appropriate. You didn't ask me at the time. I was assigned that without being consulted. So, I'm AMAB, which is 'assigned male at birth.'"

"Are you going to do all of the surgery?" she asks.

"Maybe." I can see her try not to sigh. Or cry. "Being a woman is everything, Mom. You should know—being one yourself." I could see her struggling to keep it together. "Ever notice in a movie how when a grieving widower finds a pair of his dead wife's underwear, he smells it? It's the best smell in the world."

She gives me that look. That look that screams, "This person could not possibly have come out of *my* body."

Back into the kitchen I go to forage for lunch. At 4:30 p.m. And the two are *still* there.

As I stand over the sink chowing down leftover Chinese, I glance out the window at our huge, leafy palm tree, my favorite thing about the house. Mom put white lights around it, making the tree look like an ongoing California party just on its own. Her ridiculous car sits nearby.

"Oh noooo," I playfully scream to her. "The aliens ate your Buick!"

"What?" But it's that short, cute, quick, playful *what* like comedians do. Fun!

"No, wait, it's still out there. Unfortunately."

"You crazy kid!" But she's laughing.

"That's an album from the eighties, *Aliens Ate My Buick*."

"How would you even know about that?" Mom's still snickering. But then, she starts doing her sneezing thing, which she does a lot.

"Why don't you give up wheat and dairy for a month?" Gram asks her. "You might be allergic to them, which could be why you sneeze so much."

Mom does put half a cow of cream in her coffee. And she does have quite a love affair with cheese. And every meal of hers involves wheat, maybe even an entire wheatfield.

"If I gave up wheat and dairy for a month, my allergies would most certainly stop. Because I'd be dead."

Gram shakes her head. "I can't even walk down the bread aisle in the regular supermarket. The smell makes me want to pass out."

"Oh, dear Lord, Mother. I swear. If it's not one thing, it's another."

My good mood dematerializes. I hate it when she lights into Gram for no reason. "MOTHERFUCKER!"

Mom's good mood evaporates too. "Language!"

"However do you cope?" I ask her, stabbing the last of the tofu with my chopsticks.

She leaves. She's so good at that.

Except Mom and Gram are yet again doing their thing at the kitchen table when I arrive home later that night, a new friend by my side.

"This is Vision."

Again, Gram smiles and Mom moms.

Vision takes her right on. "In answer to all the questions all over your face, I'm genderqueer, an enby. N.B. Non-binary."

"Oh." Mom looks like she sat on a rabbit.

"I don't fit into the male or female thing. Non-binary, like I said, so not a one or a zero. I'm outside the box—like, literally. Outside balls, too. Ha!" Mom clearly doesn't understand, so Vision continues. "Not identified by a twat or a dick. I'm totally fluid—not one way or the other."

"What are your preferred pronouns?" Go Gram!

"They and them. Thank you for asking."

Mom looks like the rabbit has shapeshifted into a porcupine. "How did you two meet?"

"At a party in San Francisco," Vision answers.

Mom nods. She's trying to check Vision out without being obvious about it. Epic fail. Yes, Mom…whatever *is* Vision—or what did they start out as—under that hut (*à la* the aliens in *Twilight Zone*) they love to wear?

Mom certainly wouldn't be alone in her wondering. Vision started out life as a dude, like I did, but isn't as into the whole female thing as I am.

They put on their gender each day in the same way some people put on clothes. Casual attire one day. Formal enough to give a presentation another day. Total comfies the next day.

Not that one gender is the formal one and the other is the informal one—it's just a metaphor. And Vision would never say there are only two genders anyway.

"The future is non-binary," Vision says to Mom. "We're the most diverse generation in this country, probably in the world."

To Mom and her very thin smile, I say, "Don't worry. It's not anything most cis people would understand, least of all you." Okay, that was uncalled for.

"That was uncalled for." Except when you tell me it's uncalled for. "Try me," she continues.

"Want some dinner?" Gram intervenes, rising to rescue whatever's on the stove.

"No, thanks." I sniff. "This room smells like some unfortunate dead animal's burned flesh. And we're both vegan."

Mom and Gram try—unsuccessfully—to cover their surprise. "Oh," they say in unison.

"We're just going to head up to my room." Vision and I head to the hallway.

"Vegan? When did that happen?" I overhear Mom asking Gram.

"As if they could ever keep up with us anyway," I snort to Vision.

A little while later, we trek back down to the kitchen. Mom's still battling paperwork., Gram's scrolling through some old-timer's platform like Facebook or something.

"So, what do you do?" Vision asks Mom.

"I'm a nurse."

"Why not a doctor?"

Chapter 8

Alice

Listen, you creature from the black lagoon with your black lipstick and three-inch gauges and umpteen hundred piercings up the side of your ears and chains crisscrossing your body, in your black potato sack, usurping the Frankenstein miscreation's look, if I wanted to be a doctor, I would've been. But I didn't. I wanted to be a nurse.

How can this uppity little shit (Lord, please forgive me!), just waltz into *my* house and judge *my* life choices? This…this…this *character*, to put it nicely, makes the regular goth kids look like angelic light-bearers. Does this thing even have flies buzzing around it?

While I'm trying to think of a polite way to respond to the hirsute hominid's question, James grabs some food for the two of them.

I only realize how wide my eyes must've gone because Vision looks at me, obviously finding me deficient. James then quickly pulls them (hey, I can be with it every now and again) out of the kitchen and up the stairs toward his room.

"Here," I hear my son say. This old house can be an echo chamber. Voices carry. "Put this on. That looks great! Now, move around a little in it."

I can only imagine what my child has put on this…individual. Cancel that—I don't want to imagine it.

Did I pick up the wrong newborn at the hospital? I'm horrible. Lord, please forgive me.

"Work it, work it!" James sings out.

"What century is she in?" I hear Vision ask.

"Well, Gram is still in the sixties and her nationality is one-hundred-percent hippie. But that's okay—better than a lot of other mindsets. I'm not sure where Mom is."

"Single, straight, middle-aged, white, cis female is its own category altogether."

"Although it's probably a dying breed."

Wow, is the fridge always that loud? I'm only noticing now because James finally shut his door—he was probably done having me "accidentally" hear everything they wanted to say about me—and my shock has filled the room.

"I didn't want to be a doctor," I finally say to Mother, choosing just one of those snippets of conversation to respond to.

"No one said you had to be."

"Why do kids assume that being a nurse is second tier to being a doctor? No one complains when a land surveyor isn't an engineer." Mother just nods. "And I don't want to be made wrong for being straight and cis. There's not a whole lot I can do about the white part. Or the single part—for the time being, anyway."

"They're not really making you wrong. They're just making themselves right. This is the first time the world has encountered this kind of thing on this scale, and they can finally be themselves. It'll calibrate itself into society."

"Wonderful."

A little later, I call up the stairs. "James?"

A muffled answer comes from behind the door. "There's no James here! Quit deadnaming me!"

"Deadnaming?" I ask Mother.

"Referring to the name she had before she transitioned. It can be very invalidating to a trans person to not use his/her/their chosen name." And to what must be a mystified look on my face, she adds, "Learned it at the shelter."

Couldn't he have chosen the name Jamie, so I could at least catch myself before I completely make that ever-so-egregious error? I'd at least have that extra half a nanosecond to catch myself. I need everything I can get.

Kaaaaaa! I stab the ground with the trowel. I appreciate that dramatic intrigue in a gardening tool. Okay, maybe that stabbing is a little too exuberant. A little pallet of annuals sits ready to add some bright colors to the otherwise xeriscape yard. Small circles of rocks and wood chips surround the trees and bushes, so no grass needs to be watered. Summertime in Petaluma can be exceedingly hot and dry, and watering a lawn is ludicrous in a state often stricken with drought.

A gentle breeze carries the scent of the jasmine, bougainvillea, and geraniums from their planters on the front deck. Those sweet smells can lift me even higher than the incense in church.

As I stab, I mean dig—once again—I review my life—once again. What is all this? How did this all happen? This…this…this…this *this* that I'm living!

Regarding that conversation we had the other week, I honestly didn't mean to tell James that I think *he* was the failure. *I've* been the failure. But I even failed in telling him that!

After James, I got pregnant two more times and lost them both. The pain of that was bad enough then; the pain now when my child turns out to surpass his grandmother in lunacy is sometimes too much to bear. With more than one child, the chance of one being somewhat normal is much greater. I can't tell anyone I'm feeling all this. I can't let people know what a horrible person I am.

Maybe, I'm not so horrible. Just human.

I'm sorry. I'm so sorry. I just…I don't know.

Over the last twenty years, since Mother was MIA most of the time, my father was some far-off mystery, I didn't have any siblings, and the man I married went rogue, I gushed my love on James. He's all I had, family-wise. I thought we were so close.

And this is all in addition to being a divorced woman who gets lonely. I've dated some here and there, always when James was out of the house. Now, I can't even handle the thought of dating. Life is complicated enough at this particular moment in time.

About that rogue husband of mine who went rogue. I could handle our drifting apart but not the books. I started finding odd titles around the house by people with hard names to pronounce: Eckhart Tolle, Deepak Chopra, Thich Nhat Hanh. Oh, then there was something about a guy named Zen and fixing a motorcycle. Just kidding—I know the real title and what it's about. But this was all very far from our usual Catholic fare.

And then came this one day out of the blue: "Wanna go to Harbin sometime?"

"Oh, that's a great idea!" I really thought he was joking. Harbin Hot Springs is a clothing-optional retreat center just up Highway 101 a little ways. The very idea—yuck! He knew I was being sarcastic, and as I looked at him waiting for him to crack a smile, it dawned on me that he was serious. Who on God's green Earth was this person? How long had he been slipping away from the church-going, devout, solid man I had married? Bang! Yes, that was the final nail in the coffin of our marriage.

I had to practice different versions of my divorce story for different crowds: close friends, fellow church members, the men I dated, coworkers. The first group patiently sat through the "What a cad! How could he just up and change on me?" earful. For the second group, all I had to say was he didn't want to go to church anymore. Nothing else needed to be said to this group of fervent churchers. Dates got something along the lines of "different religious interests." Since I only went out with Catholics, they completely understood. The last group, coworkers, heard a nebulous "Oh, we'd started walking different paths" spiel. Well, just one of us started walking a different path, perhaps even a naked one, but I didn't elaborate.

Meanwhile, back in the present.

"Whatcha lookin' at?" James asks.

My attempt to hide my laptop screen has obviously failed miserably. "Pinterest. Just getting some ideas for a book nook with a built-in bookcase."

I love all these neat, orderly Pins. Not a chicken coop to be found. And it beats Facebook where all my classmates post pictures of their ultra-successful kids who are somehow happy with the way they were born. Pang.

"To go where the window seat is?"

"Well, if I decide to do this, yes, that's where it'd go."

"That's a great idea." James looks at a couple of examples I'm studying. "Here, try this." He takes my mouse and types a few extra words in the search bar. Dozens of book nooks surrounded by bookcases appear. "You want one with a window?" He adds *window* in the search and a bunch of windowed book nooks with bookcases appear. "Wow," he says, pointing to one particular pin, "that'd look great in there."

Who is this kind, patient being? Who are you and what have you done with my son? And how do you know so much about Pinter…? Oh, right. Even still, I sometimes forget.

Mother looks over our shoulders. "Lovely."

Is she talking about the book nook or the cozy coffee klatch that's happening here? But then, the creature appears at the back door and my once-kind kid remembers he has to be that sassy, sarcastic spitfire again.

He and his human pet slither up to the crypt.

Oh, dear Lord—please give me strength. Hail Mary, full of grace.

I can't both fix him and save her at the same time, so the next evening after the creature's visit, I decide to start with one. "Turn to Jesus, Mother. Let Him into your heart."

Oh, does she ever shoot me a look! If I were to translate said look, it might go something along these lines. "I don't know how this person and I could even live in the same galaxy, let alone how my genes stream through her blood."

My son sashays into the kitchen just then. Oh, dear Lord, it's getting worse. Long, blonde hair pulled back into a perfect French braid. Probably more makeup than I've had on my face in my whole life altogether. Eyelash extensions. Where does he get the money for stuff like that? Probably gets it done by a friend. Black lipstick. Black miniskirt. Black, black, black. Blech.

Those strikingly beautiful, blue eyes rimmed in those multitudinous layers of black blare, "I dare you to say anything to me."

So, I don't. He does.

"Off to do some necromancy with some of my peeps." He prances out the back door, and we hear his car start up.

"Please tell me this is just a phase," I say to Mother after I look up *necromancy* on my phone. I show her the definition because she isn't sure what it means either.

"I can't tell you that. I don't know if this is a decision that's just for the next two minutes, the next two weeks, the next two years, or one that'll stick for life. Jaye doesn't even know that."

"But I wanted a son. And I got one. He can't just go changing on me."

"Well, she is. Just changing on you, that is."

"I can't handle this!"

"That's just a whole lot of wackadoo hooha."

"I had to look up the "I" and the "A" in LGBTQIA+. I'd just gotten used to the first five. I might be the only one in my church and my Republican group who knows what those letters are."

"Probably not. The Republicans have probably experienced most of those letters firsthand, all while praising Focus on the Family."

Ignoring that swipe, I groan into my hands. "I'm so scared, too. I keep thinking of that suicide rate you told me about."

Mother once informed me that over forty percent of transgender people attempt suicide. That certainly led to more than a few nights of no sleep and days of dancing on eggshells.

"So, I try to be as outrageously loving and accepting as possible." Mother lets out a little sputter, which I ignore. "Plus, I have to handle him with kid gloves."

"Her."

"He changes his mind all the time," I plow on.

"She. Her."

"When he was in college for part of that one semester, I had to look on Snaptwit or InstaChat or TwitFace or whatever it is—I can't keep up—to see what major he was thinking of at any given time. Sometimes, it seemed to change by the hour, that is if I could follow his loopdeedoo Spirograph designs for that day."

"That's actually one of the common traits of many transgender people, changing their minds frequently."

"How in the world do you know so much about all this?"

"The homeless shelter. You wouldn't believe how many kids come through there, thrown out of their homes by parents who won't accept them."

"As you've told me." I sigh. "He's still my flesh and blood. No matter how confused he is."

"What if she's not confused?"

I don't dignify that idea with an answer.

"Are you ever going to refer to her as Jaye?" Mother asks.

"Heavens, no. Not with my dying breath."

Chapter 9

Starr

The next day, as Alice and I munch on lunch, Jaye flies through the kitchen and out the back door without saying a word. That's flying not as in fast, but as in feet-off-the-ground happy. I swear, despite all of the bickering in the house, this is the most joyful I've ever seen my grandchild.

Plop! That's Alice's head dropping onto her crossed arms on the table. "I have to fix him," she mutters.

"Her. And you don't have to fix anyone. You just lift people up with your love and light, just by being with them. And letting them be them."

She looks up at me, practically cross-eyed. Plop! There goes her head hitting her arms again.

Alice's voice is muffled as she leaves her head on her arms. "You are so out there."

I can't resist. "Farrrrrr out!"

Later comes this from Alice to Jaye: "This whole thing is just a choice you're making."

"Right, like we choose to be a social pariah. Like we choose to need hormones. Like we choose to be hated by haters. Like we choose to have to make an agonizing decision every time we have to go to the bathroom. I have trans male friends who've been assaulted when they've tried to use the men's room."

"They don't have to use the men's room!"

"They do!"

"I won't ever understand this!"

"You won't!"

SLAM! That was Jaye.

And the next day, I overhear, "Mom, gender is so last century!"

SLAM! That was Alice. Like mother, like daughter.

Om Tare Tuttare Ture Soha....

From my room, I watch Jaye arranging her crystals and stones in a pentagram. On a black scarf on the black rug. Alice walks by and as she clearly finds another aspect of Jaye's life with which to find fault, she crosses her arms.

"Why don't you just sit in judgment of everyone right now from your throne on high?" Jaye asks. "You do it very well."

As Alice sits in the living room reading the Bible, I walk by and, hardly realizing it, cross my arms.

"Why don't you just sit in judgment of everyone right now from your throne on high?" she asks, repeating Jaye's exact words. "You do it very well."

Whoosh! Phhhht, phhhhhht, phhhhhhhht! Do you hear that? Is it just me or are things boomeranging around here again or what?

"Must you? What is that stuff?" Alice wrinkles her nose at my rose oil and me, then continues down the hallway. "And must you? What is that stuff?" She wrinkles her nose at her daughter's lavender oil and her. "Smells like a cramped, closed-in florist around here."

A few minutes later, Jaye and I walk into the kitchen, where Alice is microwaving (don't even get me started on that!) a TV dinner that smells like a garbage heap.

"Must you?" we both say to her.

And a dozen other examples occur in just the next few days. "She has bats in her belfry!" "She's two witches short of a coven!" "She's just a little confused sometimes, but she'll be just fine." (Spoken by Alice, Jaye, and me about me, Alice, and Jaye.)

Maybe those boomerangs aren't just boomeranging around here. It's more than that. They're bazoomeranging—coming around and around, again and again.

Bazoomerangs. I like it. If they weren't a thing before, they are now. Phhhhttttt, phhhhhhttttt, phhhhhhhhhhttttttttt—there they go again! Lord, love a duck! (I'll explain that one later.)

I can't wait to tell my progeny about my new word. Alice, of course, just shuts her eyes as if the word is an assault on her nervous system.

"Hey, if it involves bazooms, I'm all in," Jaye giggles.

That's an even worse assault on Alice's nervous system, and she shudders.

○

Meanwhile, stepping into a nearby Tuesday morning, Jaye and Vision—still up from the night before—join Alice and me for breakfast. The two youngsters quickly get lost in their phones.

"Oh, look!" Jaye shows Vision a photo on Instagram. "That's totally dope."

"What does that even mean?" Alice stage whispers to me.

Vision shoves their phone in Jaye's face. "Look at what this dude is writing on your page!"

Jaye takes a look. "Oh, wow. I need to throw some serious shade on that troll."

"What language is she speaking?" I stage whisper back to Alice.

"I was going to ask you." Alice picks up her phone. "Siri, could you please translate some Gen Z for us?"

Jaye purses her lips at her. "That's so…lame."

Alice turns to me. "That's so…random. Who does that?"

"I know, right?"

Jaye puts her hands on her hips. "You're both trying to speak millennial and Gen Z, and it doesn't sound right coming from you. At all."

"Gnarly," Alice says.

"Do they still use that one?" I ask her.

"I think so."

I chuckle. "Notice how they still use *cool*, all these years later? Although *hot* means the same thing, apparently."

Vision nudges Jaye. "Ouch! Look at this dude."

Alice can't resist. "Ouch?"

"It means he's gorgeous," Vision explains, far more patiently than Jaye would have.

Alice turns back to me. "Notice how we have to reverse everything these days? 'Drop the mic' means delivering a great line. 'Killed it' and 'the bomb' mean great…" But her phone rings, and she answers it. A minute later she hangs up and groans, "I have to go fix a fiasco."

"Your life?" Jaye says.

"Mind your own fiascos."

"Hashtag Ihateyou. Mean it."
"Hashtag I'mnotsocrazyaboutyoueither. Mean it."
"Children, children!" I holler.

Not that I want to leave such a lovefest, but as soon as I possibly can, I return to work at the shelter. Sure, I'm pretty much volunteering at the shelter known as this house, too, and being of great use. But I also need to get out of here from time to time.

Really, I'm feeling fine and could go back to my cute, cozy, little life in my cute, cozy, little RV, but I'm called to stay at Alice's restaurant. Did you know you could get anything you want there? Heh!

The shelter I volunteer at provides a temporary residence for women and their children, although it'll take kids of all genders (more than just the usual two genders, that is) ages eighteen and nineteen who've been thrown out of their homes. We take them in for a short time until they can find someone to stay with or a job and their own place.

And the stories they tell! How could their parents throw them out like a piece of refuse? Literally, they're refusing them. Some have even been tortured or exorcised! I tried telling Alice that, but I'm not sure she believed me.

One night, a young girl, who I don't think started life that way, came in.

"How old are you?" I had to ask her. She wouldn't answer. "I have to call Child Protective Services if you're under eighteen. That's our policy here."

"I have friends who've had worse times with foster parents than they did with their own parents," she whispers. "What am I supposed to do? I can't go with CPS. I can't go home. And as uninformed as my parents are, I don't want to get them in trouble. It's not like they hit me or anything."

No, they only make you feel so unwelcome that you want to run away. Oh, I wanted to take so many home with me and love them all up.

Some of my beatnik, draft-dodger friends, back in the day, were tossed out of their homes, too, but it seems like we all had so many more options for housing back then, including for this particular dazzled duckling with her own duckling on the way. My shelter doesn't have any pregnant teens, as there's another place in town specifically for them.

Most of the kids I meet at the shelter are quite resourceful and street smart, far more than I was at their age. But I must've had invisible Hell's Angels or some other beings around me offering protection, because I was nowhere near as savvy as these kids are. We hippies were just cruising on the currents and living on love. Times are not so innocent anymore.

As the ambulance sirens wail in the distance, growing louder as they approach the house, the stench of blood still assaults me. How could this be? How could this be?

"Please, just let me wake up from this horrible dream."

Chapter 10

Jaye

I don't know if Mom's happy I volunteered to go along as she drives Gram to her specialist, because that means she won't get any Age of Aquarius lectures coming and going, or she's unhappy because that means more time with me, too. Oh, well. Too bad, too sad. Sorry not sorry. I snort to myself. (Oops! Thought I'd moved beyond that.) Really, I want to protect Gram from the Jesus lectures.

On the way back, Mom suddenly decides to do some off-roading. Not on purpose, of course. She had decided on purpose to take a back road to enjoy the beauty…and some cows, apparently. We round a bend, and she swerves to avoid hitting one.

"Nice ditch," I grumble after we land in one.

"What?" That, too, is a short, quick "What" but not the fun kind.

"Nothing. Not a thing. No. Thing."

A dairy-cow truck had broken down. Apparently, the captives had become restless and somehow busted out of the truck, and now the fine black and white ladies are wandering all over the road. Mom has a fit. And a flat tire. She looks at me over that last one.

"You want me to break a nail?" I put on my best utterly aghast face. "Just kidding. Where's that jack, Jack?"

But in addition to the flat tire, the car also needs to be pulled out of the ditch. So, we wait for AAA to handle both. Cows can be great company I discover.

"Well, the cows look very happy," I say to Mom and Gram. "They're munching on the lush, not-so-very-green grass here in this ditch we're suddenly all sharing." The grass in California turns brown by late May, so it's really brown now. Some might call it golden, as in the Golden State. Nah. It's brown.

Mom pops the trunk and climbs out of the car. She needs something from back there now?

"Ack!" comes her all-too-familiar scream. A cow had gently butted her in the… well, butt. If she ever really does need to scream for help, I hope it sounds a little different from her usual as I've become habituated to it.

The dairy-trucker's version of AAA arrives and helps him fix the truck and gather up the cows. Mom grouses (love that word) for, like, the thirtieth time. At what, I have no idea.

Gram's had enough of it, too. "MOTHERTRUCKER!" she shouts. "How do you cope?"

"Mother! I swear to God…"

"Hey!" I shout. "Don't have a cow! Or be one!"

At that, the three of us laugh. And laugh. Feels good. Better than all those hidden tears.

○

I play with Vision's curls. Then, they braid and then unbraid my tresses. This is as sexual as it gets with us. Maybe because, in all of this wild-'n-wonderful, this-'n-that with identity and trying sex with a him or her or them, here and there, we just decided we needed a home base to come back to. A true bestie. So, sex has never come up with us. We're way too young and feral to have a serious, long-term relationship. Neither of us want to lose what we have, which is a lot.

"What's your favorite thing about yourself?" I ask as Vision braids my hair again.

Actually, they've been going a little crazier than usual tonight and gone full Daenerys Targaryen on me. Daenerys is ye good olde Mother of Dragons from *Game of Thrones*, and what that means is I have a head covered with tiny braids in intricate patterns.

"My favorite thing about myself? Oh, so many to choose from," they laugh. "Where do we begin?"

"How about the way we present ourselves?"

"Yeah, that and how we dress and walk our own path and forge a new frontier and shit."

"Hey, don't forget we're dealing some striking blows to the status quo and the patriarchy."

We fall asleep in each other's arms, dreaming of those new frontiers.

○

"Jaye," Gram calls up the stairs a few mornings later. "You have a visitor."

Who in the world comes by without texting first? I stumble down the stairs, as it was well before my personal awakening hour, and on a Saturday, no less.

Sarah. My old girlfriend from high school. OMG. I pull my black silk robe around me a little more tightly.

"James?" she gently queries, looking at my smeared makeup, long hair full of braids, robe, and downward…probably checking to see if things are still intact there. Yes—for the time being.

"It's Jaye now." Nothing. "My pronouns are she and her, to the question you should ask."

"Oh. Well, I guess you could teach me the proper protocol."

"I don't wanna. I'm not some science experiment or your token trans person. Google shit."

She looks like she's about to cry, and I feel bad. "I'm sorry," I sigh. But not too sorry—after all, she's waking me up without any warning. Who'd even think of doing a thing like that? "Maybe I should've told you. I thought you might've seen me on Insta or heard the word somewhere."

Vision's face appears at the top of the stairs. Sarah goes white.

"Just a friend," I say.

Sarah can't make her excuses fast enough and rushes out the door.

"Sarah was so nice," Mom sighs as I join the dynamic duo at the table later. "You had so many girls swooning over you."

"Too bad I wanted to be their girlfriend, not their boyfriend."

Mom ignores that. "I don't see a problem with taking her out…"

"Mom," I practically scream at her, "what if *I'm* not the problem?"

"I wasn't saying you're a problem," she lies through her teeth. And she continues, moving on to the psychoanalytical aspects of being trans. And then come the motheroanalytical aspects.

"Mom, stop momsplaining my life to me!"

"I'm not momsplaining anything!" She puts her face in her hands, then: "I was twenty once, too. I know what it's like."

"You know what twenty was like in 1990, almost thirty whole years ago. You don't even know what it's like to be young in the new millennium."

"I'm still young, really. Young is relative."

I ignore that. She's old. Like, so old. "So, yes, you were twenty once, but you weren't a twenty-year-old trans female in the digital, social-media age. You were twenty in 1990, which called and wants its naive innocence back."

"Honey…"

I think it's easier to call me that than trying to get my name right. "I'm not here to live your life!"

She grunt-sighs. "I'm not telling you to live my life. I've already got that one handled."

I grunt-sigh right back. "Oh, really?"

SLAM!

I'm surprised the window in the back door doesn't break every week.

"More bags in the car?"

Mom nods, clearly touched by my warm offer of help. I do go all soft and gooey when I can tell it's been one of those days for her. She looks like she's been crying in the car again.

Not that I could ever tell her this, but sometimes I get it. I do. James was here and now he's not. This other person has taken his place. She misses him. I really do get it. I'm not, like, an ogre or something. Except when I want to be.

We carry the rest of her groceries into the house together. I still have amazing arm muscles under these lacy things I wear, and I can put them to good use sometime, like for lugging grocery bags and, even now, when I wrap them around her in a hug.

Actually, today's been another hard one for me, too, and tonight's not getting any easier.

The hormones. The confusion. The alienation. The looks, although they make me hold my head higher. But here and there they do tear me down, although I never let that show in front of the looker. Hell no! Those who give me looks get the full me.

Sometimes, I've actually forgotten for a minute, and I pass a mirror. Who's that? What a babe! She looks familiar. Then, I remember. Ohhhhhhhh, that stunningly gorgeous, foxy, lit woman I see in the mirror is…me! Right. Me. I'm *her*. Wowwwwwwww!

James? Oh, he's pretty much left this earthly realm. Sometimes, I recall him, especially when I go to the bathroom. This member thing I hold in my hand makes me re-member (ha!) him, although I generally sit down to pee. Not in the woods or at the beach, though. Sometimes, this member thing is convenient. Still thinking about that surgery thing, though.

Most of the time I'm fine with it all, even the not-so-easy parts. Other times, tonight in particular, I cry into my pillow. For hours.

WTF, life? Why? I know I'm finally letting myself be who I've always been, but why did it have to be this way? Why wasn't I born a girl? If we choose these life situations, as Gram's alluded to, why did I choose this one?

Maybe this one's easier than being born a girl in a country where girls are less than second-class citizens. Maybe. At least, they got to be girls. That's tops on my list. Okay, that's my privilege poking through. Sorry.

Sometimes, I talk to Vision and other friends about this. We seem to take turns being solid in our new selves, so we can pull each other through the less-than-solid times. But, tonight, it's just me and the pillow and Ratness scuffling around her cage. I pick her up for some company, and she covers my face with little rat kisses.

Maybe, if I'd been born a girl in one of those non-girl-oriented countries, I'd do everything I could to fight for education and equality and that whole thing. Like Malala, the Pakistani activist. She's such a rock star.

At 5 a.m., I pull out my Tarot cards and turn just one card over. High Priestess. Yep, that's me. I'm such a rock star, too.

The card makes me think of Emma, my galpal from my days at Venice Beach. Oh, woah-man! Talk about lit up. She was about my age, but she was already totally steeped in Gram's brand of "Ah, isn't life fabulous?" and way beyond breathtakingly beautiful from being so happy.

"Oh," Emma gushed after turning a card over in my Tarot spread. "High Priestess. Of course, because that's who you are. She even looks like you."

Seen! Truly. For the first time, maybe?

I look up Emma on Insta. There she is, still with her boho wrap around her head and belly dancer skirt swirling. She'd take me shopping for threads on Melrose Ave, sneaking a few of her colorful, swishy things into my shopping bag. I graciously took them but would never put them—not black enough—on my body, I thought. Maybe, when hell freezes over.

I look at the High Priestess card again. Hey, maybe, I can start doing Tarot readings for some extra buckolas.

Pressing the card to my heart, I slip off to sleep and dream of Malala and Emma and the strength, beauty, and magic they hold for all us women.

When I wake up, I'm back. I'm here to hold that strength, beauty, and magic, too. No matter how hard this can be at times, I'm in it for the long haul, in it to win it. Game on.

Especially with Mom.

A couple of days later, after a bunch more "especially with Mom" moments came along, Gram gazes out the kitchen window and watches Mom gardening.

"Something happened to her at some point," she sighs. "I think it was late in nursing school or right when she started working. She completely changed—she withdrew, went full-monty Catholic. Okay, that's a bad use of an adjective if ever there was one."

"Really bad!" I laugh.

"I didn't see her very often during those years, since my van and I were crisscrossing the country. But when I'd swing back through to see her—which didn't exactly thrill her, of course—I would probe, as gently as I could. Nothing. Ever."

"Holy fuck!" That was my super chill response to Mom pulling her usual bullshit the next day. Gram's words from yesterday still float through my head—about something happening after my mom's college years or so.

"Language!"

"Mom, what in creation happened to you to make you all cray-cray like this?"

Chapter 11

Alice

"I had an abortion!"

Only the sound of that loud fridge fills the room for about five minutes while they sit, stunned, with that information, and I beat myself up, over and over and over, for opening my big, fat mouth. Where in the world did that brilliant idea to divulge the deepest pain of my soul come from? It just popped out.

My head spins yet again. Why would I tell these two particular individuals—who enjoy beating up on me—about the most painful event in my life? Why would I open myself up like that? I can't trust them with this information. But they might be wondering why I took that event so hard, for all I know. Oh! That makes me want to scream. Okay, maybe they're not thinking that.

After those five minutes, I start talking. And talking. And talking.

If I could have conjured up the image of the perfect man for me, it would've been him. What with his banking job and BMW, he was a model of solidity and sanity after all those years of crazy.

Shortly after graduation from nursing school, I was still trying to figure my way around the San Francisco ER I found myself working in. One night, there he was, clean-cut and still in his suit, with some strange stomach ailment. As I hooked him up to the IV to handle his severe dehydration, I noticed he wore a cross. Under normal circumstances, it would've been tucked under his shirt, but in this less-than-normal-circumstance, it was lying on his neck. I looked up from the cross and into his big, blue eyes and fell in love.

It was the early nineties. Grunge rock was making its move on society, as were designer drugs. Us? We went to church.

A nurse and a banker. We had two of the most dependable occupations there are. He was financially responsible, as was I. He was slow and careful, as was I. He was cautious and circumspect, as was I. What a pleasure!

My first time. How could I have gone all the way through college without having done that? I didn't want to. For one thing, I'd started my religious journey. For another, I never met anyone remotely appealing enough for me to consider experiencing that major life event with. I wanted to get as far away from a fling in the mud at a hippie music concert as I could possibly get. Anyway, I find it so strange that both my mom's and my first times resulted in a baby...or what could've and should've been a baby, in my case.

So much for all that religious and pro-life ideology he espoused. He wouldn't stay with me if I didn't end the pregnancy. Oh, would I rather have had the baby than even that beyond-perfect boyfriend, but the call of the stability he had was just too enticing. Completely abandoning myself and slaughtering my spirit, I had that precious life destroyed. How could a lifetime of so much subsequent pain come from a moment of so much love, or what I thought was love? Silly, stupid me.

Of course, he didn't stay with me anyway. Young (or fairly young) love rarely lasts, especially when something as traumatic as that happens.

Oh, those endless tears I shed for my sweet angel, my baby—never for him, the lout. How could I have ever made that choice? Every single second of every single day delivered ever new pain to my heart, for years. Much to my surprise, in all that time, no one ever asked me why my eyes were so red.

One day, Jesus appeared to me. Sure, I'd been attending Catholic and other churches for a while by then, but I hadn't had any visions. I don't want to sound like my mother, but that's what it was—a vision. I crawled into His arms and let Him embrace me, with all my faults and foibles. The love that emanated from Him was a healing balm to my broken soul. The grace that came over me when I took His love into my heart was beyond words. I'd never known a love like that in my life, and I doubt I will ever again. There's no human counterpart to Divine love.

"You certainly have a thing for bankers," James gently joshes after I finally stop talking. When neither Mother nor I respond to that, he mutters, "Sorry. Bad timing."

"I'm so sorry, darling." Mother takes my hand,

"Me, too, Mom." James holds my other hand.

"But, just one thing: your soul never breaks."

I don't reply to Mother's words. We're all quiet again for a few minutes, lost in our thoughts.

Then, I turn to James. "Yes, I guess he was like your father in many ways, what I was looking for: stable, circumspect, deliberate, a Catholic. My yearning for those things didn't go away."

"One thing, though," Mother says after another moment of silence. "Not that I have anything against Jesus, but Divine love has so many names and faces. Buddha. Krishna. Kwan Yin. Life. Universe."

"Mine was Jesus," I state. "It might seem hypocritical, but that's why I'm so pro-life, because I know how it feels to terminate a life. And it's not right to just make that decision on behalf of another soul, just kill a human being."

Mother wipes away a tear. "But life is eternal. That being will come back another way. Maybe they just came in to teach you compassion."

"This is a human being we're talking about. It's not like it's a cockroach in there."

"Technically, even killing a cockroach is bad karma."

"Then, how can you be for the killing of a child?" I ask my chimerical mother.

"I'm not. I'm for safe abortions for women who *will* go that route no matter what the law says, so you might as well have other laws in place to keep them safe and not dying from botched back-alley abortions or self-inflicted wounds. As you can well see, I didn't have an abortion."

Crickets. The silence seems to last forever.

"Why didn't you?" I finally ask.

"I really, really wanted you. Plus, it never crossed my mind, after watching a close friend die from a hatchet job."

More silence. Then, "Well, this room would be mostly empty if you had," James notes.

"You two would've figured out a way to get here."

More crickets come after that comment of Mother's.

"Do you understand why I'm distraught over the killing of unborn children?" I finally ask.

"Yes," Mother answers. "Do you understand my concern over the women who would resort to butcher-like methods if abortion were not legal?"

"There are alternatives." Then, I respond to something else that's long been weighing on my heart. "In my mind, the pro-abortion people honestly don't believe it's a baby, a human being, yet. So, they think they're killing something else. Well, they're in denial. I killed a baby, and I'm going to have to pay for that for the rest of my life."

"Karma can be worked out." I glance at Mother sideways, but she carries on. "Or penance or forgiveness or being let off the hook or whatever you want to call it. The release comes with intention."

James joins in. "The moment you decide it should be released, with a truly atoning heart, which you have, it'll be released."

Mother and I look at him in amazement.

"Is this why you became a maternity nurse?" James asks. "So, you can hug your baby all day?"

I'm sure the tear slipping down my face answers him.

"Hey, Mom, lemme take you out for dinner."

"Oh, you don't have to do that." Really. You don't.

"I want to. Chinese sound good?"

As long as it's in China. Oh, can't we wait a couple years until this outrageous whatever-you're-in passes?

I'm a horrible mother.

And it's not uneventful. Nothing with James ever is these days. A long line snakes around the restaurant, since some recent review made it the biggest thing since the advent of potstickers. And, of course, we just *have* to come to this particular restaurant.

The older man (older than me—now that's old!) in line ahead of us keeps turning around and looking at us. His stupefied expression announces he's not quite sure what he's seeing, what with this six-foot-two person with that large Adam's apple…in a black dress and long, loose blonde curls. "Beach waves" I think is what James calls them. I'd find them quite beautiful…on someone else.

Finally, the man isn't subtle anymore. He's outright staring.

"Why don't you pull your codependent, non-boundary-oriented tentacles off of us and back into you where they belong?" James's super friendly, inquiring tone does not match his words at all. The man turns around and stays turned around.

As I try to suppress my sheer mortification, something new seems to want to make an appearance in that bottomless pit of endless emotions in there. Pride? Nah. Couldn't be. Not of him. Maybe, in bygone days of another gender or so ago. Certainly not today.

And then, it comes from the other direction, literally. Of course—of *course*—another one of those alpha moms, this time from James's kindergarten days, has to be there standing in the line behind us.

"Alice?" she singsongs. "Is that you?"

No. Alice doesn't live here anymore. (So sorry—had to.) "Yes. Jane, how great to see you." Ever hear that computer answer how often humans lie? It's more than even we generally honest ones want to admit.

Jane looks waaaaaaay up, as she's quite short next to my once-upon-a-son. "This must be…"

"Jaye," James says, holding out his giant paw with genuine genteelness for her to shake. She looks like she's about to faint from surprise.

Yeah, well, imagine having this surprise walking around your house.

"Jaye, how nice to see you. Look at you, all grown up."

She looks over at me and does that thing. That thing. Yes, that very thing. The look in her eyes says, "Have you thought of locking him up?"

Hey, that's my child you're talking about! You…you…you…well, it rhymes with witch, and I'm too polite to say it even if just in my head. Witch…well, funny, a witch is what my child happens to be, too, sometimes these days. Haha! My head is spinning.

"You're *such* a good mom!" she whispers to me.

Ack. She's far from the first other mother to do that to me, arm-clutching thing and all. My arm still stings from her tight grip.

$$\bigcirc$$

Oh! My hand flailing wakes me up. Again. I roll over and try to fall back to sleep before my thoughts divebomb me. Too late.

They all say it the same way. "You're *such* a good mom."

Yes, indeed, when I started appearing in public with James-as-Jaye, people who knew him as James would take me aside and pat (or clutch) me on my arm, or even take both my hands, and say to me, "You're *such* a good mom! You're so supportive." Meanwhile, their eyes are saying, "How can you possibly live with this?" Or, "Why are you humoring him?" Or, "Haul him off to a doctor!" Or, "Thank God, *I* don't have to deal with this. Let those statistics I scroll past include you and not me!"

Or I could be making all that up. Everyone has secrets behind the closed front door and curtained windows. All of us. And if they don't kill us, those secrets and heartaches can turn us into phenomenal people. Or mental cases. I'm raising my hand for that second one.

James doesn't want to be labeled anything but a trans woman. Actually, counting my (few) blessings here, he's relatively easy, just wanting that label, the feminine pronouns, and the name Jaye. His friends seem to shift all the time. Well, not the creature so much. (Yes, I know the creature's name is Vision, but said person treats me like I'm less than dirt, so this moniker at least makes me smile on the inside so I can better tolerate said person. A bit. I never said I was a saint.)

But some of his other friends who come and go seem to, well, come and go with the pronouns, too. So, as I mentioned earlier, I quickly learned it's all about the name, the pronoun, and the label. Except when it isn't. And when isn't it? I don't know, but they'll tell you. They're not shy about it. Heaven forbid, I should ever get a pronoun or label wrong when yesterday they were something else entirely. Sometimes, I need an operations management flowchart.

"Please don't call me tone deaf," I want to say to him (and to Mother). Please just call me a confused woman. A distressed mother (and daughter). Human.

Oh, don't mind me as I fall apart at the seams here. I'm trying to stitch them back together as fast as I can, but they're ripping too quickly for me to keep up. Maybe, I should just let 'em rip.

I can't. See, there's this high-level job to go to, a beautiful home and yard to keep up, a floundering life to live. Nice idea, though.

A few days later, I bring up the abortion again. "You know what really does me in? That line from the song about ever really loving a woman, when he talks about being able to look in her eyes and see his unborn children. Whenever I hear that, I actually have to pull the car over, as that's the only place I ever hear it. I've stopped listening to the love-song channel for that reason alone. And why in the world do they have to use the word *abort* when you're trying to close out of something computer related that's gotten stuck or something. Can't they just use *end* or *escape*?"

Mother nods. "I understand."

Then, and I have no idea where this has come from, "You're more me than you want to admit, you know." She looks horrified.

James jumps all over that. "I couldn't be more different from you if I was born on Mars. But you and Gram *are* more alike than you realize."

"And you're more me than you want to admit," Mother says to me. I'm sure I look just as horrified as she just did.

"And you're also more me than you want to admit," I say to James. Now, it's his turn to look horrified.

"If that's true, just kill me now, and let me start over again," James says. "Mom, I'm just kidding," he shouts as I burst into tears.

But what I'm really crying over is this ultimate betrayal, to and by myself, and even more to this being I would've loved, loved, loved to have known, raised, spent a life with.

And then, there are the tears of relief from finally talking about it. I had never said a word about it to anyone, in all these years.

Chapter 12

Starr

"You hush about that," I say to Jaye as Alice's tears subside. "Besides, you can't short-circuit your soul's journey. If you did that—left this life before getting your lesson, that is—you'd just have to come back to get the lesson all over again."

"What lesson is that?" the two women ask me in unison.

"Whatever lesson you decided to work on when you chose to incarnate. And you two obviously chose each other as teachers."

They look at each other, at first, with curiosity, given what I'd said. Then, it turns to that horrified look again. Then, all three of us burst into a fit of giggles.

Oh, Life, you wild, wondrous, topsy-turvy, magnificent, perplexing, de-light-filled, flabbergasting, sumptuous thing, you.

It's pretty peaceful for, oh, a day or two. Then, they're back to bickering in the kitchen…and on the stairs…and in the hallway.

"I can't do my meditating with all this noise!" I holler from the top of the staircase.

"Isn't the point of meditation to be at peace with whatever's going on wherever you're at?"

Well, Alice has me there. And then, they're bickering again. I fall against the wall.

"Mother!"

"Gram! You okay?"

"Mother, are you having another stroke?"

"No. But a stroke would be easier to handle than you two. And I'm not even joking."

"Yuck! What is that smell?" Alice surveys the kitchen, trying to find the offender. I look down when she glances in my direction. "Why are you suddenly looking so guilty?"

"That smell is from the composting container."

"Composting container? What compost?"

"I started a compost pile, and I usually remember to take the container outside before it gets this pungent. I never meant for you to find out. The pile's behind the garage. You never go there. I might get some worms, too."

"Worms!" Her word isn't a question—it's revulsion.

"How in creation can you be a gardener and not appreciate worms? Or compost?"

"I appreciate the flowers. Not the creepy crawly and smelly things."

"Oh, well, I started a vegetable garden."

"A vegetable garden!" She expresses almost as much revulsion at that idea as she had at the worms.

She follows me out to a part of the property she never has reason to visit as it's basically just bare dirt—or was, before I came along. This barren, unattended behind-the-garage district is a little hard to get to and no one can see it from the street or house anyway. I'd set up several compost bins, and I'd ordered my worms, who (not *that* or *which*, since worms are people, too) are on their way. I'd also started the veggie garden.

"That's squash over there, tomatoes over there…"

"Mother!"

"What? It's great exercise, plus it keeps me out of trouble and out of your hair."

"Just how long are you planning on staying here?"

I shrug. "I can leave tomorrow if you want."

"Oh, I don't know if you're fully recovered yet, I mean, recovered enough to hit the road with your rig on your own. I was just wondering about the future. Ohhhhhhhhhh, whatever!" She spins around and hurries back to the house.

My beautiful, beloved worms—oh, they're so dear!—arrive later that day. Luckily, Alice has already left for some errand or other, so I can welcome them without her less-than-complimentary commentary.

I could go back and live in Arissa, my RV, while tooling around, I suppose. She doesn't like being just parked by the garage. She told me so. My Social Security check keeps me fed and the remnants of Tim's money keeps Arissa gassed and housed in the odd RV park. Plus, I still have mystery money show up from time to time in my post-office box, just like the travel money did.

Why, just last week there was a check from a guy who worked for

George Lucas. I actually gave him the idea for one of those movies that made it really big.

Oh, Lord love a duck! I haven't even mentioned Tim yet.

Isn't that a great phrase? I picked it up from Tim, an English poet who was the one main love of my life. Every now and then, he'd shout out this decidedly British phrase with a fake Cockney accent, because he knew it'd make me laugh.

He came along just as Alice headed off to college and my nanny gig ended. Meeting him was perfect timing. I got to move in with him instead of having to look for a place on my own.

He lived in a ramshackle cottage in an old hippie surfer town on the Northern California coast. He had a lawn-mower motor in the middle of the dining table. I didn't want to push anything on him, so I didn't say anything for a couple of months until I could no longer eat my beautiful (hippie-store-bought) food with this machine as a centerpiece.

"Hon, can we move this motor to the shed?"

"Sure, Love!"

Whyever did I wait so long? Well, mostly because he was a moody poet. He wasn't abusive—I would've lived in the streets rather than put up with that. Many a day he'd wake up and, no matter what the weather was, say, "Oh, what a beautiful day!" But then, he also had many a personal thunderstorm roll in, and I just gave him his space. When the thunderstorms rolled out, he'd assure me it was all just part of his creative process.

He died in a car accident a few years later. I thought I'd die, too.

In those initial, overwhelming moments of "how in the world am I going to deal with the rest of my life?" a friend said something so simple. "First, you make a meal."

It breaks that whole lonely rest-of-life vista down to the initial most important thing—me, in this body that needs my attention. I've remembered her words in every heartbreaking moment that's come along since. I'm not the most food-oriented person. I can live on nuts and smoothies for days. But making a wonderful soup or hearty stew is a good place to start the journey back to today, to start the rest of this life.

Tim left his cottage to me, so I lived there for a couple of years. I didn't even know he had a will—his lawyer told me. He must've known he was going to check out sooner than later.

I took to taking long walks on the beach during that time. I watched sunsets from the cliffs. I heard music from the clouds and wisdom from the Earth. My father died, and I discovered that he and my mom left all their money to Alice. I think I saw a spaceship or two.

After a while, I got the traveling itch and sold the place. (STUpid! That tiny cottage and land is worth millions now. I should've just rented it out.) That's when I bought the van.

To be honest, I *thought* Tim was the love of my life. And he was, for that time of my life. But before and after, there was always this lingering presence. Hmmmmmmmm.

I call him Ted, because that's an easy, comfortable name for an easy, comfortable guy. Plus, he was definitely in the Teddy Bear category—those big brown eyes, brown curls, all cuddly, so big and built.

He just appeared, it seems, as I look back now. We just disappeared into the tent, it still seems. He then just disappeared into this thing called life. No "seems" about that.

The next thing I remember is walking down the road with my friend in search of her car. I looked all around for him, just like I still do, in a way.

He was a loss, too. So, by middle age, I lost my brother, my mother and father, Tim, so many friends from drugs and Viet Nam, and this mysterious Ted. Can you lose someone you've never really known?

Oh, regarding that tidbit about my parents leaving all their money to Alice? I talked to them about that (yes, after they died), and they told me they couldn't trust me with a dime. Thanks, Mother and Dad. But I'm sure—or, at least, I hope—they figured that if I ever needed anything, Alice would certainly help me. I didn't know if that was really true until the stroke, but she has been taking wonderful care of me. For her, anyway.

If only she'd…well… She's on her path, I suppose.

While I'm still on the topic of men—or, at least, not too far from it—no, I definitely haven't had the best of luck with men in my life. I guess I have my reasons.

When I was growing up, my father was so distant, and my brother was so…dead. Oh, my beautiful brother. Adam didn't want to go to college, and he ended up fighting that useless, nonsensical war. He left when I was fourteen and, other than one quick visit, never came home again. My fun, laughing, loving, big brother was gone. Gone! How could that be? How could that even be in the same universe as fair? He'd been so alive.

He'd sent us a postcard from an R&R trip to Phuket, Thailand. That was the last we heard from him before…nothing.

Nothing until two uniformed young men showed up on our front porch and rang the blasted doorbell. My mother answered the door and burst into tears as soon as she saw them standing there. The cold December wind whipped through the house.

"Ma'am," I overheard one start to say, "we have an important message to deliver from the secretary of the Army. The secretary has asked us to express his deep regret."

Her sobs escalated to screams. That was the last time I heard her cry. What did she do—tuck all of her emotions away? Completely put them on ice? Well, yes.

The flag-draped coffin was transported from the Air Force base to the military cemetery. I wanted to tear open the casket and shout, "See? It's not him. My brother is on a beach in Thailand."

Yo, hey, LBJ
You know you killed my brother today?

Whenever I think of him, I picture him sitting on that beautiful, luscious beach on his postcard. I still talk to him here and there. Sometimes, I think he answers.

I dated a lot, but there wasn't anyone too profound, other than my poet. I'm surprised I let him in to my heart so deeply, after the searing pain of losing my brother. Between each dating jaunt, I'd think about Ted. I'm not much for "if only's," but that's one I certainly do have.

One night, I said to Alice, "Jaye could do the DNA thing, you know, and find out who her grandfather is and if he's still around."

"Is James thinking of doing that?"

"I have no idea."

"Oh, sure. What if he's an ageing hippie like you, and I end up having to support you both?"

I ignore that. "It's Jaye."

"What?"

"Your daughter's name is Jaye." I let out a long sigh of exasperation. "How would you have liked it if I still called you Ambrosia after you told me you wanted to be called Alice? Of all things—Alice! The name I threw in the garbage!"

"You think my name is garbage?"

"Of course not. Just wasn't me. How interesting all three of us changed our names in order to live as our truer selves."

"Mother!"

Wish I could throw that name in the garbage. But at least she calls me something.

Ah, Alice, Alice, Alice. She's at a major turning point, whether she knows it or not. Something's cracking in her foundation, so something's gotta give sometime.

Oh, life. What a mystery you are. So up, so down, so far in, so far out, so this, so that, so back, so forth. So boomeranging. So bazoomeranging. Soooooooooo....

Back in the house with the bickering. I breathe in love. Breathe out light. Breathe in light. Breathe out love. Repeat, repeat, repeat, repeat the repeating.

The bickering eases. Maybe, I'll stay a while longer. And definitely not just for my worms.

Chapter 13

Jaye

What happened? It's actually been okay around here for a little while. Maybe even entertaining.

"Did you know there's a blob that has no brain, but it does have seven hundred and twenty sexes?" I ask one morning. Noon thirty, really.

"Jumpin' Jupiter!" Gram giggles. "I always thought it was seven hundred and twenty-one. What happened to that other one?"

Mom crosses her arms. "Where in the world did you ever hear that?"

"Reuters." Oh, the look on their faces! "I don't always just get my news from Snapchat and Instagram, you know."

"That's a relief." Mom bites into her non-lunch.

"Anyway, away from your glyphosate goodies and back to the blob. It can find its way out of a maze. If you cut it in half, it'll heal in two minutes."

"I'm more impressed you're reading that much news than I am with the blob," Gram says. "And I'm *very* impressed with the blob!"

Mom uncrosses and then crosses her arms again. "Seven hundred and twenty sexes?"

"Makes my friends and me look pretty tame now, doesn't it?"

She stands up to get another cup of coffee. "Not so much." I guess my face fell a bit because she returns to the table, cups my chin, lifts my head, and looks into my eyes. "And that's okay."

Wow.

○

A few days later, I take off to hang out with Vision and some of our homies. We stop at a convenience store where a bunch of old timers—age fifty, sixty, or so—in the car next to us do a double take. And then, a triple take. And then...

"Take a picture—it lasts longer," I tell them. "Never seen a woman before?" I should grab one of their phones and snap a pic, but I don't need the police being called or anything like that.

They don't respond. But they also don't stop staring. I have thick, black eyeliner around my eyes and going off to my temples, Egyptian style. Vision had braided my ever-getting-longer locks again. Vision's hair is its usual curly cluster f, and they're wearing all black, like I am, complete with black chains and a black choker. They also have a drop of blood near their mouth, near their lip ring.

Vision flashes the old folks their tongue piercing. "It's really good during oral sex."

The oldies turn white(r). Hey, which part of this scenario do you have the problem with? The face hardware? The clothes? The color? The attitude? The inability to guess what sexual organs lie under these clothes? Meanwhile, are they really all in tennis gear?

A response, finally! "You're young for a really short time, you know," one of the women says to us.

Oohhhhkaaaay. Get a life, old ones. You obviously were young for a very short time and got way old, way too soon, a very long time ago.

Vision calls out to the woman, who happens to be wearing a very, very—did I mention *very*?—bright fuchsia top. "That deserves a ticket for loud!"

I poke them. "Hey, my grandmother would love that color."

"Of course, she would." Vision pokes me back. "But not everyone has a license to wear it like she does."

Okay, I take that back, about the entertaining times at home. Oh well. It was good while it lasted.

I slice myself a bit, along with my tomato and yell, "Jesus!"

"Don't say that!" Mom shouts.

"I thought you liked the guy!"

OMG, you would've thought WWIII started. She starts railing about the Lord, and I just want to throw up.

"Oh, sure," I finally scream. "Let's just keep going with those old, desert religions that were totally based on lack—because it's fucking hard to live in a desert, you know—and keeping women submissive. They'd kill each other over water. They'd sacrifice their children to appease angry gods." I'm on a roll and hardly stop to breathe. "And then throw on some of that biblical nonsense about not being as good as a man or having to follow your husband's lead or that basic bullshit.

Heaven forbid, you should ever let a woman be president, because, if you did, you might have to admit you were wrong about keeping women down all along and, hell no, you can't ever admit you were wrong. That would just be so…wrong!"

Mom bursts into tears and rushes out of the kitchen. Gram and I sit in silence for a bit.

"I'm not wrong," I finally announce to her.

"No. Though perhaps you could work on your delivery a bit."

But then, Gram just has to start in on me, too. After floating into my room and alighting on the bed, she starts talking once, twice, three times, until I finally semi-shout, "Out with it!"

"What's with all this dark stuff you wear and keep around you?"

"Just stuff I like."

Out of the ethers, where she usually hangs out, she pulls, "I have spirit guides, you know."

"No surprise there," I laugh. "And just what do your spirit guides say?"

"Your sincerity is overwhelming."

"No, seriously. What do they say?"

"They don't really give me answers. They just sit me down in their circle of energy and raise me up to their vibration of peace."

I start belting out "Good Vibrations" by the Beach Boys, which I only know from, yes, Gram.

Ignoring me, she continues. "At that vibration everything is answered. All is well. All is unfolding as it should. Everything I want will be here in its divine right time, or it isn't mine to have."

The kettle on the stove whistles. I follow her downstairs to the kitchen where she pours her cup of tea.

"And who decides that what you want isn't yours to have?"

She stares out the window as the silver steam from her tea swirls in front of her face. "Ultimately, I do," she answers. "You do. Your mom does. We all do."

Gram knows more than anyone I've ever met. Except when she doesn't. But she usually does.

○

Oh, but that daughter of hers. Mom starts in on me one day when

I'm just sitting at the table doing nothing else but being me. That can really get to her. She's also been talking about church, and I'm sure I'm totally fucking up as the receptive audience she wants.

She sighs. "For someone who's into live and let live, you're not very into live and let live."

I'm not sure if I heard what I think I heard. "Say what?"

"For someone who wants those around you to be very live and let live about you, you're not very live and let live about us. And you should talk!"

"I'm a do and let dudette." Mom doesn't think that's anywhere near as funny as I do. In fact, she grimaces. Are we back there again? "Mom, being trans is, like, just another experience. Just another experience. Isn't that what we all came here for?"

Gram chuckles. "It's the story planet. Once upon a planet, or once upon a universe, or two, or eight trillion. Oh, what a tangled Indra's net we weave."

Mom ignores her, but not me. "Aren't you sabotaging yourself?"

Gram speaks up again. "Maybe, those times of so-called 'self-sabotage' weren't that at all, but the soul pointing us to a higher path. Maybe, they were calls from our soul to go in a different direction."

"There's a lot of that going around." I turn back to Mom. "I'm done flububbering. Done! Don't ask me to be less than who I am!" I leave before she can say anything else.

Flububbering? I like it. Yes, as I just said, I am my grandmother's granddaughter, after all. And proud of it.

Who should I bump into at Whole Foods but Sarah and her mom. Yes, that Sarah—my old girlfriend. I don't know which is worse, Sarah's dismay or her mom's disapproval. Actually, it's way more than your regular disapproval. How about disparagement? Reproach? Out-and-out censure? Hey, I can pull out some big words—bigger than usual, that is, even for me, sometimes.

Sarah's mom wraps her arm around her daughter's shoulder, part comfort, part shield. She'd be looking down her nose at me if I weren't so much taller.

"Nice to see you, Ja…" She stops herself, unsure of how to continue that thought. Oh, it's just the all-important name.

"Jaye."

"Nice to see you." But, even though she now knows my name, she doesn't use it. She shepherds Sarah out of the store without waiting for a reply.

Later that night, I lose it—completely lose it. WTF, life? What the fucking fuck? I don't know why I was born into a body I didn't fit in. I don't know why if, as some people say, our higher selves don't even have a gender, it's so important to me down here in my lower self.

I ugly cry into my pillow so Mom and Gram won't hear me. Huge hacking, racking sobs shake my whole body from head to toe.

Fuck this shit. It hurts so much. It hurts so fucking much. I put up a good front most of the time, especially around Mom, but it hurts so fucking much. Quite a bit. Have I mentioned it hurts so fucking much? Quite a bit? My heart aches some days. It doesn't hit me *this* hard very often, though, but when it does, I just let it go. My whole body appreciates it when I do. Sometimes, I think a good cry is our body's best way of coping with life on Earth. I didn't think that—never even occurred to me—before I was Jaye.

Mom. Even with all her toils and troubles, well… at least, she tries. Her version of trying, anyway. I'm so pissed at her for not just shifting into the trans gear, but at least she's pushing in the clutch and has her hand on the shift stick. (I tried driving one of those once, so I know how hard it is.) That's a lot more than I can say for other people. Thank you, Sarah's mom, and so many parents and relatives of so many of my trans friends. Not.

Other days, when my heart isn't aching from the confusion and the ostracism, I can deal. Here's something wild. I've heard even some trans buds talk about their own ostracism—of themselves. At least, I don't have that. This…other person…even if she was simmering under the surface…has been with me my whole life, whispering to me and patiently waiting. It was just a matter of time.

I fall asleep so grateful that the time finally came for me. No matter what assholes from yesteryear I run into out there in the world, I'm so happy I can finally be…me. Jaye.

I finally love my life. Mostly. Way more than before, anyway.

Mom's landscapers chat as they work on the yard. I remember enough from my high school Spanish class to know what they're talking about—the meaning of life! I go out to join right in with them.

Before I can even brush the dust off my Spanish, Mom comes charging out. Is she trying to protect them from the likes of me? Oh, Mom, they can handle me.

A spider crawls onto my flip flop. I scream and scream and flip that flop right onto the roof. Two men and a mom all look at me. If I could read their thoughts, they'd probably be something like, "Why is this big, tough guy dressed up as a girl screaming at a spider?" Okay, that's probably just Mom.

I disappear into the house. I can get my flip flop later.

From my window, I watch Mom chat with the guys about the work she wants done. She's actually really good at speaking Spanish. Sure wish she could speak Mom-of-trans just as well.

But she's starting to have her moments, I suppose. I'll give her that.

The EMTs shut the door to the ambulance and tear out of the driveway. We follow close behind, not speaking a word. But a lot is being said.

Please, please, please, please, please, my mind races.

Chapter 14

Alice

There it all is, going along just fine and…bang! Suddenly it just doesn't stop, from either direction. Over nothing.

Such as…minding my own business, munching an apple when James asks, "Is that organic?"

I want to throw the fruit at him. "I'd think you'd be happy I'm eating something healthy!"

"Pesticides don't make for healthy apples. Might as well eat a Twinkie."

And then, later, when I eat three cookies in a row, Mother says, "You know, when I eat a commercial cookie or piece of chocolate, I want more, more, more. That kind of food creates a vicious cycle, where it just wants more of itself. But one piece of organic dark chocolate does it."

"Grrrrrrr."

"Darling," Mother continues, "why don't you go to the gym? Or maybe just start taking walks around your sweet neighborhood. You'll feel healthier, sleep better, eat less."

"Is that a crack about my weight?"

"If the crack fits…." James says.

Trounced. Trammeled. Trummeled. Is trummeled a word? It should be. That's how I feel around here. And it's myyyyyyy home!

Oh, dear Lord, please give me strength. Now. This very minute. Please.

It bothers me all the more because I know they're right. Why, if it's my body, the only one I'll ever have, don't I take better care of it? I do take beautiful care of my outsides—my hair, skin, clothes (at least, for church), home, garden. These two don't even know how many cookies I actually do eat because I don't bring most of them into the house. Yes, emotional eating. No, not proud of it.

On the rare occasion I do work out, I love it—at least, right afterwards. The screaming of my body for the next few days, because it isn't used to such activities, isn't so much fun. But that'd go away if I worked out more.

Oh, just let me have my cookies. I'm going through a lot.

Did opening up about something painful, being so exposed, diffuse the tension? The house was peaceful—for an hour, okay, maybe it was a week, okay, maybe longer—until they started in on my eating yet again. After that, if anything, the mood around here has been getting worse.

There are crazy people living in this house. This is, well, crazy-making.

"Oh, Mother. When will this all get easier?" A few mornings later, I don't ask what I *really* want to ask, "When will this all go away?" We're at...well, I don't even have to say where we're at.

"This very moment. If you decide so, that is."

"If you were a soothsayer, what would you say?"

"Sooth!"

That sends me into a laughing spasm. "That was really quite funny." Sigh. Again. "Oh, Mother." Again. I sure seem to say that a lot. "Your life seems to be one long, fun carnival ride."

"Yours can, too."

"Oh, shut up," I don't say to her.

"What do you love about her other than that she's your own flesh and blood?"

"He's clever, intelligent, funny, playful, his own person. Why are you asking me this? I could go on all day about what I love about him."

"Her."

"Oh, shut up," I don't say to her, yet again.

The kitchen smells heavenly from the bread Mother's baking. I do appreciate the hominess—hey, better late than never—but not her endless, unwelcome, extra-terrestrial verbiage. Well, I suppose I do ask her a lot of questions. I should know better, as her answers are not the ones I want to hear.

Mother pulls the bread out of the oven. She breaks off a chunk and hands it to me smeared with... "Pasture-raised butter," she says, "and the bread is gluten-free."

Mother bites into a chunk of bread, raised on a pasture. Oh, sorry—

no, that's just the butter. What?

James shwooshes through the kitchen, talking into his phone. "Okay, sure, let's set up a sesh." He's out the door.

Mother looks at me. "Sesh?"

"It's a word in the dictionary. Look it up." Her jaw drops a bit at my tone, which is abrasive and laden with attitude, even for me. I chuckle. "That's what I received the other day when I asked the same thing. No offense intended. In fact, I take it back. *Session* is what it is."

"What are these seshes?"

"Tarot-card readings. Of course. Don't you know?" She looks at me. "That was the answer I got when I asked that question, too."

Tarot-card readings. Oh, dear Lord. The sin of the occult. Hail Mary, full of grace. Soooooooooo…noooooooooo…it's not even just the trans thing. There's this whole…um…vampire thing still going on, too, that's not fading away as a phase either. The whole goth thing is all about shocking people. Can't they get a more productive hobby? If they have to be in the shocking game, can't they pleasantly shock us by discovering the cure for cancer or something like that?

I once passed a young man in the hospital who had enormous gauges in his ears. I did everything I could to keep from doing a double take, but I couldn't help myself. Oh, look what a strong, independent thinker you are, I wanted to cluck at him. Making certain that people look at you but being mad at everyone who does. Why are you using such a shock-and-awe attention-getting thing, then being upset with the attention you're getting?

James is saying to me, subtly and not so subtly, "Love me as I am. That's all I want. Now and ever."

Okay, fine. I can do that. But, at the same time, he's trying to shock me—and anyone who sees him—as much as possible with all the goth stuff. So, how in the world am I supposed to be completely accepting and totally shocked at the same time? I just hope he feels the love that's underneath all of it, because that will never die.

I'm not usually philosophical or existential, but…the thing about approaching fifty is you can see the whole gamut. Twenty-five seems like just a few breaths ago. Seventy-five seems just over that next hill. At this age, you can see both ends of your life with increased clarity. I don't want to see the end of my life with so much…disheartening information.

"I wanted grandchildren!" I, yes, sigh to Mother one day.

"Who's saying you won't have them? She might marry someone with children or adopt..."

"He would've made a great father."

"She'll probably make a great mother."

"He's a man."

"She's a woman."

"He has a penis under that miniskirt."

"She's wearing a miniskirt over that penis." Mother shakes her head. "It's what's in that gray matter of hers that truly matters—pun intended. She came to help rewrite the conversation on gender."

"Who says it needs to be rewritten?"

"She and everyone like her say that every day."

"Well, I resent having all these so-called women walking around who will never know what it's like to conceive a child and grow it inside."

Of course, he just has to walk in at that exact moment. "Hey, no TERFs."

"Huh?"

"Trans-exclusionary radical feminists. They think trans women don't count as women. I might not have the experience of being a female from birth, but I do have the experience of being a trans female since age eighteen. That's just as valid an experience, too."

"No one would ever accuse me of being a radical feminist!"

"True that. But not all women have the full-blown experience of being a woman. Like, they can't have kids or they have other things wrong. No one yells at them for not being a full woman."

I'm about to respond—with what, I don't know—but he mutters to himself. "Oh, forgot something." He spins around and heads back to his room.

Mother continues the conversation we were having before James came in. "Your job is just to love. Her."

"Him." I remember something I want to say to him and holler from the doorway, "James!"

But he's right out in the hallway, on his way back in. I nearly faint. "It's Jaye! It's not that hard. Everyone called Snoop Dogg that when he wanted to change his name back from Snoop Lion, which came after Snoop Doggy Dogg. And everyone called Dwayne Johnson The Rock when he wanted that. Respect my choice, too."

"I doubt Dwayne's mother calls him The Rock."

"Well, call me what I want. Like I said, it's not that hard. Just cut off the mmms!"

"Fine. Just don't cut off your schlong!"

Siri takes that opportunity to butt in: "I missed that. Could you please say it again?"

After a beat, where all three of us look at each other and then at the errant iPhone in Mother's hand, which had delivered that snippy comeback, we all laugh. And laugh. And laugh.

Oh, does that ever feel good. I've almost forgotten how, but it seems to be coming back to me.

○

One of my happiest happy places? The supermarket. I love the shelves stocked full with food and supplies. I even love all the rings, pings, and dings at the register. I usually go through the line with the cashier, not the self-serve, because I prefer the human contact. But this time, the cashier's chatting with the previous customer, even though she's already paid, and her bags have been loaded back into her cart. And they're chatting. And chatting. So, I start screaming. And screaming. Suddenly, the manager's holding my hand.

"Ma'am? You okay, ma'am? Should we get you an ambulance?"

"I'm fine," I insist. Then, I start crying. And crying.

He leads me to a chair near the front door and mumbles something about getting my items from the cashier. I hand him my credit card, and the next thing I know my cart of bagged groceries sits beside me.

"Can I call someone to come get you?" he asks.

"No, thanks. I'll be okay. I'm a nurse." I hiccugiggleburp at that one. Translated: I can help others, but clearly not myself so much. "I'll be fine, really."

Fine? Will I ever be fine again? I slump in the car for about an hour after that. Okay, maybe I didn't have to scream. But how could the cashier be engaging in ongoing inane babble when my life has been upended? My son. My mother. My house. My life.

I ask Mother about her timetable for leaving when she's gotten on my last nerve, but that's just...I don't know. Frustration? I have no idea why her parents didn't leave her a dime. I've tried to give her money over the years, but she turns it down. Perhaps, I could set her up in a senior-living situation somewhere. Or, maybe, I could at least get her RV set up in a stable place for a while, until she grows tired of living that way.

I drive my groceries home—thankfully, no one was in the house to ask me about my state of mind—and then, I drive to the Point Reyes lighthouse. I love lighthouses, and this one's a beauty. I also love seeing the whales making their way up or down the coast, depending on the time of year and if they're heading for warmer or cooler waters.

After loving on the lighthouse, I wander through the little town of Point Reyes Station and come across a kooky clothes shop.

When the saleswoman asks me something, I want to say, "What? I can't hear you. Your clothing is too loud!" Mother would love it all. So, I buy her a jacket.

Then, I wander across the street to a little thrift store and buy a lacey black wrap for my former superjock son—quite a perfect find, if I say so myself. I also purchase a simple dress for me to wear to church and, oh, maybe on a date.

A date. Would I ever date again? Truthfully, I don't miss it. My life is still quite complicated, and I certainly don't need any more complications. I just want to keep it simple for right now. God. Work. Family. Oh, this funky family that's just shown back up in my life. As I climb into the car for the drive home, my lips start moving in a silent prayer to Jesus to help me. I could sure use another vision of/with him right about now.

Since I'm still in no hurry, I meander along some back roads. There's a sweet, tiny church in the sweet, tiny town of Nicasio—St. Mary's, almost a hundred and fifty years old. I pull up in front of her. It's dusk, but I can still see the steeple and the steps going up to the one-room church. Oh, it's such a beautiful building, beloved by filmmakers and photographers from around the globe.

As I gaze at the little church, I think there's really no difference between having Jesus as your savior and believing in the whole panoply of gods and goddesses of the Hindu religion. Or bending to touch your forehead to the ground five times a day in prayer. Or having spirit guides and burning sage to clear away bad vibes. Or… all of these myriad, multitudes of divergent beliefs that we have can meet—somewhere.

Rumi wrote, "Out beyond the ideas of wrongdoing and right doing, there is a field. I'll meet you there."

Truthfully, though, I'm sometimes still so triggered by James just walking into the room. I don't want to go meet this "her" version of him in a field. I want to meet someone else—the him I used to know—in that field. I know we don't choose our children...we kind of get who we get and make the best of it. But this person is not my person. If I wasn't related to this individual, I would have nothing to do with him. I mean her. Oh, the heck with it, it's my brain and saying that still bothers me, even now. Him.

I try to imagine what she, *that* she—and I do picture her as a she—would be like now, if I hadn't ended her life. She'd be twenty-six. She'd probably be tall and beautiful, like her father. She'd probably be smart and wise like her mother. Haha! Sometimes, I think if I'd had her, I might not have had James. And lately, I think that might not have been such a bad thing.

I'm evil. I'm bad. I'm awful. The evil isn't out there, after all. It's in my heart.

Good people can think bad thoughts, can't they? Please tell me I'm not the only one. Lord, please forgive me.

Isn't it absurd? James is turning into this woman I wish I knew! But I didn't really, really, *really* start into serious wistfulness about my first pregnancy until James was turning female.

He could never be her anyway. In my mind, she's so sweet and kind and loving and...

I'm an awful mother. I'm so sorry. I'm so lost. And so sad. And so scared. The night terrors still attest to that.

With any miracle, my meltdown and then being out in all this fresh air will help me sleep tonight. I head home...

...where over the next few days I try to be nicer to my one-and-only child to atone for my evil thoughts, but it backfires.

"Oh, I love that dress," I say to him one day. "I had one like that and..."

"It's all about you, Mom. All. About. You."

"Are. You. Kidding. Me?"

"It is! You don't know there's anyone else on Earth!"

"Are you serious? It's alllllllllll about you! When it's not about you," I say, turning to Mother. "This drives me insane. It's all about the parents. It's all about the kids. My generation got the shaft. The boomers don't know there's anyone else alive, and Gen Z isn't much better.

And then, comes this on another day: "You cis people cannot control what it means to be a person, what it means to be female or male, from now on. It's not one extreme or the other anymore. It's all shades in between. It's not binary, one or the other."

"Being happy with what we were born with doesn't make us wrong!"

"Talk to the hand. In fact, talk to the back of the hand. In fact, talk to the back. I'm outta here."

And outta here he goes. I turn to my mother. "We're not allowed to have a natural reaction to something that's been a given our entire life. It's all our problem. If we ever hesitate or falter at all…"

"Of course, you can have your reaction. Just not around her."

After returning home from another shopping trip, I help Mother put her yogurt-and-granola groceries away.

"That's just plain wackadoo." Dear Lord, those words flew out of *my* mouth, not Mother's! And about nothing in particular at all. Maybe I was just speaking to the air…about my life.

Mother couldn't be happier if I'd spoken Pleiadean. "Wackadoo! Look at you using my word!"

Maybe, I did speak Pleiadean, come to think of it. "I'm just trying to speak your language. But you're wackadoo. I'm wackadon't."

We crack up at that. Even after Mother stops, I keep laughing. Too much.

"Don't mind me," I say when I can finally catch a breath. "I have to laugh, or I'll start crying."

"Oh, hog potatoes. I keep on telling you you're making this so much harder than it needs to be."

I burst into another laughing jag again. "Hog potatoes?"

"Just accept it. It's not going to go away."

"Hog potatoes!" Completely slap happy, I laugh some more…and some more…until I start crying. Not enough.

Mother wraps her arms around me.

"No more wise witticisms from the cosmic jet stream?" I ask her when the tears finally subside.

"Not right now. Just cosmic love from these arms and this heart."

I don't know how long she holds me, but it sure feels good.

So much for feeling good. As James slumps around one afternoon, I say, in an attempt to be beneficent and altruistic, "You're going through all the pain that's turning you into a phenomenal person. There's no way around it."

"You've had pain. You're not a phenomenal person."

Who is this person, who's probably acting far loopier than he'd otherwise be due to female hormones surging through his exceedingly virile male body? Where did my son go? Where is he? I want him back! Plus, what with all my studies of the hormone therapies he's probably involved in, it doesn't help that I found out that brain tumors and blood clots are just two of the many possible side effects.

He's been seeing counselors and doctors all over the place during his transition, but I don't know how reputable any of them or their protocols are. The one time I brought up my concerns about this to him was the last time I brought them up to him. He told me in no uncertain terms that it was none of my business. At all. And never would be.

"Not to you, perhaps," I say in reference to me not being phenomenal. "But I am. Ask my coworkers, patients, and their families." I pause. "What are you waiting for? In life, I mean."

"What are *you* waiting for?"

"Oh, rapture," I joke, then turn to Mother. "And you?"

"Special, divine dispensation from the Galactic Federation." After all three of us smile, she adds, "Well, you asked!"

I smile, but more to humor her than anything else. I think she was kidding. I hope so, anyway. With her, though, you never know.

I turn back to my child. "What is it that you want? With your life, I mean."

"I'm trying to play a bigger game."

"You could start by thinking bigger of yourself first."

"You didn't help me much in that regard."

I'm sure my glare could melt Antarctica. "I've apologized. And I've apologized. And I've apologized. I surrender. It's time to stop blaming me and take responsibility for your own road."

Chapter 15

Starr

Alice spins around and catches me looking at her—just...oh...looking at her. Tears spring to her eyes, and she runs from the room yet again. Having it from both sides must be hard.

Plus, this whole life-movement thing is, well, yes, wackadoo. Up, down, backwards, sideways. Three steps forward, two steps back. Two good days, three bad. A touch of acceptance in the mind followed by a full-body revolt.

Om shanti, shanti, shanti...

"Why do you have to ride her so hard?" I ask Jaye later. "She's not perfect. None of us are. But you seem to hold her in special contempt."

"She doesn't get it. And it seems like she refuses to get it."

"Give her time." When Jaye sighs, I add, "Time goes so slowly at your age. But it speeds up. For us, well, we just blinked our eyes, and you went from an infant to twenty. She'll get it, though. She has to. That's why you're in her life—to make sure she gets it."

I putter around the house, doing my laundry, doing Alice's laundry, doing this, doing that. No matter what I'm doing, though, I think about this wild and wonderful life of mine. Alice. Jaye. The way things bazoomerang and bite us in the butt. Funny how that works.

I know Alice's religion cage (did I just say that?) could be a backlash to her way-too-far-out-there childhood, because she was headed that way long before her abortion. And Jaye's betrothal to the dark could be a backlash to her way-too-far-in-there childhood.

I hear, over and over, that there is no cause and effect (sin, karma, and the like). But I don't know about that. Like Jaye said recently, we really do know what's right. And we eventually do what's right, not because it's right, but because it's the right thing to do. There's a difference. And we, ourselves, determine the effect.

I've seen so many things. And now, I see the end isn't that far away. My mother had a stroke from which she never emerged. Her health condition weighs on me sometimes, especially since I had a stroke of my own, even though mine was significantly less severe. I could be gone tomorrow.

Or, I could have maybe another twenty or even thirty years. That's a whole lot less than what's behind me, though. So, what am I going to do with the rest of my years? What's my legacy?

I know I'm leaving two amazing beings behind me. That's enough in many ways. I'm not afraid of dying; I just don't want to die unbaked, if I can help it. Oh, that crazy stroke opened up this whole onslaught of questions. Is there anything else I was supposed to do while I was here, something that'd put me in the well-baked category?

Do I want to be free to move around the world? Or do I want to stay near family? Do I want to...? So many questions. So strange for one who used to not care about answers.

○

Alice and I sit at the table. Again. And we are talking about Jaye. Again. And Alice, really. Again.

"We tend to believe in a God who reflects our level of understanding. If we believe in a punishing, vengeful God, that's where we're at. If we believe in a God of All Love, that's where we're at."

Completely missing my not-so-subtle point, Alice asks, "My church friends don't have children who've gone to the Dark Side."

"And what about the other Hitler Youths?" Okay, that was uncalled for. Or maybe it was called for. Either way, she ignores it. "She's just going to an extreme overreaction to your Jesus stuff," I continue.

Jaye walks in just then. "No, I'm not. It's the judgmentalism I object to. I wouldn't bash your religion so much if you weren't trying to bash me over the head with it so much."

"But you have it, too," I say to her. "The judgmentalism, I mean." Oh, is she not happy to hear that!

"And where did I get it from?" Jaye asks, looking at her mom.

"And where did *I* get it from?" Alice asks, looking at me.

"You're saying you got it from me?" I mean, I know I have it, too, I guess, but I didn't think it was that obvious. (Heh!)

Alice nods. "You can be just as judgmental as anyone—believing that people just *think* themselves into bad situations and can then just *think* themselves out of it."

"In many cases they do, they can," I say.

"Thinking that way can be a form of ableism."

Jaye looks at her mother in surprise. "I'm very impressed you know that term."

Alice's squirm and mouth squiggle show me she's restraining herself from making a super snippy comeback. She tones it way down. "I might know a thing or two."

I let out a long sigh. "Life requires a whole lot of this and that: surrender, right action, discernment, getting appropriate advice. But most of all, it requires right thinking. That's where it starts."

"Hah!" Alice smirks. "That's nonsense. Look where it's gotten you."

Beautiful Life, please give me strength. But instead of saying anything, I just radiate love at her.

"Mom, that's not nice."

"Are you kidding me?" Alice's eyes shoot darts at her daughter. But then Alice obviously realizes that it really isn't very nice. In fact, she probably finds it quite James-like—in her book, that is. "I'm sorry, Mother. You've had an amazing life."

"I'm not dead yet!" I laugh.

But thoughts clearly continue to cluster around Alice's head, as they always seem to. Finally, she speaks again. "It's just that…you've lived this hippie-dippy lifestyle all these years, and I'm the one paying for it right now. You can't be flat broke *and* enlightened."

"You can be both." But she's cringing and twitching slightly. So, I know she's thinking about her inheritance and my lack of one. I also know Jaye has no idea about it. Alice probably wants to keep it that way, so I don't ever bring it up. But she's probably thinking my parents' money is beside the point—of my life—anyway. She'd be fine financially even without those funds and probably thinks I should be, too.

"You live in a van."

"That was years ago. Now, she's an RV and her name is Arissa."

That breaks the ice, and peals of laughter circle and soar above the table. But then, a thought comes through that seems to shock her, and her subsequent words shock all three of us: "But maybe it's not that bad having you with me, either." I watch the thoughts continue to swarm around in her head until she visibly softens. "You and your worms. I know they arrived."

"Oh, my little darlings," I smile. "Okay, now that you've warmed up to the worms, I'm thinking of getting bees."

"Bees!" Just like with the worms, it's an exclamation instead of a question. "Bees!"

"You'll like them—they're yellow," I smile. "So is honey."

She shakes her head but laughs again.

As I head out on a few errands, my iPhone sends Scott McKenzie's "San Francisco" to the car stereo. That certainly sends me into a life review, which has been happening much more often since my stroke. I'm all over the map. It's who I am and what I do: physically, emotionally, conversation-wise, all ways. But the roamings aren't because of my age or the stroke. I've always been like this. I drove my parents and brother bonkers. "These are the voyages of Mary Alice Anderson," my friends would tease me, starting back when *Star Trek* first came out in 1966 and continuing through, oh, yesterday over herbal tea at Copperfield's Bookstore. Now, my friends say Starr, of course, as they have since 1969.

Woah, there's that year again, the one that changed everything.

I couldn't tell my mother about my, uh, situation. I just couldn't. I especially wouldn't be able to say, "Uh, well, I don't know his name," when she asked me who the father was. Oh, minor detail.

"Mary Alice!" would've been her response, like it always was. I had to get away.

Age eighteen. Very little money. Late 1969. Where else but California?

My yellow Beetle and I hit the open road. Somewhere along the way, a few giant psychedelic flower decals made their way to the car doors, and I covered the seats and the dashboard with some psychedelic fabric. It was very…well…yes, psychedelic.

"Wow, groovy! I can dig it!" said the dozens of hitchhikers I picked up all along the way.

I was led to San Francisco—probably, in no small part by Scott's soulful song about gentle folks with flowers in their hair—and headed straight to the Haight-Ashbury district. Wow, was that Jerry and the rest of the Dead, just walking down the street? Even though I'd just seen them live at Woodstock, so I knew they were real people made of flesh and bones and all, somehow I pictured them sitting on a magic carpet or something like that when they moved about.

I bought some hippie-esque takeout for lunch and sat on a bench in Golden Gate Park to eat it…and my pack of friends found me. Kids these days are so into having their packs, but we definitely had our packs back then, too.

Home, finally! Everything that made me a misfit back East was what made me gel with my new crowd. A little spacey? Heh! I seemed grounded, relative to most. Into words like *cosmic* and concepts like *consciousness*? I was far out and far from alone in talking about those.

A bunch of us lived in a huge house on Masonic Avenue, right around the corner from the actual intersection of Haight and Ashbury and all the action. Our rent was something ridiculous like twenty dollars each because it was divided by something ridiculous like twenty people. Drugs flowed like water, but none for me, being pregnant and all. Plus, I was high enough being in such a vibrant place with my people, at last.

I had boyfriend after boyfriend (full-fledged relationships came and went quickly) who really dug that I was pregnant—probably because someone else was already on the hook for that! Lots of us young women were, and it was treated like a great gift.

I'd often dream of him, though. Yes, *that* him.

By Thanksgiving, just a couple of weeks after I found my tribe, vibe, and crashing pad, I summoned the courage to call my mother.

"Hi. I'm in San Francisco. I'm pregnant." That's it. Get it all out of the way right up front.

"Will you be home for Christmas?" The question was not as warm and loving as it might sound—not coming from her, anyway.

"I doubt it."

Long pause. Then, "Are you eating enough for you and a baby? Do you need money?" That, too, was one of the warmest of questions delivered with the coldest of tones.

I don't know which was worse for my mother—the Army men showing up at the door to inform her that her son had been killed in action or me calling her to tell her I was knocked up. I'm not trying to be a smart-ass. There was a nobility to dying on the battlefield (at least in her mind). There was none in my situation. She probably thought I got pregnant to punish her. Actually, I have no idea what she thought because she was such a closed book, or a padlocked freezer, as the case was.

And I was one of the lucky ones. My friends couldn't even call their parents, let alone have money wired to them, because of their long hair, torn jeans, or whatever other excuse their parents chose.

Beautiful, perfect, cooing, laughing Ambrosia was born at St. Mary's Hospital, not far from the house. Was she ever a good baby— slept through the night early on, no colic, not a big crier. When the pad became a little overwhelming, we moved north to the famous (or infamous, to Alice) converted chicken coop in Petaluma.

My baby girl and I were inseparable for her first five years, but she doesn't seem to remember this "best friend" part of the story at all now. Selective recall is a powerful thing. I do hope she holds some sunny, warm memories of those days somewhere deep inside that aching heart of hers.

When my mom died in the late seventies, I was wracked with guilt. Had I helped to cause her somewhat early death somehow? Should I have gone home, I mean back there? But the few times I did bring Ambrosia to ice-cold Connecticut to be with her grandparents, my mother didn't exactly put out the welcome mat.

"I'm so sorry, Mother," I find myself saying as I finish up my errands. "I'm so sorry. I didn't mean to hurt you. I was young, confused, pregnant, with wild hormones flooding my body and thoughts, so exceedingly happy for the first time in my life. I'm sorry."

Then comes something that surprises me. "I'm sorry I couldn't rescue you from yourself." And then comes something that surprises me even more: "Alice, I'm sorry I can't rescue you from yourself either."

Just 'cause, a bouquet of roses and I swing by the hospital on the way home.

"Alice is assisting in a birth right now—a water delivery, her favorite," her coworker says, taking the flowers. "Can I tell her who brought these beauties?"

"Her mom."

Her eyebrows quickly hit her hairline, perhaps as she tries to put these two wildly dissimilar women in the same family line. But then, my eyebrows do the same at her next words.

"You're Alice's mom? How lucky are you? What a wonderful daughter you raised!" Since I'm speechless, she continues. "I'll add these flowers to her usual collection in the kitchen. She gets more of these and gifts and cards than any of us."

Well, just shock me Shakti—how 'bout that?

○

Back at the ranch, I happily lug some items I retrieved from my storage unit up the stairs. Okay, yes, perhaps those roses were a peace offering in case she notices how much more I've loaded up my room. I hope she doesn't flip out, thinking I'm moving in forever.

Alice does do "home" very well, and she does *not* have me to thank for that. She's created such a beautiful nest after growing up with a mom who was escaping any semblance of a roost—chicken coop notwithstanding. Heh! Making this cozy, comforting, charming home could be from a longing for the home she felt she never had. For me, this whole, magnificent blue marble floating in the firmament of forever is my home. She clearly wanted just one acre of home with solid flooring under her. And a God who holds her hand every day. And a political structure that provides steadfast answers.

I've said as much to her on many occasions, and her retort is always, "Don't play armchair therapist with me!" But then, she'd say, "You ran away from structure and floated off to a distant dimension and galaxy!" Well, she certainly isn't wrong there.

If only she'd treat her body like her home, too. If only she'd dress like her house. Actually, she does dress like *a* house, in a way, in these blah-colored, oversized sweats and shirts. But if she'd tend to herself as well as decorate herself as beautifully and tastefully as she decorates her house, she'd be something else. Well, she is something else. She's my daughter, I love her and…still, she's something else, although on the job she's obviously another kind of something else. Hmmmmm.

Oops, Jaye and I are out of TP again, so I slip into Alice's bathroom for some. Why does it always smell so medicinal in here? She doesn't take any medicine, as far as I know. And hope.

The bathroom Jaye and I share smells like a hillside of lavender or a rose bush in full bloom. I'm so happy Jaye enjoys essential oils as much as I do. When we first started sharing this space, though, she put in a bunch of black—towels, curtains, soap dish. I replaced those items with purple and indigo ones, the darkest colors I can handle. She never said a word, thankfully, nor did she try to slip the black back in. I'm grateful she sometimes puts age before beauty.

The next time Alice is at work, I wash a few of my fabrics, hoping some lavender-scented soap will remove that storage-unit smell. Once they've dried, I drape them on my bedroom walls. The largest piece of fabric, pink silk tulle, gets affixed around the light fixture in the center of the ceiling and then out to the edges, harem-tent style. I hang some white Christmas lights along the billowing fabric, plus a light curtain over a wall. I string green lights on the wall behind my altar.

I switch on the lights and the room turns into a fairy's den. Luminous and numinous. The firmament is alive and well in my space.

No one has to tell me Alice stands in the doorway. I'd know that winded, bullish breathing anywhere, plus there was that stomp up the stairs. Have I really been at this decorating all day?

"Like it?" I ask.

She shrugs and heads to her room. Coming from her, that's high praise.

Alice and I, along with quite the merry, gregarious goth group, celebrate Jaye's birthday at a vegan restaurant. The way this bunch is dressed, I feel like we're at the wedding of Dracula and Elvira.

The waitstaff doesn't seem to know what to do with this band in black until Vision tells them, "We don't bite. At least, not people who don't want to be bitten, that is." Even the folks at the surrounding tables laugh at that one, and, perhaps, they breathe a sigh of relief, too.

Alice doesn't eat anything. But she's there and she's smiling. Mostly.

And after the kids head off to their adventures, she doesn't even complain on the drive home. Much.

Swoon. I love Love—the magic panacea. It's all getting better. Thank you, Life.

Chapter 16

Jaye

Burning Man bound, yo!

Really, I just want out of this house, out of this county, out of this world, and into a bigger creation than I've ever experienced so far. But, oh woahman, the look on Mom's face when I tell her I'm going there. Where's my phone so I can snap a pic? This is so totally the wrong moment for it not to be affixed to my hand.

"How about France? Or New Zealand?" Mom suggests, desperately trying to press the undo key for that aghast look on her face. "Those are relatively safe places."

"How about Burning Man, France, New Zealand, and everywhere else I can get my delicious derriere in?" I suggest back.

"A desert full of dust is not exactly what you need, six months out from TB."

"Probably not."

"If you get sick again, I'm the one who'll have to take care of you again."

"I won't get sick again. I promise." I'd rather die first.

"At least you're young and resilient," Mom mutters, although the way she says it makes it sound more like an insult than the praise it should be.

What better way to spend Labor Day weekend? At least, if I go, there'd be no more FOMO about it, no more wondering. At least, if I go, I'll have gone. At least, if I go, I got to see that look on Mom's face...

Which is only beaten by the look on her face when Gram announces she's going, too!

"Besides," Gram tells her oh-so-recalcitrant daughter, who stands there with her arms crossed as if Gram is her oh-so-recalcitrant daughter, "your time is your time. If I'm meant to die, I'll do it at Burning Man or here in the bathtub."

"The bathtub is slightly tidier and easier," Mom says.

"I'll be dead! I won't care."

"That is just so you," Mom grumbles.

What a trip—literally. Gram's RV delivers us and a few of my peeps to the Burn in great style…well, she delivers (drives) and I navigate. To music.

"Woah, Gram, that's the Lumineers, not the Grateful Dead!"

"Well, I have to keep up."

"You're so beyond cool." She smiles. "And so friggin' adorable." Her smile grows.

"Dozens and dozens of my friends have been to Burning Man," Gram says, "but I just haven't made it yet. There's something about a brush with death—even if it wasn't all that close—that's making me want to do everything I've been meaning to do, to check every single item off my bucket list. This is definitely one of them."

I take her hand. "I'm so glad you get to make this major checkmark, Gram. And with me, no less."

Gram's home for the week is her RV, of course. The friends I'm hanging with own a crystal shop, and they've brought a huge sampling of their wares, but not to sell. The only items anyone can buy are ice and coffee. Everything else has to be brought in, and in this gifting society, people freely give away all kinds of things: stickers, necklaces, a wide assortment of food, clothes and costumes, plane rides. Really anything you could imagine. So, after watching my friends give away their crystals and in turn receive alcohol and drugs, along with beautiful artwork, household items, and decorations, I jump into action.

"Hey, I'll take a Tarot reading," this gorgeous babe says, after walking by my table and then backing up. "Want some ecstasy for my fee?"

And then, comes the fine lady who exchanges one of her goddess-y scarves. And then, the couple dressed in faux-leather boots. The guy runs back to their tent to get me my own pair in exchange for their (very long) reading.

Our digs are pretty close to Center Camp. My buds have decked it all out like a harem tent (although not quite as lit-up-harem-y as Gram's room), what with rugs, cushions, wall hangings, and pottery (and ever more of those objects as the week goes on). I'm sure they would've had plants, too, if those and other sundry items didn't increase the potential for MOOP—Matter Out of Place—also known as trash. Burning Man has a delicate relationship with the Bureau of Land Management, so everyone's super diligent about leaving no trace of ourselves after the event is done.

Unlike what the name conveys, Center Camp is not in the center, but at the bottom of the loop that encircles the little city. The forty-foot man—yes, that one, the one who gets burned for, well, Burning Man—stands atop his twenty-foot base in the actual center, as well he should, I suppose.

Fun fact: Burning Man is an art festival, more than anything. While there's so much artwork on display, though, to me, the real artwork is the people. Oh, the makeup, hairstyles, costumes, and personas! I might look so far out there on the streets of Petaluma (let alone, say, Dubuque, Iowa), but I'm pretty tame compared to my compadres at the Burn. There goes a woman in a flowing scarf—just a flowing scarf. There goes one in just a veil. There goes a doll in just a fur (fake, to be sure) vest. And there's a group in costumes made of lights. Many roam around in nothing at all. Well, maybe in a few tattoos or henna designs.

There goes a dude on stilts. There goes a car made up as a spaceship, and then another as a dragon. For most, though, the main mode of transportation is the humble bicycle, sometimes decked out in fabrics, furs, lights, you name it, to be not quite so humble.

Nighttime's my fave part—when the people, art, and sky light up with lasers, lanterns, torches, flames, fireworks, pyrotechnics. The whole scene is one huge lightscape filled with music and dancing and more music and dancing, from live bands and DJs.

"What's on for today?" someone asks every morning. Well, every noon.

"Wanna go to that TED talk?"

"How 'bout that yoga class?"

"Hey, there's that zip lining deal."

"Let's go make sand angels again!"

Everyone has to carry goggles and scarves for the random dust storms that arise. Actually, that stuff flying through the air and getting absolutely everywhere—including all bodily openings and crevices—is neither dust nor sand, though. It's the alkali residue from the area being the bottom of an old lakebed. Even peskier than the flying stuff (at least, to me) is the temperature extremes: from hotter than blazes during the day to literally freezing at night.

But nothing—no thing, not one thing—can dim my joy. Happy? This is by far and above the happiest I've ever been. I can be me. No judgment from anyone, at all, in any way, shape, or form. Blisssssssss.

I'm just so happy to be doing something I've wanted to do ever since I first heard about it in, oh, preschool or so. Dust be damned! Now, I can check it off my much-younger-than-Gram's-bucket-list and, well, that's it. I'm here every year for the rest of my life, barring something ridiculous like a global pandemic—would those even happen anymore?—or other unforeseen catastrophes along those lines.

What a scene! My Bay Area friends run the gamut of single, poly, pan, group, as well as every needle stop on the male/female spectrum. Did I once hear that there are, like, two hundred stops on that spectrum? I think there were more than that just in our little Burning Man cul-de-sac. This is my tribe. Of course, most of my homie tribe is here, too, including Vision. But we've found our bigger tribe.

One night, my peeps and I slip out for some electric groove jam. Blue lights flash around us as we slither and slide around the dance floor.

I feel someone's eyes on the back of my head, and I turn around. This ultimate fox puts his hands on my hips. The electricity's not just in the music, nor is the grooving. With those amazing eyes fixed on mine, we move together in time to the tunes. At dawn, we disappear to his RV. (Yes, I totally know Gram's story. History does repeat itself, but I knew this wasn't going to be a one-night thing.)

"Uh, Jaye? About your new boyfriend," Vision giggles later after I introduce them to Charles, and he's turned away from us for a minute.

"Okay, okay, he looks on the straight and narrow, but he's not. He's so not."

Yeah, Vision and some other friends are more than a little surprised at me, but, hey, we're the last ones to judge anyone (usually).

Besides, it's always good to have someone around who could pass as an average Joe to talk to the cops—if ever needed—on our behalf, LOL.

During the all-night, explosive, celebratory, blowout bash of the actual burning of the man, Charles and I have our own bash out in the dark...also all night, explosive, celebratory, and, well, yeah.

Gram and I don't see each other at all until the very last day when I bump into her on the Esplanade—the innermost radial street of the whole Burning Man city—on the way to the burning of the temple. Of the seventy-thousand-or-so people, maybe only five percent are older than sixty, but even given that huge throng, Gram found her gang.

As she folds me in her arms, she announces to her friends, "This is my granddaughter." OMG, she says it with such pride I almost melt into the ground with gratitude. "So many of you colorful kids make this your annual...oh, I have no idea what to call what you make it. Pilgrimage? Thing? Event? Those words seem so small for what this is. Happening? Hajj? Twenty-first-century barnstorm?"

"Those all work," I smile. "Well, maybe not the barnstorm so much."

"It's amazing how many of your peeps center their lives around this. Many have linked up here, as I've seen more than one wedding/union/joining together. So touching."

The very early mornings have the least amount of dust, so that's when Gram would be up and walking around, she tells me. "I figure most of the thousands of folks passing by me haven't been to bed yet," she laughs. "Just like home."

Gram and her group walk next to my brood of "Whatever we are," I laugh quietly as we approach the ritual.

"Well, I was going to say 'kids,'" Gram whispers, "but I didn't want to be impolite and belittle the wisdom you incredible young beings have brought in with you."

Nobody makes me feel as seen as Gram. I know I dis oldies from time to time, but Gram will never be one of them, no matter how old she gets.

Every time I passed the temple all week, I saw folks in there grieving for their people and even dreams and situations they'd lost over the past year. So, I'm not too surprised to see the burning of the temple is quite somber, in complete contrast to last night.

Gram and Charles each take my hand as the temple goes up in flames. I feel all that grief, along with the building, get consumed by the fire. The relief is palpable.

This temple thing really stays with me, like it's poked a soft finger into my heart. I'm loathe to miss a moment of the activity and being with my crew, but I feel compelled, called, coaxed, coerced, whatevered to walk off at sunset and be by myself for a bit. Who should show up in my desert vision? No, not Satan, like he supposedly did for Jesus and all, but…Mom! Woahman, I thought these drugs were better than that!

"Mom?" She's not there, of course, but I can practically see and feel her. "Mom." It's almost as if she sits down in front of me and gazes into my eyes. For a minute, I could see her life from her point of view: the early-childhood craziness, the longing for sanity, the pain of the abortion, the divorce, what it's like to have her beautiful son become her—no! No, I don't want to see that. Stop. Is somebody messing with me? Is somebody casting a spell or something? I'd almost think it's Mom doing it, but she'd never go near anything like that.

Fuck it. I don't want to see her point of view about me. She should love me just the way I am, fake tits (at least for now) and all.

But I do. See her point of view, that is. And this is more than other times, such as when I had this feeling about her after seeing Sarah and her mom. I do. I don't want to, but I do. My heart has melted here in the heat of the desert…even for Mom. Shit.

On the drive home, my peeps fall asleep, and I find myself listening to Gram gab esoterically. I'm not even sure what she's talking about, as my mind is still out in the desert.

I doubt she's looking for any particular answer, though, so I don't have to say anything. But then, she's quiet for a minute.

"That whole thing was so profound," she finally whispers. "And so am I, even more than before, as a result of it."

"Me, too."

Chapter 17

Alice

When James told me he and Mother (Mother!) were going to Burning Man, I really wanted to say, "Well, if you're both well enough to do that, aren't you well enough to go find a life outside of this house? And, perhaps, go start that life right now?"

He said something about altars and his tribe. Funny, Mother said something about the exact same thing, although then she retracted the word *tribe*, mumbling something about it being cultural appropriation. I can't keep up! Re the Burn, as my two call it, I just picture a whole lot of dust flying in oppressive heat. Not my idea of a grand old time, that's for sure.

Some high school and college classmates of mine (no current friends, though, of course) go every year. They post pictures on Facebook with their heads wrapped in bandanas to keep the dust out of their facial orifices. Oh, what a blast—not!

Seriously, though, Mother and James had recently been very sick and may be still convalescing a little. Since I work in a hospital, I hear many a thing about Burning Man, like it's really tough, physically, even for young people (Mother, what are you thinking?) who are very healthy (James? Mother?). Heaven forbid, I should bring up such a trivial subject as health.

"Well, we all have to go sometime," Mother said, after saying something about her preference for dying in the desert rather than in a bathtub. "I'd rather go with my boots on, off experiencing some grand adventure."

"Hasn't your whole life been one long, grand adventure?"

My own adventure calls—to the City, as we still refer to it, not for anything mystical but for a mere, mundane errand. As insane as my San Francisco years were, the Golden Gate Bridge still thrills me. Thankfully the sight of that amazing orange-red structure doesn't trigger bad memories. It just brings a smile.

The blue waters of the bay were and are a calming analgesic to my jangled nerves, back then as a confused child and still now as a confused adult. The spikey spires of downtown, changing as the years went by, have always been a sight to admire, from afar, anyway. I'll take my nest in the country any day. Back in my middle and high school years, the downtown was called the FiDi (Financial District) and the mayor was DiFi (Dianne Feinstein, who became the long-term senator). Cute.

Since I'm in no hurry whatsoever, I find myself driving around town, even to the Haight Ashbury, an area I've never particularly liked. The "painted ladies," as the old Victorian houses are called, are still just as colorful. Mother used to take great pride in pointing out the houses where the Grateful Dead, Janis Joplin, Jefferson Airplane, and others lived, as if the structures were some shrines to the holiest of holies. I could've cared less.

I stop at the McDonald's near the entrance to Golden Gate Park. Some kids, James's age, are playing frisbee. I try to picture my mom there, pregnant, back in 1970, at a Be-In or something like that. Okay, yes, the Be-Ins had stopped by then, but Mother would've been in...whatever there was to be in.

Almost as if it has a will of its own, my car climbs the hill to Twin Peaks, the two summits right smack dab in the center of San Francisco. The usual summertime grayness whorls and tumbles off the ocean to the west, moving my way as if it's an act of God—this big slate-colored hand with fingers of fog reaching toward me. Looking the other way, I see the sun's still shining on downtown and the East Bay cities, including Berkeley and Oakland.

And then, as if that will-of-its-own continues to take over my car, I find myself driving through the old neighborhood itself. The gay pride flag is embedded in the pavement now.

I wonder if that organ player still works at the Castro, the movie theater. He'd always play as we'd wander in, ending his extravaganza with "San Francisco, Open that Golden Gate." The organ would start to disappear into the floor as he performed his flavorful, finishing flourish, to uproarious applause, and then the theater would darken.

Mom dragged me there for a presentation against female genital mutilation by Alice Walker, based on her book on the subject. Ugh! But it did stick with me. Almost ninety-eight percent of the women in Somalia and a number of other countries undergo that. Crazy planet!

I drive over the crest of Divisadero Street and down into Noe Valley, which was really my old neighborhood but didn't impact me as much as the Castro did. I stop in front of the house we shared with the family

Mother was caretaking. She was supposed to just be taking care of the daughter, but I think she was taking care of the whole family, really. Sure wish she'd thought to take a little more care of me.

I look up at the window to the attic bedroom and try to imagine myself at age ten, twelve, sixteen, staring out the window and dreaming of the life that lay ahead of me. What a shock it's all turned out to be. I'm grateful for so much of it...and want to scream about some other parts of it.

On the drive home, my thoughts return to my son. Truth is, he's almost always on my mind. From the moment James was born, my check-child light came on, and it doesn't, probably under no condition until the end of time will it ever, go off. I thought it would at least flicker out sometimes once he became an adult, but it's only gotten worse over the past couple of years since...yes, that. Even at work, if I'm handling an urgent matter for a patient, he's in the periphery, waiting until the crisis passes to come careening back into my mind, front and center. The trip down Memory Lane served as a brief respite.

Did I not see it coming? I hear that sometimes when people come out, their friends and family say, "Oh, sure. Of course. We knew that."

But I was completely blindsided. No, I didn't know. I remember seeing a TV show where a fairly young child came out as a trans boy. The dad was flabbergasted, but the mom said she knew, had known all along.

I remember wondering what my reaction would be in that situation and then being thankful that I'd never have to find out, being the mom of an ultra-masculine, supersonic track star. Then, six months later came that moment.

James walked into my room and sat on my bed. "Mom?"

"Yes, darling?"

"I'm a woman."

I laughed. I regret that, but that was my honest reaction at the time. Of course, I'd noticed my missing underwear before that, but didn't pay it much heed, thinking it was just a phase. Or maybe I'd misplaced it. Although, it happened several more times...

But...he wasn't kidding. After my heart stopped and then restarted, after my blood drained from my veins, my mind played a few tricks on me in that moment. Is that tree in the front yard okay? It looks a little droopy. My brain wanted to do something, anything, to stave off this rising wave of horror that was about to crash over me and rearrange my life from everything it had ever been.

Yes, it was horror. I'm so sorry. That's where I was. That's what it was. I wish I could say I was somewhere else, and it was something else. But I wasn't, and it wasn't.

The mind does play those tricks sometimes to buffer the blow. Otherwise, we'd go crazy. His eyes flashed intense hurt when I laughed. A cold, clammy dread filled my body from the inside out. Sweat sprang out of my forehead despite the chill of the gloomy, foggy Saturday, when I'd really wanted to enjoy one of his last weekends home before he left for college. I suppressed the urge to scream. Can we please rewind this movie by a minute or two? Can Superman fly around the Earth and make time reverse itself? It worked to save Lois Lane.

Then, denial, that ever-useful ally, filled my brain. He doesn't mean it. It's just a phase. He's been watching too many TV shows. He's the most unfeminine being I've ever met. On the spectrum of male-y male to female-y female, he'd be ninety-nine percent male-y male. I'd be his parallel at the other end of the spectrum.

"I didn't do this to you, did I?" It just popped out. I didn't mean to ask it. Or maybe I did. Maybe if I could take on all the responsibility, then it might somehow be easier to see this dazzling young man throw his dazzling young life to the winds of change, peer pressure, fads, craziness.

Was it his father? Did he have anything and perhaps everything to do with it? Did something happen that I'm not aware of? I thought Dan did an okay job as far as dads go. Of course, I didn't have anyone to compare his dadness to, just like I didn't have anyone to compare his husbandness to.

"Can't you be happy for me?" James asked.

My throat was beyond parched. "Yes. Of course." And then, I said what I once said I said, but he doesn't remember this part: "Whatever you desire, sweetheart. Whatever your soul yearns for."

I know he doesn't remember because he's brought it up more than once that I should've said such a thing. "I did!" I stress to him. Sometimes, I wish we could have security cameras running on our entire lives so we could play these important scenes back when our loved ones don't remember things the right way.

At that moment back then, though, my foot suddenly started cramping. Better than my brain cramping, I supposed, although maybe

I had some of that, too.

Hey, maybe James is bipolar, I thought. If I'd truly realized he was sane and serious and this wasn't "just some phase," I might've considered my life ended that day. I'm not kidding. Nothing could make this easier. Nothing.

I thought my life was complete because I'd had a child. A partner doesn't matter to me anywhere near as much. The only thing that matters more is my relationship to my Lord, because without Him none of this is anything.

One time, when the overwhelm was too much, I mentioned to Mother, "I just want to lie down one final time and be lifted up in the arms of the Lord."

"You could do that right now," she said. "You don't have to die to experience that." Then, she told me of some near-death experience or another that she'd had, where she was swooshed up in Love (her words, not mine, of course). Oh, Mother. I doubt it even happened.

Oh, James. Oh, how I've always adored him. Him. HIM! My son. My SON!

When he was born, I was just so happy he had all of his fingers and toes and other parts intact. It never, ever dawned on me that some of those precious parts would ever come into question.

I'd feel very wistful—as well as very guilty for feeling so—at Christmastime, as my friends swept their daughters off to the Nutcracker. Wait, did James once ask me to take him to that ballet? I must be imagining that.

Oh, I'm being punished for being so wistful. I'm being doubly punished because now it looks like I won't ever have a granddaughter to take, either.

I find myself talking to him. I gave birth to you. I held you in my arms every single, solitary moment possible. I read you *The Little Engine that Could* every day for a year because you loved it so much.

We picked out your toys together, in this order and at your request: a Simba lion, those rock and sock 'em—or whatever you call 'em—robots, a soccer ball, a football, dozens of video games, a drone helicopter for inside the house, some virtual-reality game/thing that you played endlessly.

I coordinated your birthday parties with *Toy Story* and, later, *Star Wars* themes, also at your request. You even thought of going into the military. You could do that as a she, too, of course, but statistics-wise…

If there's anyone in the world I felt close to, it's you, my one and only child. No, I didn't know. If this wasn't you, then I have absolutely no idea who you are. I miss you—the you I thought I knew.

You say you've been this way your whole life, but that was news—literally, a breaking story—to me. I didn't see it.

I do miss him, my son. I miss him so much. But if I say anything about it, at least to him…well, that's *verboten*. So, I'm in mourning, but not allowed to mourn. Sometimes, I want to have a memorial for the son I lost. But I can't.

And what about all my grief—vats and vats of it—over losing my beautiful son? This person I carried in my womb and raised and took to soccer practice and did his homework with. Where did that person go? Why am I not allowed to grieve and mourn for him? I miss him!

There's a snippy, snarky woman-wannabe suffering from hormone imbalance in his place now. Why do I suddenly have to stand at attention, jump to it, and get with the program that I didn't know existed until a couple of years ago? I'm sure even some of those most with-it parents have their moments of doubt and fear. It's brand new for most of us.

I thought time heals all wounds. This seems to be getting worse as the months go by, maybe because this whole situation is not going away like I was positive it would.

Oh, James, you're the biggest area of pain in my life, even bigger than the abortion. That's the first time I've said that to myself. I thought nothing could ever beat that. But it's not your fault. You're just who you are, doing your thing.

A brand-new idea occurs to me. I guess it's not up to you to come around to what I wanted. I have to come around to who you are and what you want. I have to look at family and grandchildren and all of those things in a different light now. There are so many new ways to be a family these days.

Two steps forward, three steps backward. And again. Sure, I have that momentous minute of positive acceptance, but then my stomach lurches, and I have to pull the car over to the side of the road.

Oh, sure, heap it on, Lord. I can handle it. I'll keep being grateful for this miracle of a life I have, this fucking messed-up miracle of a life I have.

Language, Alice! And don't talk to the Lord like that.

Oh, for fuck's sake! Just let me be in this one minute! Just give me this one minute to vent and rend my garments and ask what the hell did I do wrong? Why do any of us deserve this—least of all him? Where did he go? Why am I stuck with this sarcastic, sassy spitfire (his words, but very appropriate) who took his place? I want my James back!

I scream. And cry. And scream some more. And cry some more. And…

The rest of the time they're gone, at least, when I'm home. I curl up in the window seat, just feeling my sweet home without their strident personalities searing through it. Ah, peace. Bliss.

It's quiet around here. Really quiet. Quite quiet. Very quiet. Really quite very quiet. *Zzzzzzzzzzz*

Chapter 18

Starr

Jaye stumbles into the kitchen at her usual non-witching hour of high noon. Whichever friend—or friends—had spent the night was/were still asleep. Honestly, I don't think it's all a sexual thing as much as it's a litter of puppies bonding.

I do like her new beau, though. Charles seems a little sedate for Jaye's crowd, but he also seems genuine and doesn't have to ruffle the feathers of everyone around him to determine who he is and where he stands in the world.

Oops—did I just say that? I do adore my granddaughter, and even her penchant for panache. But sometimes that seems to come about just to come about. Ah, well. She'll find her place in the scheme of things. I've certainly had my moments. And I love her in all her moments.

"A touch of the morning vapors?" I ask Jaye. Alice harrumphs.

Jaye smiles. "Something like that."

After she blends her smoothie and plops down at the table, I lean in. "Did I ever tell you about your great grandmother?"

"Yes, two thousand times," Alice moans as she finishes her lunch. I ignore her.

"A bit," Jaye says. "But you can tell me again. You mean anything in particular?"

"She came of age during World War II. She was in love with a young GI who was blinded in a firefight and ended up marrying his nurse. She says she would've walked to the ends of the Earth for him."

"Wow."

"She married the first man who came along after that, probably to wipe that earlier experience out of her mind. But that didn't work, of course. She had my brother at age twenty-four and then, a couple of years later, she lost a baby at eight months' pregnant."

"Wow."

"Then, she had me a couple of years later. So, that's, in part, where her perfect house, the fixed smile, the coldness came from."

"Hmmmmm." Jaye fidgets with the straw (stainless steel—I bought a few, plus cleaning brushes, for everyone in the house) in her breakfast smoothie. "But sometimes these awful events that happen to us can be the very things that catapult us."

"Jaye, you are so wise."

"Do you miss her?" Alice asks me.

"In a way." I'm more than a little surprised at the question, considering the source, and even more surprised at my initial answer. "We had hardly anything in common."

"I know exactly what you mean." Alice none-too-quietly deposits her lunch dishes in the dishwasher, and heads upstairs to get ready to disappear on one of her off-workday errands. And church, probably.

"I know exactly what you mean, too," Jaye says to me but looking through the kitchen doorway, where her mother had been.

"I can appreciate that. But…you know what? After your mom goes, right before every Mother's Day for the rest of your life, you'll have an urge to buy her a card. My mom died decades ago. And yet, still, every time I see a Mother's Day card display, I have this automatic, innate response to buy her one."

Jaye doesn't say anything, and I'm not even sure she heard me. Ah, youth. Well, I certainly didn't listen to anyone over the age of twenty-five when I was twenty, either.

◯

Well, since I had indeed recovered enough to go to Burning Man—although if I died there, that really would've been fine, I'm pretty loosey-goosey about where I die at this point, although that uncooked question stirs me up—I thought maybe I'd recovered enough to do more than just volunteer at the shelter.

Jaye's spending more and more time doing her Tarot seshes or hanging out with her pack, and I have to have some place to lavish this love of mine. Alice sure doesn't want it. Well, she does, but that doesn't mean it's easy for her to take it in.

As I've said, having the stroke made me appreciate this life even more than I did before, and that was a lot. But I don't think dying is the end of the journey. It just goes on from here after we lay this body down. So, I'm grateful. Not attached. Loving life. Looking forward to new adventures here. Or somewhere else.

Anyway, back to the present. Hmmmmmm, what else could I do?

"If you're well enough to volunteer even more, you're well enough to work and pay me some rent!" Alice grumbles. "Or you could move out on your own."

"And what would you have me do?"

"A little old man I know lost his wife recently. He used to own a restaurant, and he's quite a people person. So now, he's a greeter at Walmart."

"Okay. I could do that." That's definitely a you-get-more-flies-with-honey move. Who needs more vinegar around here, anyway?

It works. She softens. "Oh, frig. Your parents gave me the money knowing I'd take care of you. And I will. But I don't need to do that in this house. Can't you find your own place? I'll help you find a senior-living condo or something."

"Sure." There, even more honey for the flies. She softens even further. I don't mean to be manipulative, but, well…this particular fly loves honey. She loves being in charge and getting to call the shots. We all do, for the most part, and it *is* her house.

Despite the oodles of silly squabbling, I love all this family time, especially with Jaye. I love Alice, of course, warts and wackadooness and all, but Jaye is really quite the masterpiece.

◯

"I started a radio show at the local station!"

"You what?" Alice seems nowhere near as thrilled as I am, but probably more thrilled than she would've been a couple months ago. "Whatever will you be talking about?"

"Peace."

"Peace!" She sounds as mystified as she did about the worms and the bees at first.

"Go Gram!" Jaye is by far the best cheerleader I've ever had in my entire life.

I've also started hanging out more with friends myself, including some I'd bumped into at Burning Man—even a fella. Oh, on second thought, cancel that fella. My patience for such humdrum efforts has evaporated. I love hearing about what people have done with their lives, but I don't particularly appreciate the judgment that creeps in when they hear about mine.

"You did what? How recently?" come the common questions.

For so many years, people would gush about my lifestyle—being free to go here, there, anywhere, on a whim and at a moment's notice. But what with my age and these adventures not being so far behind me (plus not having a flush retirement account), many a furrowed brow appears.

"Well. That must've been…interesting."

Oh, go furrow someplace else. I had a life to live and live it I did. Still do!

It was as bad as that one blind date long ago where the potential gentleman caller said, "I just can't handle someone with numerous bumper stickers." He'd picked me up downtown and had no idea what any vehicle of mine looked like. Or maybe one look at me told him I was definitely the numerous-bumper-sticker type, and he was looking for a way to quickly end our night.

"Could you please take me home now?" I asked politely. "To my van?"

At least, the furrows are lessening on the home front.

"Did you know you can rent clothes now?" Alice scoffs, looking up from an article on her laptop as I return home from the (natural) grocery store. "Just a hundred and sixty dollars a month will do you."

"Holy holograms!" That's me, of course.

"We're not as into the material world as you all are," Jaye says.

"Tell that to your phone and your car and the furnace and the coffee pot…" Alice starts.

"Clothing, in particular, has a very big effect on the environment," Jaye continues, "especially synthetic fabrics. Millennials and my generation even score clothing companies based on their social impact and carbon footprint."

I reach into one of my (reusable) shopping bags and pull out a jug with a cap. "By the way, here's a reusable laundry detergent container we can refill at the store. I'm all over the Zero Waste Initiative."

"Of course you are." Alice returns to her article reading.

"They found a plastic bag at the bottom of the Mariana Trench, and it's raining plastic particles in Rocky Mountain National Park, fourteen thousand feet up. Those particles are probably at Mt. Everest, too."

Alice grunts. "I already have enough in my brain without worrying about what's at the top or the bottom of the world."

"Okay, boomer," Jaye says.

"Boom!" I just have to.

Alices sputters a bit. "I'm not a boomer."

"You act like one." Jaye turns to me. "And you don't."

Alice and I both look at her and then at each other. We decide not to continue in that direction. Not going there.

Hmmmmm. Oh, cancel that. Yes, I am. "That's an ageist thing to say, you know."

"Huh?"

"I guess 'Okay, boomer' is the younger generations' response to us seemingly not being sympathetic to their concerns and struggles. That's understandable, especially given how we've polluted the Earth, that we could go to college with very little debt, we never had to spend half our paycheck on rent, the list could go on and on. I actually don't blame you. But some of us do care."

Neither of them responds until Alice speaks first. Well, actually she makes a noise first. "Uggggggghhhhhhhh! Where have I ended up?"

"Are you on a lost timeline or is something going on in a parallel universe?"

"Oh, Mother, honestly! What planet are you from?"

"You really want an answer to that?"

Alice shakes her head. "If you say anything other than Earth, I'll scream."

"Arcturus, probably."

"I did not just hear that."

"Very good. Carry on. As you were."

But laugh lines crinkle around Alice's eyes as we say these things these days. It's becoming a game. At least, with Alice and me, and with Jaye and me. But the two of them, while relaxing somewhat, obviously still have some hashing to do...

"Could you please drive me to the shelter tonight?"

"Aren't you driving just fine these days?" Alice grumbles yet again, although not quite so grumbly about it. But drive me she does, and I invite her in.

"What?"

"Come in with me." I climb out of the car and stand right in front of it, so she can't just drive off without running me over. Perhaps, I was taking too big a chance there. Heh!

Alice turns off her car and then accompanies me into the shelter. After greeting the staff and introducing my daughter to them, I hand her a children's book. "Here. How about you read to them?" I point to a circle of children who are impatiently awaiting reading hour in a corner of the lobby.

Certainly not one to turn down a couple dozen young, eager eyes, Alice—none too gracefully—sits down on the floor with them and starts reading. When she finishes that book, one of the children hands her another.

Alice notices a teenager sitting outside the circle of children. After her voice starts to tire as she's not used to speaking loudly to a group for this long, she looks at me. I pick up a book and start reading.

Alice sits next to the teenage boy (Assigned Female at Birth). This gender change becomes obvious to her as the boy starts chattering.

After I've finished reading a few books, bringing reading hour to a close, I join Alice and her new friend.

"Where are your parents?" Alice asks him.

"I'm with my sister," the boy explains. "My parents threw both of us out since she didn't go against my change like they did. She's nineteen, so she could be my guardian. We're working on that and getting a place to stay and all. She just started a job at the Sonic over on Apollo Way, so taking care of me is a big possibility."

Clearly touched by the tender words coming from the tender boy of such a tender age, Alice puts her hand on his shoulder. "I wish you the best with your sister and with your life."

I think she really means it. Why couldn't…? Oh, never mind. It's a process. Sometimes a long one, at that, and often with no clear eureka moments. Just a circling path to the center of the heart.

The siren's wails subside as the ambulance arrives at the hospital. Several doctors and nurses rush out to greet the EMTs, who shout medical stats at them.

Meanwhile, my own words continue: "Please, oh please. I'd rather die. Take me."

Chapter 19

Jaye

So, like, here I come back from this super cosmic event and Mom's…Mom: walking on eggshells but still getting everything wrong. And then, turning it backward and upside-down to disengage herself. Back to the Matrix we go. You want the red pill or the blue pill? It's still…a pill.

I'm counting the hours until I can leave and never come back. Charles and I are talking SoCal, a lot.

I'm still trying to figure out what the hell Mom made of Charles. When she walked in on us just chilling in the kitchen the first time he was over, it was like she saw a ghost. I think he's really cute, if a little clean-cut looking. It's a nice change of pace. I just don't know what her trip is. Plus, he's tall and super built, which goes great with a big-ass woman like me.

Soooooooooo, seems like as good a time as any to finally hang with Dad, as I've been meaning to for a while. Seeing him is great, even despite noticing this definite dad bod he's sprouted. Seeing his wife Brenda? That'd be no.

Brenda hadn't met me before. They'd gone off and gotten married at City Hall, with just a witness. Then, they had a baby, who is now a toddler. Of course, I knew all this already, but it didn't really, really hit me until my visit. He has this whole life thing happening without me, and he's not even a dozen miles away. Teardrop.

Come to think of it, I haven't seen Dad since I came out to him. I left for college right after that, then went to SoCal for a while, then got sick so I couldn't be around his new family, then…time passed. Maybe…maybe, Dad didn't want me to meet Brenda? Could that even be possible?

Wifenstein, I mean Brenda, doesn't even want me in the near vicinity of their little girl, let alone touch her. Hey, that's my half-sister, lady! And I'm sure it isn't because I had TB. The doc cleared me of any remnants ages ago, and I keep telling her that over and over. Maybe, I should tone the outfits down. I could at least wear red lipstick instead of black, possibly.

Or not. This is who I am. If she can't handle it, that's her problem.

Oh, do I love having a sister! Okay, okay, my half-sister, Joy. I always wanted a sibling or two or twelve. I once asked Mom why she and Dad never had more kids, and she said, "You were enough for me." Well, that could certainly be taken a few ways! Thanks, Mom.

I accidentally leave my pentagram necklace on the sink after a shower, and I find it later with the string neatly wrapped up around it, sitting on my suitcase. Subtle hint.

And the longer I'm here, it's getting less and less great to see Dad. Maybe he can't handle me either, after all. (Insert that wailing emoji here.) Dad! I thought you were better than that. I thought you got...*things*.

Plus, their house is pretty cozy—meaning small, crowded, too full—and they really don't have room for me. I could tell Dad has been trying to keep some peace for Brenda, although I've been on my best behavior, for me.

Since my own mom can be so inept at being a mom sometimes, I think part of me was hoping Brenda would step in and be that mother figure I was looking for. Ha! Hardly. She makes Mom look like Lady Madonna.

For years, I couldn't figure out why Dad ever married Mom in the first place, with all her Catholic-crazy stuff. I totally understand why they broke up, and I even did back at the time, as I mentioned. I mean, sure, he was a Catholic, too, but I can't picture him ever as crazy as Mom. Now, I'm not sure why she ever married him in the first place. He doesn't have her crazies, sure, but she doesn't have his schleppiness. She might be, oh, just a little opinionated, but, at least, she has opinions. Oh, Dad, I thought you were better than this.

Fuck it all. Now, all these other feelings are flooding me, too. Delayed reaction? Having your parents split up is not exactly the best thing to happen to a kid. Even though at Dad's I had a break from Mom's crazy shit, and even though the two of them had that fun-activity competitive thing going, it still sucked, as I look back at it now. A ten-year-old kid needs a dad at home, not across town. Funny how the whole situation didn't make me want to emulate a man more, being that I was kind of deprived of him. But I had the female thing going long before all this went down, at least on the inside.

Oh, the female thing, now on the outside. I'm getting the impression that Dad must've thought I was just "going through a phase," as so many people think of it, thoroughly misunderstanding the whole LGBTQIA+ thing. It's not a phase—it's a life. Ours. Anyway, I'm picking up that he must've been on the phase-y train when he was giving me all that support when I first came out. So much for that.

I overhear him getting something from the fridge and go into the kitchen to join him. Suddenly, the backyard needs his attention. I overhear him laughing and playing with Brenda and the baby. But in I walk and he turns to insta-sad.

Teardrop again. Dad! Where'd you go? Do you wish for your son back so you and he can talk sports? Find a beer buddy for that.

"Any thoughts about going back to college?" he asks.

"No. My boyfriend and I are thinking of moving south."

No response. At least, not from his mouth. His eyes say all kinds of things. At first, he seems to wonder if he heard me correctly. Boyfriend? Then, as it dawns on him that, yes, he did hear me correctly, he's obviously saying to himself, so what does this all mean? Does it mean… oh, to hell with it. I'm not in the mood for mindreading.

"Your only job is to love me," I tell him, "just as I am."

He nods. "I do love you," he says. That's it. No second part of the sentence. Well, that certainly speaks volumes, too.

Also, much to my chagrin, I am my father's son, a bit, even now, to this day. Time after time, I find myself sitting forward with my arms hanging between my legs somewhat, twiddling my entire hands. Yikes! That's a major Dadism and women don't do that, I say to myself. So, I correct my posture and hand occupation, only to do it again a few minutes later. I also find myself using his phrasing, intonations, and inflections sometimes, too—in ways that a woman wouldn't. Shit.

One afternoon, as I head out for a run, I notice Brenda trying not to stare at my shaved legs and shortish shorts.

But she's not the only one staring. Some random dude about my age walking down the sidewalk calls out, "Hey! Running my way?"

Ewww, gross. As if the whole family thing isn't bad enough. I could deck him if I want, but I decide to tamper my temper a bit instead.

As I return to the house, I hear Dad and Brenda arguing. I can't really make out words, but I can definitely make out the tone. Then, I hear Brenda say one word clearly, "Ja-aaye!" She says it with so much derision, there's no confusion what they're arguing about.

Fuck it! To hell with all this. Between not wanting to see myself as my father's daughter (translated: the masculine parts of him I don't really want) and not being allowed in the same galaxy as little Joy, I leave.

And back to Mom's I go. I can't even call it home. It's such a darling place, at least, visually, but it's not mine. I need my own universe where there's no judgment, no wistfulness, only acceptance of what is.

I wish Burning Man could be year-round. Maybe, whenever I have to be at the house, I'll just hang with Gram as much as possible until I leave for SoCal with Charles.

Not long after I arrive back at the rancheroo, Mom takes Gram and me to doctors' appointments, so we could carpool and be green. I show up in my black fishnets.

"Must you?" she asks. She turns around to see Gram in tie dye. "Must you?"

We look at her in her waaaaaaay oversize gray T-shirt. "Must *you*?" we ask. Then, we all laugh.

"You know, even though you're both recovered, you two sure don't seem to be going anywhere anytime soon," Mom says after our doc visits. "For whatever reason, you're both still here. And you don't seem to be in any hurry to change that."

"Are you in what should be our hurry?" I ask.

She shrugs and doesn't continue.

Charles flexes his arm, making his biceps and then his triceps bulge.

"You're not fawning enough," he says, because I'd turned to attend to a ding on my phone. We're lolling in his bed in his tiny cabin up in the wilds of Humboldt County, just outside of Garberville.

"Oh, let me make up for that." I pull his face toward mine.

After, uh, lots more of making up for that, we lie together just gazing at each other. All of each other, that is.

"You look good in stark naked," he smiles.

"That's Lady Starke naked to you," I smile back referring to another character in *Game of Thrones*. "Cocks are so crazy weird looking," I say, looking at his no-longer-standing-at-full-attention-but-now-puckered pecker.

"Thanks a lot, dude!"

"Dudette."

"Dudette."

"Not just yours," I assure him. "All of 'em. I think they're designed to be weird looking."

He looks at mine. "Yours is friendly looking."

I look down. "Shit! What's that thing still doing here?"

After we both laugh, he turns serious. "Going to do it?"

"I think so. When I have the money, that is. What do you think?"

"It's what you think that matters. It's your choice. Whatever you want is what I want." He kisses me on the forehead.

"Do you have a preference when it comes to fucking?"

Charles shrugs. "Not so much. You?"

"Not really. It's all good."

"That it is. With you, anyway."

I really love this guy.

"You're from a town where everyone prides themselves on looking like random mountain people," I say, looking at some pedestrians as we head out of Garberville. "Why'd you decide to rock this wholesome shit?"

"Stands out when your friends are all into the dark stuff. You noticed me more."

I smile.

"Southern California," Charles chuckles as we pass a sign for San Francisco. Folks up north consider San Francisco and its environs as Southern California even though there's another whole half a state below us.

"So, ask me more getting-to-know-each-other shit," I say.

"Hmmmmmmm." He thinks for a minute. "Ever wish your parents had stayed together?" he asks.

"Nah. I know lots of kids of divorced parents long for that oh-so-ever-elusive reconciliation, but I never did. One of them would've had to have been a completely different person, and I knew that even at age ten."

"Yeah. Same, kind of."

"Doesn't mean the whole divorce didn't hurt like hell, though."

"Yeah. Same. Totally." He turns to me. "What is the deal with your mom?"

"Where do I begin?" I laugh, but he doesn't. "Well, which part in particular?"

"Every time she looks at me, it's like she's trying to figure out where she's seen me before."

"Yeah, I've noticed that, too. Just another one of her Momisms, I guess."

Mom and Gram have stopped asking me about my future plans. That's certainly very wise of them. Every time they asked me in the past, I felt like I slipped a few feet back on the ladder of choices—maybe out of spite, but mostly out of confusion.

"Just let me figure it out," I want to say to them. "I'll get there."

My Tarot readings are still going strong, but I definitely need to get out of the house a whole lot more. I land a way cool job at the store Vision works at—a second-hand shop that sells everything from old, vintage, even Victorian, clothing, to funky jewelry that looks great on me as well as any of my vampire friends, to furniture that would go well in Mom's parlor, to blue-glass bottles I buy to put in Mom's kitchen, although I'll take them to my own one day.

I especially love helping customers try on the antique clothing. Some of the old ladies transform into child brides when they try on a wedding dress from the forties. My goth gal pals transform into Dracula's bride when they slip into the same dress. Go figure.

Sometimes people—who aren't particularly goth—come in and want goth clothes. I point to the general collection of goth garments. They usually then ask if there's a section for male or female.

"It's never mattered to us in the slightest," I answer. "One section works for all of us."

After they recover from their surprise, they go over to the rack. Of all things to get hung up on for all these centuries.

Chapter 20

Alice

By this point in my ever-astounding existence, I thought absolutely nothing could possibly surprise me anymore. But that was before I found Charles sitting at my kitchen table the other week, just before James went to stay with his dad.

Charles comes with a coating of confidence, power, even some intrigue. He's tall and somewhat built, very athletic, with shoulder-length blonde hair and blue eyes. James has glorious blonde hair that most women would kill for. Oh, right—he *is* a woman. And he did have to kill...something...for it.

So...this new young man is...James? Yes! He's James! Or is he who James might've been...could've been...or, perhaps, was supposed to be but was hidden away because James was too beautiful and powerful and couldn't handle it? Am I just being an armchair therapist and missing the whole point of my son's choice? But I do know...things...sometimes. This could be one of them.

"Mom, this is Charles. Charles, my mom."

I shook the young man's hand, unable to believe my eyes. I probably made both of them quite uncomfortable, but I also knew they had not the slightest idea of the reason behind my staring. I unpacked my grocery bags for something else to focus on.

"Want some cookies? I got some organic vegan for you."

James choked on the water he was drinking. "You feeling alright, Mom?"

He then kissed Charles right then and there, in front of me—a big, long, sloppy, drink-in-your-face kind of kiss. I'm sure they were trying to get my goat, but somehow I actually thought it was quite beautiful. Maybe, I was channeling my mother at that particular moment in time once again.

Then, it struck me. My James, still in there, somewhere, deep inside, was kissing...who was he kissing...himself? His higher self? (There's my mother again!) Even the name Charles is similar to James, and not just for the *es* ending, but also in that they're both rather formal. Neither went with the nickname version.

○

Oh, that Charles, Charles, Charles. Oh, my James, James, James. Oh, this life, life, life. Oh, my new best friend (not) midnight, midnight, midnight. Once again, I turn to the ceiling for answers, but, once again, it's not very forthcoming.

When we look for a partner, who and what are we looking for? Is it someone to complete us? Is it someone to aspire to? Is it someone to abuse us, if that's how low we think of ourselves? Of course, the answer comes from wherever we're at.

From what he probably thought he could tell from the outside looking in, I'm sure James thought I was experiencing something far different than all the machinations I actually was going through. But what I said above was my experience of my being on the outside of this Charles person and this kissing occurrence, looking in, and the machinations I had were from valid feelings as well as brand-new philosophical ideas.

Oh, I have to tread so carefully because the super-whatever-phobic, ostracizing people (fellow church members and fellow political party members) have persecuted them so much. I'm not trying to be hurtful. I'm just trying to understand it, assimilate it, and have it make sense in my head.

I just can't keep up. It's impossible to have to be hip to all the enormous changes going on around me. As in, who in the world are all these new movie stars? As in, where was that music made—in a sheet-metal cutting warehouse? As in, I should've known all about gender dysphoria and its ramifications and effects...on *my* child. I've been so lost in this world I had no idea about and have suddenly found myself living in, and not by my choice.

Oh, sure, every generation of parents has to come face to face with whole new ballgames that weren't in their worldview. And somehow, we're supposed to just snap to it and love and accept this new lifestyle.

I'm sure the parents of the baby girls born just after 1900 were appalled when their daughters became flappers and smoked cigarettes. Then, there was what the pot-smoking, draft-card-burning hippies did to their post-WWII, triumphing-over-Hitler, by-the-book parents. Mother, I'm talking to you.

I'm just trying to do an honest exploration of...my heart, I guess. I'm trying to forget what most of society says, plus what my friends and my priest have said to me (without knowing what I'm going through), at least for the time being.

As a matter of fact, when Father Moore was speaking against same-sex couples in a recent church service, my mind went to a new place: "Well, if those couples are happy, I'm happy for them. True love is such a rare gift." That surprising new place felt good to my whole nervous system.

So...I gave birth to this child of God, and no matter what he does, I will always love him. If he wants me to love him as a her, fine. I can do that—when he's in earshot, that is. I have my own world that lives outside of his earshot. Does he just want acceptance no matter what he does? Is that what he's looking for? Is that what this is all about?

I'm starting to understand the trans thing, I suppose. But, as I've said, James was never, ever—not once—interested in anything female-related as he was growing up. Dan played ball with him. They went to sporting events. Am I even wrong for thinking those things are more male than female? What happened to the world I was kind of used to? I want it back. What do I do?

Yes, I truly thought James was going through a phase, and if I ignored it, it'd go the way of most phases: away. Silly me. Stupid me. Maybe if I'd known—really known and really understood the ramifications—about all this sooner, I would've helped him start hormone suppressants, so he wouldn't be a woman with that deep voice and Adam's apple. I didn't know. I didn't want to know. I do know that since he told me, I've been lying in bed, driving my car, weeding my garden, living my whole life wondering if it was my parenting—or lack thereof—that did this. I've wondered if the whole gender dysphoria in so many of the kids will be just a short-term thing, a passing fancy for a whole generation as well as my own child.

But...many years back, I remember a friend of mine moaning and groaning about her gay son. "Why, oh why, did he have to jump in on the gay fad?" Even I knew it wasn't a fad—just a way of being that was finally allowed out loud in society.

And that's what James is—finally allowed out loud in society. Not fully yet, but more than ever before. Even the whole bathroom issue has become a national conversation, and I'm starting to see both sides. That's a lot more than I could say a year ago.

Something definitely happened when he went to visit his dad and new stepmom. He came back nowhere near as combative and contentious as usual. I'm not sure why he's still hanging around. He's all better, and I've offered him plenty of money.

How could my grandparents leave almost all of their money to me and none to Mother? I understand their reasoning, I think, but still can't believe they did that. Maybe, it was their ultimate FU to her for getting pregnant, for the whole hippie happening that they probably took as a personal affront. They probably also figured I'd take good care of her whenever she needed it. I do give her a hard time, but I'm honestly considering how I can set her up for her final years. I did Google a few senior-living centers when I returned home from Point Reyes that time, when her situation was really on my mind. She certainly can't stay with me forever.

This night is certainly lasting forever. I give up on trying to sleep and head to the coffee maker.

○

Then, there's this other thing. Before I can even wrap my head around it, the DNA test sits on the bathroom counter. All I have to do is send a saliva sample to some lab somewhere in some distant place. I picture young men with man buns and black-rimmed glasses looking like they're about to take over the planet.

But I find that I can't bring myself to touch the kit. Do I want to know? Or would I rather avoid this man for this whole lifetime? Maybe he's dead. Maybe he died of an overdose around the time Janis and Jimi did.

Or maybe he sports a man bun, too…although at his age at most it'd probably be a man crouton, if that. Haha!

Or maybe he loves Jesus, and we'd have a lot to talk about. He probably doesn't even know he has an almost-fifty-year-old daughter. Or maybe he thinks back on that night—and other nights, other hookups—and wonders if he has any offspring wandering around the world. He could certainly do the DNA test, too.

Truthfully, I did one a few years ago and threw the report package out before I even opened it. Maybe I'll do that again. Maybe not.

Chapter 21

Starr

There's magick afoot.

Is it my imagination or has Alice been sweeter to Jaye since that night at the shelter, when she met her new little friend?

Jaye's been somewhat subdued since her return from her father's house. I never really took to that man. I thought Alice was settling—not that Dan was beneath her, per se, but that she just took the first halfway decent guy to come along. He didn't have the greatest sense of humor. But then neither did, nor does, Alice. And Heaven forbid, I should ever give her my opinion about a landmine topic, such as a boyfriend/ fiancé/husband/former spouse. I keep my mouth shut about him.

Throughout her life, Alice has been so sad at times. I still wonder, did I do that to her? Was it even up to me or did she come in like that, of her own volition? When I look back at the effect my mom had on me…well, there is an effect, of course, but I'm mostly just who I am, which totally pissed her off.

And yet, is something changing in Alice? Could it be? Yes, there's definitely magick afoot in the house.

"You know, the more the past passes, the less future we have."
"How very profound, Mother."
"But the future is infinite, really."
"In Heaven?" Ever my Alice.
"In all the places we go after here." Ever her mother.
"I just want to see my Lord."
"And so you shall."
She seems surprised I just took her at her words there. Well, who am I to say who she's going to meet or not meet when she's done here? But the spiritual-v-religious truce only lasts a minute, thanks to a glance at my news feed.

"Criminy, we're in a fall the likes of which haven't been seen since Atlantis."
"Mother! Honestly!"
"Oh, honestly yourself. Is what I'm saying any crazier than Adam

and Eve hanging out in a garden with a snake? Or that ark? There are two hundred sunken cities in just the Mediterranean, and countless more around the world."

"Where on God's green Earth do you get information like this?"

"*Ancient Aliens.* On the History Channel."

Alice decides to ignore that. "What do you think of Charles?"

"They seem madly in love."

"Or just mad."

"Couldn't that be said about us all?"

She glowers, but at a lower wattage than her usual glower. Yes, something's definitely shifting in her.

Now, about this DNA thingamajig on Alice's bathroom counter (I had to go in to grab some TP. Yes, again. She's chided me over that. I do have to remember to get some from time to time). I just don't know. Part of me wants her to do it and part of me doesn't.

I've thought of that young man so so so so so so so so so so many times. I have a clear snapshot of him in my head, but that doesn't mean that's exactly what he looked like. So many memories morph over the decades, and we often remember what we want to remember. I've pored through scores and scores of photos from Woodstock, trying to find him, but he was somehow invisible, as was I.

I still wonder about him. Who was he? Who is he now? Where is he? I've always been more curious about him than Alice ever seemed to be, but it's up to her to instigate this.

A couple of weeks later, Alice drops a report on the table in front of me.

"Michael Templeton," she says. "Ring a bell?"

I shake my head.

"He's my father."

Hands shaking, I pick up the report. My reading glasses slip off, but then my eyes fill up so I can't see the words anyway. Tears slip down my face, as they do Alice's.

"Oh, do I love me a good tearfest," Jaye faux-sighs but with a smile as she walks into the kitchen.

"Can you please find him?" I place the report in her hands.

After the quickest of glances at the words: "My grandfather?"

Alice and I nod. Jaye races out of the room and up the stairs, heels and all, and then races back to the kitchen with her laptop to start sleuthing.

Still wiping away tears, I turn to Alice. "Apparently, law enforcement can get your DNA results, you know."

"Well, here I am. Being me. I haven't done anything wrong. And if they find a third cousin twice removed who committed a crime, that's fine with me."

"Ah, ancestry," I say. "Did you know in our lineage of our little family here, we have some (males, as per the time) who went to Yale when it was a pup, some who are from some vague European aristocracy, and some who've invented things? We also hail from hearty peasant stock."

"Love that part!" Jaye giggles. "Hey, maybe we're related to Vlad the Impaler."

"The not-so-distinguished dude who started the whole Dracula deal?" I ask. "Lovely!"

"That kid will be the death of me yet," Alice says when Jaye rushes upstairs to get her computer charger.

"Maybe, she's from the Pleiadean side of the family."

"You might be the death of me yet before he is."

I turn to the list of our heritage included in the package. "This is fascinating," I say. "We're as white and WASPy as they usually come…"

"So. White," Jaye mutters as she returns with her charger.

"But we're also point two percent Ashkenazi Jew, point zero two Native American, and even African. How cool is all this?"

Alice shrugs. She has other things on her mind. Well, so do I, but it's not keeping me from babbling. Or maybe, it's the cause of my babbling. "These DNA tests can certainly erase some racism in the world." Alice doesn't say anything, so I go on. "I'm a little racist— against whites, that is."

"Oh, Mother."

"For the most part, I think racism is just confusion, elitism, with some fear-of-the-other thrown in. In my case of being racist against my own group, I just hate the privilege people have without even realizing how privileged they are. White privilege doesn't mean that life hasn't been tough. It just means that our race wasn't one of the reasons it's been tough."

To all that wisdom, Alice simply says, "Slavery ended a hundred and fifty years ago."

"Apartheid ended fifty years ago. And, in some areas, it's still going strong."

"We didn't have apartheid."

Where in all of the creations did this daughter of mine come from? "Oh, didn't we? We most certainly did! What else would you call having to use separate bathrooms and even drinking fountains? And not being allowed to marry someone of another race and being killed…"

"Okay! Alright already! Whatever. You win."

Whaaaaaaat?

Chapter 22

Jaye

Woahman! I could so not believe my eyes when I walked into the kitchen and found Mom and Gram at the table, as is usual, but both crying, as is not usual at all. Mom's usually so tightly wound up and Gram's usually firmly planted on a cloud; so, open tears are somewhat of an anomaly around here.

It doesn't take long to find him. That dude. My grandfather. Why they didn't look for him, I have absolutely no idea—they're both more than tech savvy enough to do a basic Google search, which is all it takes.

"Here he is. He lives in Boston."

They both stare at him, for very different reasons, for a very long time.

I finally break into their breathless silence: "He's an attorney for indigent asylum seekers from war zones."

"That's certainly noble," Gram says, her voice hushed.

"He was also in on the ground floor of Google, apparently, so he's loaded."

"That's certainly convenient," Gram smiles.

"There's an article about his philanthropy, which explains where he got his money," I tell them. "And his wife is apparently loaded, too."

Mom just stares and stares...and stares and stares...at his picture. At last, she speaks, also in a hushed voice: "A seventy-year-old gentleman is looking back at me—with my own eyes!"

"You certainly do have his eyes," Gram murmurs. She lets out a long sigh. "All these years, I thought that you did, but I wasn't completely sure I wasn't hallucinating."

Then, she chuckles, snapping herself out of her reverie. "The picture I'd carried in my head for fifty years remained of a twenty-year-old man. And here he is, age seventy or so, of course. But those brown eyes haven't changed much at all. Oh, sure, they're surrounded by crinkles and laugh lines, but the warm glow is the same. As all this time was passing, I thought I'd imagined that warmth and shine, just made it up, but there it is."

Gram looks at Mom, who's still lost in those eyes, those beautiful eyes. Finally, those same beautiful eyes look up at her mother. Yes, I guess she does have beautiful eyes. Funny how I have to see them in someone else to see how beautiful they are in her.

"What should I do?" Mom wonders aloud.

"That's entirely up to you," Gram shrugs.

I'm so crazy flustered I can't talk for a minute. "Are you kidding?" I finally blurt out. "You've got to get in touch with him! Get right on that!"

Mom doesn't respond.

"Or I will." They both look at me. "I'm allowed that. He's my grandfather. I could've just as easily spit in a tube to search for him, too."

"How would I get in touch with him?" Mom asks.

Well, that's a start. "You can call or email him at his work. Here, all that info is in this tab." I switch to another screen, which has his law firm's website already pulled up.

Mom reads a few of the rave reviews he's received. "He's certainly well loved. Strange he's still working at age seventy when he apparently doesn't have to."

"I'll meet him with you, too," I say.

They both look at me again, and I look right back at both of them. "You're not even going to tell me you're not going to see him. Of course you are, and I am, too." Then, just to Mom, I say, "He couldn't possibly have a worse reaction to me than you did."

Mom smiles and takes my hand. Woah, part *deux*. This day keeps getting more and more amazing. When's the last time she took my hand?

Mom emails him, and he answers right away. I mean, how could he not? Wouldn't he be curious?

"He's open to meeting," Mom reads to us, "but wouldn't be able to take a trip for a few months as he's dealing with a complicated legal issue. But if we don't want to wait and instead want to come visit him…"

Oh, what to pack to see my long-lost-and-never-seen-before grandfather? I decide to tone it down a touch. Charles and Vision come by to help me pack a few of my more understated outfits.

"I can't believe this story!" Charles says. "From a fling at Woodstock fifty years ago and here you are, going to see him."

"I can't believe I'm finally going to meet him. My grandfather! I can't even imagine what my mom and grandmother are going through. I wonder what he'll make of me." I'm blabbering, but I can't help myself.

"If he's cool, he'll be cool." Charles couldn't be any cooler about all this.

I notice Mom passing through the hallway outside my room. She hesitates when she overhears that last bit but continues on without saying anything.

I do wonder how my grandfather will receive me. Will he accept me for who I am? That's all I want.

I signed up for a killer of an issue but, yes, I can practically hear Gram telling me that it takes a killer of a person to take on a killer of an issue. Oh, and I wouldn't have signed up for it if I couldn't take it on. Yes, Gram, you've trained me well. And, yes, Gram, you would've said doozy instead of killer.

Or…does everything happen to us by fate? I don't know. If that were the case, we'd all be victims of some arbitrary chance. It's much more powerful to think we signed up for our particular killer issues.

How's this for something weird? Every now and then, I'll see a car go by, and I'll try to picture the person driving that car and try to see where he or she is going…and if they're happy…and if they're going home, and if so, are they happy going home and what is their home like? Or are they going to work, and if so, are they happy going to work and what is work like? What kind of issues do they have to deal with? Would theirs be any easier than mine? What if that guy's a drug addict, in and out of rehab? What if that woman just lost her spouse? What if…and with that, I realize that we have the issues we have, and no one else's would be any better, probably.

Maybe, I'd choose a mom who accepted all of me. But then, maybe I wouldn't. She's made me stronger, more resilient, maybe even more strident. I do know she loves me underneath all that confusion of hers. Maybe, I just came along to help her up her game.

Back to my grandfather…yes, just love me. And, yes, just let me be me. That's all I ask.

I wander into Mom's bedroom the night before our flight and plop onto her bed. "I wonder about his life. He's had so many years. What's he made of himself? Yes, he's a lawyer and a philanthropist, of course, and that's the bomb. But what's he like inside? And what made him fall for Gram all those decades ago? Did he ever look for her? Did he ever even suspect he had a whole branch of a family tree sprout from that union?"

Gram wanders in, too. "Well, we're about to find out."

Mom doesn't respond. She barely notices we're there, she's so lost in her thoughts as she packs. Don't blame her, but…

"Mom, stop leaving me on read!"

"What?"

"Stop leaving me on read. It means reading my message, but not responding."

She sits down next to me and wraps her arms around me. Gram sits down and wraps her arms around her. Wow.

The three of us descend into and onto Boston. In the cab, I gripe about my clothes. And then, about my shoes. And then, about my jewelry. And then, about…

"MOTHERFUCKER!" That's Mom. Even the cab driver turns around to look at her in shock.

"Uhhh, language!" I tease her.

"However do you cope?" she teases right back.

We laugh—even the driver.

We'd arrived the day before the big reveal. The next morning, we find ourselves with a few hours before we're supposed to meet with our mystery man. And just where do we find ourselves? A hair salon!

"My hair's a little confused today," I'd moaned. "I want some more foomph."

"So, let's go to the foomph store," Gram suggested.

We found a salon—aka the foomph store—near our hotel.

"Jeez," I report afterwards, "I had some slow-moving old thing, about forty or so, lumbering around the salon. I'm like, hey, this century, please?"

Gram laughs. "Funny, some hyper young thing, about forty or so, darted around the salon, doing my hair. I figured she hasn't mellowed with age yet. 'Hey,' I wanted to tell her, 'I know I'm in the senior category but I'm not going to leave this dimension this hour!'"

"Mine was around forty, too. I thought she was fine," Mom says.

"You're the Goldilocks in this tale," Gram laughs. "And she also happened to be closest to your age. Now, let's get this road on the show."

Neither Mom nor I correct her. Yes, right, that babbling was just to let off steam. I take their hands and smile. "We've got this."

Chapter 23

Alice

Oh, such glorious colors! The cab whizzes by the Boston Common, with its trees presenting the magnificence of New England in the fall…I'd heard about it but hadn't experienced it. Why did Mother ever leave?

"Because it's not like this year-round," she says, although I haven't even asked the question out loud. I hate it when she does that.

"You're not hard to read," she grins.

I *really* hate it when she does that!

His overstuffed office occupies the first floor of a distinguished brownstone in the Beacon Hill area. Boxes and boxes of files fill the place, but some semblance of order pervades. Each file represents a refugee, a person and, perhaps, a family. Never have file folders looked so important. Even files of medical records can't often compare to running for your life.

On the wall hang framed photos of people who originally came from all over the world, along with letters thanking him profusely for his pro-bono work. So even in his top-two profession (doctor, lawyer), he's still a dreamer, a hippie, a do-gooder, kind of like Mother. I bet if he'd become a doctor, he would've volunteered for half the year with the Red Cross or Doctors Without Borders.

His paralegal leads us into his inner office. And here he is. This complete stranger. My father. When he stands up, I see where James gets his height from, in addition to his great-grandfather on his mother's side…and who knows who else from his father's side…although now we can find out who else. His shaggy, gray curls make me want to whip out some scissors, but Mother probably loves them. Yes, my nerves are making me chatter, even just in my head.

He takes both of my hands in his and looks deep into my eyes. He suddenly blurs as I dissolve into tears.

"You must be Alice, my lovely daughter," he says, eyes misting.

What do I say? Dad, it's so nice to meet you. Haha! My mouth tries to move, but I can't say anything.

"I looked you up, by the way." His voice cracks a bit.

"You did?" all three of us ask in unison.

"Yes, not long after those DNA tests came out on the market. I wanted to know if anything had come of that night. You hadn't granted permission to be found yet, but I have friends who can find things for me."

"Are you experienced?" Mother jokes. "And from just that one night?"

He smiles at her for a second, then returns his full attention to me. "My friend even found your original name."

But then, it dawns on Mother what he just said a few seconds ago, and she turns to me. "Wait a minute! You did one of those DNA tests before?"

"I did. Then, I lost it. On purpose." Mother crosses her arms. "Why didn't you contact me, then?" I ask him.

"I didn't think that was mine to do. I figured I'd let you do that. But it was good to know you were safe and happy—from appearances on social media, anyway."

He lets go of my hands, turns to Mother, and takes both of her hands. "You're still just as beautiful as you were that day."

Her smile matches his. "As are you. You have a beautiful voice, too, which I don't remember hearing because Jimi was playing so loudly."

"Every single time I hear his version of the 'Star-Spangled Banner'…" He stops, eyes misting again.

"Me, too."

He releases Mother's hands and looks over at James.

"I'm Jaye, your granddaughter."

He takes James's hands in his, clearly trying not to look any one way—reactionwise—or the other at this granddaughter who is his height and has hands his size and the whole shebang. Literally—haha!

Cutting him some slack, James adds, "No, I didn't start out as your granddaughter. I switched a couple years back."

"So, you're trans…"

"I don't even identify as transgender anymore. I'm a woman, your granddaughter."

Mother and I exchange glances. That's certainly news to us, as *trans* has been such a vitally important label over the last two-plus years. Is that all it's been? Seems like forever.

Well, what happens when you finally find your father/

grandfather/very first love? You go to lunch.

"So, what exactly did you find when you found me?" I ask him, shrugging at the clumsiness of my question.

"Well," he says, after all four of us finish laughing, "you appeared to be well-established, along with safe and happy, at least according to what I could see on Facebook. I didn't want to intrude in case you already had a father in your life, someone who'd raised you and loved you like his own daughter. I didn't want to step on any of that."

"No. No father. Ever."

"I'm sorry."

As James would say, "Hold for the awkward pause." No, I didn't say that out loud. But, okay, let's go for more awkward. "Were you afraid I'd be after your money?" I ask him.

"Not really. I have plenty to spare and share."

Wow. That's refreshing. "So do I," I say.

"Wow. That's refreshing." No wonder he and Mother found each other in that psychedelic sea of free love and bliss—mind readers both. I did feel something or other across the table from James when I said what I just said; I still haven't told him about my (and, thus, his) inheritance from his great grandparents.

When James leaves to use the restroom, I show this all-too-familiar-but-nevertheless-still-a-complete-stranger a picture of his grandson, before the transition. "Kids these days."

He smiles. "I remember my parents saying the exact same thing about me when I burned my draft card."

"Mother said the same thing about me when I became a Catholic."

It's his turn to look slightly confused. "Mother? Not Mom?"

"She wanted something that would drive me absolutely crazy," Mother stage-whispers to him. "She certainly succeeded."

He nods in some mode of understanding, although his expression becomes far more quizzical. "Google also told me your political party, plus you were listed on a volunteer team for your church. I wasn't sure we'd have a whole lot to talk about." I can tell he's kidding with that last line.

"Maybe a lot to argue about." I tell him about having a parent and a child, with their divergent philosophies and all, as roommates for most of the past year. "It's not always peaceful."

"I bet. You're three strong women."

"But, wait!" I want to say. Instead, I ask, "Do you have much experience with transgender people?"

"Some, at least, with the LGBTQIA+ community, if not trans itself. A great niece is gender fluid. Usually she's a she, but I take her—or his, or their—lead."

I burst into tears. Over my father? Over James? I was denied the most important man of my life during my younger years, and I'll be denied the most important man of my life during my older years. I cry and cry and cry.

He takes my hands in his. Tears slip down his face, too. Mother leaves the table as James returns, to head him off. They both walk out onto the restaurant's balcony overlooking the Boston Harbor to give us some time, just the two of us.

"I just don't understand it."

"You don't have to," my father says.

"But I keep looking for understanding."

"Then, maybe, it's time to stop looking and let it come to you."

Chapter 24

Starr

Those beautiful brown eyes gaze into mine, as if fifty years hadn't passed by. Half a century. It feels like forever and no time at all—just like my whole life. Well, maybe it feels like a week from last Tuesday. A little bit of time, just to give some reverence to all these years I've lived since then.

My heart tugs for what might've been. Sure, I've had so many adventures that I wouldn't trade for anything. But what would the adventures with Michael have been like? What would it have been like to be in a real family unit? What would it have been like to raise Alice in Boston instead of Marin County and San Francisco? But then, I wouldn't have met Tim…or maybe I would've if Michael and I had broken up. Wow, now how's that for staying positive? Goodness, me—okay mind, you can stop jabbering anytime now.

Jaye tours the balcony once again, with Alice, to give Michael and me a moment. How do I sum up the tragedies and triumphs of an entire life in one sitting? The thrill of the wins, the agony of the defeats? That I feel like I failed my daughter, and she feels like she failed hers?

Oh, let's just wait awhile to talk about all that failure stuff. "You have three children, I heard?"

"Yes. And four grandchildren."

"Sounds nice."

He laughs—a little too loudly.

"Oh, you, too?" I smile. "Who are the parents of all those perfect adult children we keep hearing about?" He shrugs, still recovering from his burst of laughter. "What are your children up to?"

"I wish I had a stable nurse in the crowd," he groans.

"Well, you do!"

"True." Michael pulls out his phone to show me some family photos. "One of the three, this one," he points to a sad-looking man in his early forties, "is a recovering addict who put us through hell—sheer hell. In and out of rehab at least a dozen times. This one," he points to a somewhat cocky-looking man of forty or so, "was a Wall Street wizard and now sits in jail awaiting trial for embezzlement. He's the 'complicated legal issue' I'd mentioned in my email to Alice, but it actually looks like that should be done in the next month or so, sooner than we thought. And this one," he taps on a matronly looking woman, also around age forty, give or take, "is a member of the NRA."

I haven't been stunned into silence too often, but this is one of those times. I finally manage, "I don't know what to say."

"Maybe something about the grass always looking greener somewhere else?"

"Like over the septic tank, or something quippy like that?"

He nods. "They were a handful. Even a lifeful."

"So was my stable, Catholic, Republican nurse." He smiles.

I pause, and then, after a breath for courage: "How did you meet your wife?"

"College. She went to Radcliffe, and I went to Harvard."

So that's where my descendants get those brains of theirs. Well, from me, too, at that, although I didn't apply it quite as well as he did.

"How is she doing?"

"She was very, very sick."

"I'm sorry."

"She died a couple of years ago."

"Oh." I look away over the harbor so he wouldn't see that glimmer of hope shoot up from my heart and flash in my eyes. "Google informed us you were still married, from your website." We hadn't looked up his wife, though.

"I should get my info updated."

The glimmer has turned into a full-body tremor. How could I feel that? How could I go there? The man's wife died not long ago!

"I'll always love her, but ours was a marriage of friends, not of soul mates. We hadn't been, well, heart partners in a long, long time. And soul partners? Maybe we never were."

The full-body tremor has turned to…oh, Starr! Don't go there! What a terrible thing to be thinking about. Who does that?

As it turns out, however, I'm not alone with those thoughts.

"I looked through so many of the pictures, trying to find us," he says.

"Me, too."

"You know that picture that came out a couple months ago, for the fiftieth anniversary? You know the one, of that young, bedraggled pair famously standing in the mud wrapped in a sleeping bag. You know how they are now? They're still together! And they look so happy. That made me even more wistful over you."

"Yes, I saw them, too." Pause. "You've been wistful over me?"

He nods. "I hoped maybe a photo would have a caption with your name. I always wondered what if. And now I still do, maybe even more."

The light from the sun sparkling on the harbor maintains a stronghold on my fascination.

I finally turn back to him. The sunlight sparkles have nothing on those lights in his eyes. And he's obviously thinking the same thing about mine.

For the next day, Michael invites Alice to breakfast, a walk along the waterfront, and whatever else they decide to do, just the two of them. Jaye heads off to…Salem! House of the Seven Gables and all that jazz. Of course.

Michael loans me his car for the day and off I drive. And drive. And drive. I find myself in…Darien! I didn't mean to drive to Connecticut—heck, almost New York City, really. I hope he doesn't miss his car anytime soon.

I head down the darling main street of my darling old town. Too bad I didn't really see the darling aspects back when I lived here. I just saw the chains-around-the-ankle aspects. So much brick! And there are so many gables, everywhere. Benches sit in front of stores, inviting passersby to take a break and shoot the breeze. Or take a seat and ponder their oh-so-white existence. Oh! Oh-so-sorry about that. Well, nice to see white privilege is alive and well here. Not…nice, that is.

Here I am in my hometown and where do I go? Whole Foods, naturally. It's quite Darien-ish, what with its gables. Plus, it's like a mall compared to the Whole Foods in Petaluma. An eclectic gathering of comfy couches in the cafe area lure me over. Several of the town mavens still have that plastered-on smile. Some things never change.

I call Michael and 'fess up to my current location.

"No problem! Go wherever you want," he says.

I stop at the town's graveyard. I don't feel too much as I gaze down at my parents' tombstones, which are several rows apart, as my father was buried with his second wife. My brother lies in that far-off military cemetery. Around my parents I spy classmates and neighbors who died long ago and some who died even in the last year. Oh, there's that woman who apparently killed her husband. And there's that old man who took his own life after the 1987 stock market flash crash. Hey, come to think of it, I'm much older now than he was then. Whaaaaaaat?

I stop in front of the high school. It's so small! I didn't study much, but I was in every club possible—anything to keep from going home…yearbook, newspaper, drama-club plays. I was on the volleyball team, too, but just for one season. After that, I started hanging out with the druggies, without doing too many drugs myself for some reason.

I continue on to the middle school and then the grammar school. I know the youth these days have to deal with school shootings and climate change and so much more. Not to diminish the current fears, but I've been hearing the world is going to end for almost my whole life, too: from the fear of what lay beyond the Iron Curtain, to the Bay of Pigs, to duck-and-cover bomb drills, where we had to put on our coats and sit down in the hallway with our backs to the wall and our arms over our heads. Like that was going to save anyone from a nuclear bomb? Good Goddess, people, get real!

Oh, my boyfriend and I would park by that store over there and steam up the car windows by…just kissing. That really cute guy who looked just like Robbie Robertson worked at that gas station. And there's the old deli where my parents would stop to load up on provisions for car trips, even if just to Norwalk (a few towns over, but it seemed like forever to little me). Mother would always buy me a small box of animal crackers. I haven't had animal crackers in an elephant's age. Heh! Literally. Now, they've let them out of the cage, I hear. I absolutely love that.

I drive on until I reach our old street and park in front of our old house. It still has gables, too. The trees are so much bigger; a couple in the front yard that were so small back then now add to the canopy that shades nearly the whole road. Wait, what happened to that really big one across the way that would drop magical gold nuggets in the spring? I'd pretend I was an alchemist as I played with those nuggets while waiting for the school bus. Maybe a nor'easter took that tree out.

From the outside, the house looks like it could've been a perfectly lovely home, and it was…at least structurally. It's just that the inside thermostat was set to, yes, freezing. Compared to a war zone or extreme poverty or even the kids in the shelter who got booted out of their homes by their own parents, mine was a pretty good gig. There's nothing to pinpoint, though. That's part of what made it so bad…well, other than my brother dying in an unjust war that really was a war crime in and of itself.

But I mean before that. Well, there was Mom's abyss of sadness, but so many people lost loved ones in WWII. Was her state worse than others'?

So, I just feel guilty about feeling bad about it. Thankfully, more and more of that fades away as these years of mine pile up.

I look up at the second-floor window all the way to the right—my old room. My very first memory consists of lying in my crib, looking out the window on a very gray day. The room and the atmosphere were so void of color.

As I grew older, I'd sit and stare out that window. Somehow, I knew, even back then, that a major part of my life's purpose, in a complete reversal of that very first memory of mine, was to make this world more colorful. No more gray and ice.

I look over at the second-floor window all the way to the left—my brother's room. Mom never changed a thing in it. She left it just as he'd left it, although she'd dust and vacuum once a week.

Did she die young of a broken heart? Did I break her heart even more than my brother did? Did Dad eventually die of a broken heart, too?

After my mom died, which wasn't long after that stroke she had, and Dad got married again, was he happier the second time around? His new wife had two young kids—also a son and daughter. Maybe he thought he could start over again after losing his son and having his daughter go AWOL.

A woman walks out of the house and up to the car. "Can I help you?" she asks, as if we're at McDonald's.

Goodness me, I must've lost track of time and been sitting here for quite a while.

Sure, I'll have a new childhood to go, please. And a side of can-we-try-this-one-again? But, really, I wouldn't trade my childhood (at least, now that I'm not in it anymore). It was what it was, and it made me the person I am now. Wait, which is who again? Just joshing.

I climb out of the car. "I used to live here. Back in the fifties and sixties."

"Oh!" Wow, she reacts like Christmas has suddenly arrived. "Please come in."

What is with the millennial colors of white and gray? Except when they're lime green and brown? Or orange and purple? I do love colors, but not all mixes of 'em.

While she continues to gush over my visit and serves me iced tea in her backyard, I regale her with tales of the old neighborhood. She looks like a professional woman, and I wonder how I'm so lucky to find her home that day. And doesn't she have to pick up her kids? It's just getting to be time for school to let out.

As if she can hear my thoughts, she sighs. "I just found out my husband is having an affair. He's picking up the kids from school and taking them on a weekend trip while I figure out what I'm going to do with the rest of my life."

I'm quiet for a bit. "This house wasn't lucky in love back in my time here, either," I finally confide to her. "I applaud your honesty, though. I wish everyone could do that." She doesn't respond. "Could I make a suggestion? You don't have to decide the rest of your life right now. Just the next little while would do."

"I don't even know where to begin."

I smile. "First you make a meal." And then, I hold her as she cries.

"Shut the front door!" Jaye giggles in the cab on the way to the airport the next morning. "You were flirting with a man whose wife just died?"

"No! I was…oh, I don't know what I was doing." My sudden bout of shyness surprises me. "She didn't 'just' die—it was a couple of years ago." Totally shifting tactics, I add, "Time is of the essence at this age, you know."

Alice snickers. "I thought this was mostly for me. How wrong I was!"

"But it was for you!" I say. "It was for all of us, really, but mostly you. How was I to know I'd get such a benefit, too?"

As we walk through the airport, I watch Alice. "I can feel the eyes," she once told me. "Even though I've trained myself not to notice all the people staring at my child, trying to figure out what's what…or even what's not. This whole new world can be so confusing these days."

I see lots of people doing their non-male, non-female thing, too. How did Vision describe it? "I'm non-binary. I'm not a one or a zero." That was it. How cool is that?

Once the three of us pass through security and reach the gate, Jaye announces she has to pee. Funny how men have to take a leak (or a piss) and women have to pee. Jaye's even made that transition, too.

"By the way," Alice whispers to me as Jaye disappears into the nearby women's room, "did you happen to catch the switch about not identifying as trans anymore? Before this trip, that is?" I shake my head. "Now it's 'woman,' no 'trans' before woman?"

"Right. Totally new to me, too."

"Good to know. Glad it's not just me."

I look around the airport waiting area, which has those millennial colors of lime green and brown, as I just harangued about. It also has that conundrum of our time: long tables to gather together, but everyone's glued to their gadgets.

Alice and I settle into our books and people watching, but not for long. Shrieks fill the corridor. Of all the things people choose to be upset over. Actually, if this whole situation with my grandchild wasn't in Alice's life and face, she'd probably be upset over it, too.

"Get out of here! Get out of here! You don't belong in here, even if you and your cockamamie friends think you do!"

Alice freezes. I put my hand on her arm and say, "I'll go. You watch our stuff."

As I enter the restroom, I find a woman about my age holding her handbag over her head, about to strike Jaye with it.

"Do that and you'll be charged with assault," I tell her.

The woman drops her bag. Jaye calmly looks in the mirror to apply lipstick.

I help the woman pick up her purse items that had scattered all over the floor. She trembles as I hand her wallet and a few other things to her. "He doesn't belong in here," she says.

"She's a she."

"Think any of us have things in our lives we don't want? It doesn't get to work like that, though."

A male voice, probably belonging to a security guard, calls in: "Everything okay in there?"

We're not quite sure how to answer that, so we remain silent. We hear him speak into his radio, asking a female coworker to come assist.

Jaye looks at the woman via the mirror. "I could press charges."

"My husband just died, you bitch!" The woman bursts into tears and falls into my arms. I certainly seem to be in the high-honor habit of holding crying women these days.

"At least you're finally getting the gender right," Jaye says softly, trying to be funny.

But it's not the moment for it. I hold the woman as she weeps. Jaye pats her on her back. The other women in the room give us a wide berth and don't utter a word.

A female security guard arrives. She looks at the woman still sobbing in my arms and then at Jaye—her lipstick, her Adam's apple, her heels—and starts to speak to her.

"I'm done." Jaye walks out and I quickly follow, once I'd steadied the woman on her feet and passed the responsibility for her to the guard.

And this all happened *after* security. The TSA agent has to pick a pink button for a woman or a blue button for a man, so their software can pick up any abnormalities around the passengers' bodies. We all hate going through those blasted machines, but for trans people it can be especially unsettling. Happily, though, most agents are becoming more and more used to people expressing differently from what their machines might reveal. Jaye's agent had her step aside and she ran one of those wands around her. No unusual beeps.

The agent then looked over the three of us with our pink, brown, and peace-sign purses and roller bags—Jaye's was that great pattern by Diane von Furstenberg with the big pink hearts, Alice's was forest green, and mine had psychedelic swirls. She determined we looked safe enough, I suppose, and waved us on.

The three of us sit in a row, all very quiet, the whole way back to California. Jaye stares out the window. Alice reads a Catholic book. I shut my eyes and dream of what might have been.

But what was, was what was supposed to be. And what is, is what is supposed to be. (I mean, at a personal level and within reason—I'm not talking wars, abuse, famine, and the like. Those aren't supposed to be.)

And what is can always change.

I wish the Universe hadn't taken me so literally on that last thought. I meant change *for the better* all the way around. I should've specified that.

A doctor and two nurses wheel the gurney down the hall and out of sight.

As my heart drops to my feet, I continue my plea: "Please, please, please."

Chapter 25

Jaye

So, guess who did her usual processing her mom stuff…all over me. Meanwhile, I was chill about the whole thing. Michael Templeton—yeah, that guy, my grandfather—was cool. It wasn't as big a deal as I expected.

Salem was super cool, though. That was a bigger deal to me…or maybe I'm making that up, or something or other. But I remember being a witch. Or maybe I don't. Maybe, I'm making that up, too. Maybe, it's just in the collective consciousness like so many other events, and people who remember a past life there—or anywhere—are just plugging in to the collective memory. Woah, channeling Gram here.

Mom doesn't have to start in first thing in the morning, though. Okay, it's one-thirty in the afternoon, but it's still first thing for me. And I might be fairly young, relatively, but I'm old enough to know when whatever she's talking about isn't necessarily whatever she's talking about.

Here she goes. "Not to be mean…"

"You know that's always a prelude to being mean."

" But why are you all suddenly coming out now? Where were you all, all these years?"

Oh, Mom. I thought we were getting somewhere. And you insist on circling back here again? "We were hiding. It's not like there's suddenly a whole bunch of us coming from nowhere. It's just that it's safe now. It's safe to come out and be ourselves."

Maybe, I should go get myself adopted by a Native American tribe. They don't have just the male-and-female thing going. They have shades—all the way from ultra-masculine male to ultra-feminine female, with all these shades in the middle. Life is like that. It's not black and white, but gajillions of tones in there. Plus, they call the people in between the extremes "Two Spirits," and those exhibiting both male and female traits are considered especially gifted.

While I think about this, I notice Gram gazing out the window. She has a light in her eyes I haven't seen before. That's saying a lot, because this woman seems to eat, drink, and breathe light and then radiate it out of her body.

"Moving to Boston, are we?" My teasing shakes her out of her reverie.

"Not exactly," she blushes.

"Gram, you're so crazy cute! Meanwhile, Mom, however…" But I'm actually teasing her, too.

"Don't let the door hit you on the way out!" Mom sings to me. A few months ago, that line would've been overflowing with venom. Now, not so much, even despite her question just a minute ago.

"Now, is that what Jesus would've said?" There's less of a dig in there on my part, too. "Asking for a friend."

Gram chimes in. "I think Jesus might've said that. He probably had his share of moments where he could be a character."

"Mother!"

"I'm coming into my character," I giggle. After Mom leaves—of course, you knew she would, she's not completely cool yet—I turn to Gram. "Is she ever going to call me Jaye?"

"What does she call you? I mean, I hear her calling you pet names, but is there anything else?"

"No. Nothing, lately."

"Oh. Well…"

"That's a deep subject."

Gram smiles, but then sighs. "In answer to your question, I hope so. She still calls me Mother, though. Has for decades."

"Doesn't that bother you?"

"Well, it felt like it was something very important to her, so I wasn't going to mess with it. I think it's been more important for her to call me Mother than for me to be called Mom."

"It's more important to me for her to call me Jaye than it is to her to call me James."

"I think she'll get there. In her time."

"How would she like it if you still called her Ambrosia?" Gram laughs, but I'm not smiling. "Being called the right name is a big part of trans people not wanting to off themselves."

"You don't think about that, do you?"

"No. But being called my chosen name would still help in my life overall."

I love to hang out in playgrounds and watch the children, especially the little girls. No, no, not in a creepy way at all. I want to see what could have been. I love to see their exuberance in full expression, their swirling and twirling and shrilling and trilling and screaming and giggling. My heart, if not all the rest of me, had been swirling and twirling and all of that from a young age.

Often, these trips make me wistful. If only... What if...? Sometimes, I'm glad I'm wearing sunglasses so no one can see the tears in my eyes.

I dress way down on these days—just simple athletic wear and a ponytail. I don't want to terrify the parents any more than I probably already do. Maybe I should borrow somebody's dog so at least I could appear like I'm on an important mission. I am on one, but it probably doesn't look like it.

If only... What if...? If only I'd really known what it was I was feeling. What if I'd had someone to talk to? What if one of my friends could've been going through all this, so I had an example in my life? I certainly have found enough friends now who went through that— where were my trans peers in grammar, middle, and high school? Oh, right, Catholic school. We didn't exactly go there in there. What if I could've come out sooner? What if I could've taken hormone suppressants before puberty shot me up to the stratosphere and gave me a deep voice and an Adam's apple?

If only... What if...? I wish I could've been one of these free-spirited girly girls. Well, they're not all especially girly, though. Today, in the giant sandbox, a little girl grabs her brother's dump truck, and he starts to cry.

"Amber, little girls don't play with dump trucks." Her mother probably just wants her to give the toy back more than she really means those words.

Amber releases the truck, and the little boy runs it over to the far edge of the play area.

When the mom follows him, I say to little Amber, "It's okay, you can play with dump trucks if you want to."

Oh, if only/what if someone had come along and was able to let me know it was okay to play with dolls. On those long-ago days, when I reached for one in a sandbox, on a playground, at a friend's house, Mom did her usual, "Now, James, boys don't..." and the whole hoopla.

It's not going to stay how it was, though. We're creating a whole new world. I feel like Wonder Woman.

I stumble into the kitchen the next day, feeling a little less Wonder Womanish in that particular moment, still trying to wake up. Mom's eating lunch and Gram's doing…something. She seems to hold and let go of her fingers, and then she repeats that several times.

"Gram, what are you doing?"

"Muscle testing."

Mom waggles her head. "Of course you are."

Gram picks a bottle of supplement pills from about half a dozen on the counter, and sets it in the palm of one hand. She does the holding and letting go of her fingers again. "If it's right for me, my fingers will let me know," she says.

More Mom waggling. "Of course they will."

But for the first time I can think of, Mom and I exchange glances. Gram and I have exchanged many a glance over things Mom's said and done, and I'm sure they have over things I've said and done. But for Mom and me over Gram, this is a first.

Gram sets a different bottle in her palm and repeats her process.

"Gram, just tell me what supplement that is, and I'll look it up for you."

"No, I'd rather do it this way." She shows us that she's put each thumb and ring finger in a loop, and then has looped the two loops together. "If the circles hold tight, that's a yes." She gives an example of them holding tight. "If they don't hold tight, that's a no." She shows us that, too.

"Aren't you just telling them what to do?" Mom asks.

"No."

"Why don't you just try a Magic 8-Ball?" Mom smirks. "Or a cootie catcher? Those'd be just as effective."

"A cootie catcher?"

"Those origami paper fortune-teller things we used to play with in grade school."

"Ah."

I notice Gram's holding a bottle of Berberine, so I Google it and I read her some of the benefits of taking that.

"My hands told me already—it's a go for the Berberine."

Mom and I look at each other once more.

But our newfound special connection doesn't last long.

"Nobody's right all the time." Mom's all over me again.

"Especially those who think they are." I'm all over her, too.

"Oh, yes, I really want to be inclusive." Gram speaks as though she's each of us. "I don't want to exclude anyone for their weird-ass beliefs."

The three of us laugh. The kettle whistles and Gram pours herself a cup of tea.

Mom looks at Gram and me. "Here's a question for you. What's something the liberals and the conservatives could meet in the middle on? How about clean energy?"

Gram shakes her head. "Nah. The oil lobby is too powerful and feels it has too much at stake."

"Well," Mom says, "No one is for dirty water or air."

I cross my arms. "Could've fooled my entire generation."

"I was part of a youth quake myself," Gram says to me, "thank you very much. We were the first kids to really take a stand and say things have got to change. Although Socrates complained about the kids of his time, too. But my generation was taking on the entire military-industrial complex."

"Why'd you stop? Not you, of course, because you haven't stopped. But your generation? Woodstock generation, what happened to you? Why'd you leave this ginormous mess for us to clean up?"

"I have no idea. What a tragedy that is." After she punches in a number on her phone and gets put on hold, she stares out the window, lost in thought. "You know, there are other choices, just like in quantum computing. All possibilities exist in the same place at the same time. Just like me. Just like you."

"Stop the madness!" I hold my head. "Ouch!"

"We just have to figure out the possibility. It's right in front of us. Hiding in plain sight."

Mom walks by the kitchen doorway, and something out the living room window catches her eye. "A very young couple is moving in across the street. And his bun is bigger than hers."

I stand up to check out the new neighbors. "You did hipsturbia before it was a thing."

"Hipsturbia! I like it. Bye." She grabs her purse and leaves to go do her thing, whatever that is.

These new neighbors do look pretty hip. The other neighbors have kind of avoided me lo these many years (since my change, anyway) if they can. Sometimes, I go off to talk to them as they're gardening or puttering (a Gram word) in their yard or garage, just to see them try to wriggle out of talking. It amuses me to no end.

Gram's still on hold. "This company seems to be run by very engaging robots," she laughs.

"Gram, you're nowhere near as much of a technosaurus as other people your age seem to be."

"Have to keep up with life, of course." She notices I'm watching Mom climb into her car and then pull out of the driveway. She sighs. "You know the happiest I ever saw her?" I shrug. "When she was holding her newborn baby." I don't say anything. "Just so you know," she continues, "that love will never, ever stop."

Back I go to the store with Vision where I get to play with the goth and vintage clothing and dress more folks as Dracula's bride. Speaking of such delights, Halloween is on the horizon. Yes! My favorite holiday. There's quite the gathering of hot, happening hobgoblins like me in San Francisco the Saturday before, but then there's also an Exotic Erotic Ball in nearby Santa Rosa. Charles, Vision, a few other friends and I decide we'll go to both.

I've always had this thing about magic and alchemy. And now, I'm getting to watch lead turn to gold. It's not always bright and shiny on the surface, but I know it's happening underneath.

Chapter 26

Alice

Oh, that trip. What a trip, to sound like my mother and child for a minute. So that's my father. Interesting. The breakfast we had, just the two of us, was one awkward silence after another, until he asked me about his grandchild.

What fun I had telling him about James' infancy, his childhood, all the adventures we had.

When I finally stopped talking, he said just one thing: "Jaye. Her. She." Okay, that's three things.

Before I could stop it, a wail escaped from my heart, and he held me as I sobbed. About ten minutes must've gone by, then he said something that started me all over again: "I understand."

No, you don't, I wanted to say. I could handle never meeting you, my father—never knowing who you were, never seeing the male part of my lineage—more than I can handle this.

I do have moments where I'm all right. I'm full-on all right. But still I grieve for what I thought was so and perhaps even for what was not so. And I do grieve for this father I never got to have, I guess, especially now that I know how wonderful he is.

At least, I don't have to grieve for an understanding family. That seems to have shown up, as of recently. Thank you, Lord.

Well, sometimes it's an understanding family.

"He asked me what my purpose is," I tell Mother and James. "My purpose? My purpose is to be the best Christian I can be."

"That's a high calling if you take 'being a Christian' as the way the Christ meant it."

"The Christ. Honestly, Mother."

"'What you do to the least of my brothers' and the like," James says.

"What's your purpose?" I ask him.

As he thinks about his answer, Mother blurts out, "Oneness."

"With what?"

"All of creation in all the universes."

"Universes? Just the thought of that makes me dizzy."

"How about the multiverses?"

"Mother, isn't that a little extreme? Multiverses? You make my head swim. I can't keep up."

"Well, we do move around the sun at sixty-eight thousand miles per hour, and the whole solar system moves around the center of the Milky Way Galaxy at half a million miles an hour."

I press my hands to my eyes. "No wonder I'm exhausted."

◌

I've always loved October in general and Halloween in particular. I love decorating the house with pumpkins, witches, and skeletons. Living in such an old house, spiderwebs would accumulate on their own, and often, but I don't go as far as to just let them be. I put up fake spiderwebs complete with spiders.

"You know Halloween is a pagan ritual," James has loved to inform me ever since he learned this information at age, oh, eight or so.

Yes, I know that and don't care. Maybe that was one nostalgic remnant (*the* one?) of growing up near the Castro. Those guys sure knew how to throw one heckuva block party.

That was one of the most fun nights of the year. A group of kids from my school would gather together and mingle with the merry mob. There always seemed to be Dorothy, the Scarecrow, the Tin Man, and the Cowardly Lion stopping every few feet to belt out a song from the movie. Dr. Frankenstein, Riff Raff, and Magenta from the *Rocky Horror Picture Show* (I only saw it because a friend dragged me off to it during our college days) were frequent guests. Witches, wizards, warlocks, Boy Scouts—oh, you name it, it was there. Unfortunately, Halloween in the Castro stopped because of a shooting in 2006.

Back to the ghost of Halloween present, James isn't even all that dressed up for the holiday—for him, that is—but the trick or treaters are captivated by what probably looks to them like a goth-ish fairy princess. Their parents look at me, eyes full of questions. "Is he like this all the time or just for tonight?" they seem to ask. Maybe, it's just me.

"Who do we have here?" James sings out. "A dragon? Oh, I love your scales and tail. And who's with you? Are you a mermaid? Oh, I love your scales and tail, too!"

In between doorbell rings, my son and the wildebeest (Vision) sit at the kitchen table drinking their witch's brew. Mother sits here, too—unusually quiet for her.

"Mother, you okay?"

Mother cringes as the doorbell rings once again. The two Halloween helpers jump up to greet the visitors once again.

"Halloween, yuck." I try to hold back my surprise at her attitude, but fail miserably. "First of all," she says, "all these ghouls and goblins don't exactly light my fire. Plus, I haven't liked the sound of a doorbell since those two young Army men showed up at my parents' house all those years ago. Maybe, that's why I haven't had a real door of my own in all this time."

"Well, that's certainly understandable." I take her hand. A tear slips down her face. We haven't been together on this particular holiday in almost three-and-a-half decades, and I'm not sure I would've noticed her cringing back in the Noe Valley house. None of us kids in the neighborhood went trick-or-treating; we had a party at school and then at a community center.

James and Vision sit down to their brew, only to stand up again as the doorbell rings. This time it's Charles, joining them for the trick-or-treater fun.

Charles! I'm saying his name the same way I said worms and bees...and perhaps peace, too, when Mother told us about her radio show. It's all just something to wrap my head around. Oh, Charles—that sometimes-present reminder of who and what James could've been. Oh, dear Lord, just let me get through the night. And, Lord, help us keep you in our hearts so we can continue to have some love and peace around here. I'm starting to enjoy it.

The next afternoon, James showers, locks himself in his room for an hour, and then comes out in fishnets and heels and more makeup and lipstick than Kiss would've had on back in the day. He runs out the door. I follow not too far behind, off to my volunteer stint at the church. A couple times a month, a friend and I share a shift to set up the donation envelopes and hymnals in the sanctuary for Sunday mass.

Early the next morning, as I leave for work, James's door is open a crack, letting me know he's not home yet, which is nothing unusual. When I arrive home that evening, though, over twelve hours later, his door is shut, which *is* unusual. He's usually out and about, at least in the house if not at work or carousing with friends, in the evenings. If he's having one of his seshes, I can hear soft murmuring. No sounds this time. His door is still shut in the morning. And nothing's been touched in the fridge—I can always tell when he's been in there. Now, that's highly unusual, too.

I knock on the door, softly at first. Nothing. I knock a little louder.

This is a kid who wants to be left alone when he wants to be left alone, but my mom radar was telling me something was wrong. I start pounding on the door.

"Alice?" Mother appears in the doorway of her room, bringing with her a waft of pumpkin scent from some new oil she must've bought. "What's going on?"

"Something's wrong." I try the door. Locked. Mother blanches. Sometimes this extra weight I carry around helps out. I slam my hip into the door and the century-old lock gives way. I almost fall into the room.

Even with just the light from the hallway shining in, I can see there's something not right with the figure in the bed. Plus, I can smell the blood.

"Call 911!" I scream.

Mother and I follow the ambulance, siren blaring and all. The stench of the blood and urine still fills my nose.

Oh, James. Why? What happened? What was it? What could we have done? Yes, there are problems. Every family has problems. Every generation has new problems. You didn't choose an easy path. I remain quiet, though, with tears streaming down my face, as Mother drives.

"How can I be a nurse, with all my psych training, and have this happen with my own child?" I finally whimper.

"I don't know, honey."

A couple of doctors bombard Mother and me with questions: What was going on? What led up to this? Did James feel safe at home? Safe in the world? How long has he been transgender? Are there issues? Where'd the bruises on his face and black eye come from?

Yes, there are issues. Yes, there's that statistic of trans suicide attempts. Yes, I think he felt safe at home. In the world? I'm not so sure, but I think so—as safe as a six-foot-two man presenting as a woman could be, I guess. And regarding the bruises and black eye, he does get into fights from time to time, especially when standing up for a woman.

When they finally stop with the questions and the nurses move him from the ER into his own room, Mother and I quietly watch him sleep for the next twelve hours. The reassuring beeps of the heart monitor continue to let us know he didn't succeed at his task. Oh, dear Lord—thank you.

Oh, he's awake! My baby looks around the room, clearly in shock to… well, still be alive. Is my heart pounding with joy that he's awake or sheer terror at what could have been? Or both?

The nurses have changed him out of his Victoria's Secret outfit and into a hospital gown. They must've given him a washing, which is good because when I first found him, his face was streaked with the black gunk he wears. Without it, he looks like a wide-eyed, lost, little lamb. Well, not so little, but definitely fragile. Such a far cry from his usual sassy, sarcastic self with a touch of Egyptian Pharoah thrown in, thanks to the thick, heavy rings and extended bands of eyeliner he typically sports. The sarcasm seems far, far away, replaced with sadness and defeat. Make that a tired lamb, since he slips back into sleep's comforting arms.

My heart skips a beat, maybe two, as I look at the bandages on his wrists. From my profession, I know it's actually not that easy to commit suicide by slashing your wrists. He must've cut deep to lose that much blood, pass out, and require a transfusion. Speaking of blood, mine runs cold as I again consider what could've happened.

So much for the power of Mother's positive thinking and the freedom of James's lifestyle. So much for me. I hate myself. In this moment, I hate him, too. James, why are you making life so much harder than it even has to be, than it already is even without all this other stuff thrown in? I hate your choices. I hate that you hate yourself so much you'd try to end your life. I hate myself. I'm such an awful mother my child would choose to die.

Over my years of working in the hospital, I've seen so many suicidal kids. Some succeed. Succeed? Well, it depends what their definition of success is, I suppose. If James definitely wanted to die, that would've been his definition. But some don't really want to succeed, really, in my opinion, and in staying alive, that's their success. Oh, what if this isn't the last time he tries this? What if there are more? I won't be able to take it.

I've seen several kids over and over again. Not only would my heart ache for the pain they're going through, but also for the pain their confused and mystified parents—who are equally as confused and mystified as their kids, I might add—are going through. I don't understand why life has to be so hard.

"I don't know what to do," I moan to Mother. "I'm not equipped for all this. Whatever he throws at me, I'm just supposed to love and bless him, and I just can't do that. I'm supposed to be perfect, and I'm just not. I'm a sorry excuse for a mom in this day and age. I wasn't prepared for what came my way. I just can't handle it all."

"Yes, you can. You know you're never given more than you can handle."

"Why does the Lord have such a high opinion of how much I can handle?"

"Because you *can* handle it."

Chapter 27

Starr

I hold and comfort my baby as she sobs and sobs. Sometimes, my tears intermingle with hers.

My grandbaby sleeps for another twenty-four hours. I wonder if she can overhear us at some level.

Jaye awakens and immediately starts screaming and pulling the tubes out of her arms, which sets off some alarms. That brings several nurses running. One administers a sedative while another places Jaye's hands into restraints. And then, she slips off to sleep once more.

After the nurses leave, Alice and I sit in the sudden silence, as if that whole scene was just a very bad dream.

Jaye's awake again! Alice and I pull our chairs over to her bedside. Once more, she glares at Alice, but with less force and intensity than the day before.

"Can you talk, sweetie?" Alice asks.

Jaye shrugs.

"Is there anything you want to say to us?" I ask. My granddaughter looks so soft without all that heavy, hard makeup she wears. It's been so long since we've seen her this way. Her eyes convey fatigue and resignation...almost. There's still a spark of her fire in there, though. Is she mad she's still here or is that her indomitable spirit refusing to break completely?

She shrugs again.

Alice takes her hand. "Did something happen? Something out of the ordinary?"

Jaye shrugs once more and then looks away.

"We can't help you if you don't talk to us," Alice says.

"Who says I want help? I really just wanted to go. I hate it here."

My daughter puts her hand to her chest, as if her daughter has just thrust a dagger into her heart. Alice probably doesn't remember, but she often said the same thing to me...maybe not so much about life on Earth, as Jaye is clearly implying, but life as I was having her live it.

After my grandbaby falls asleep again, Alice and I wander the hallway. We thump the vending machine after it refuses to give Alice her treat. Once the machine complies with our pummeling, even I buy a bag of potato chips in the hope that the crunching in my head will alleviate some of the excruciating overwhelm. No such luck.

I'd called Michael the day before to let him know about Jaye, and now I call to apprise him on the status of her slow improvement. Two hours later, we're still talking. It turns out he and I have read all the same books, listened to all the same tapes (yes, tapes—we're old) and now podcasts, followed the same teachers (Thich Nhat Hanh, Ram Dass, Marianne Williamson, and many others) over the years. He's even read Thomas Berry, who's a slight detour on that road that's so less traveled. Berry was a priest—not usually our thing—but he was also an ecotheologian and historian.

Wait—cancel that "old" comment. "We're not old," I tell him. "We're gold."

"I love it," he laughs. "By the way," he continues, "my great niece is no longer a niece. They are androgynous."

"Oh," I respond. "Interesting. Kids these days. It's such a fluid situation." He really laughs at that one. "They're all over the map, in a good way."

"Well, they seem to have a much bigger map than we did."

"We helped with that, you know."

"Yes. But they're way beyond us now. The young people these days have such brilliant ideas in this high-tech world that we never even dreamed of. The whole gig and sharing economies, hoverboards, Edible Blob…"

"Edible Blob?"

"For portable water. Really, the list is endless."

"Yes, the list is definitely endless," I agree. "They're amazing."

As I walk back into Jaye's hospital room, I find Alice holding her hands out while her daughter sleeps. "Oh!" she exclaims as I settle into the chair next to her.

"What were you doing?" I ask gently.

"Holding Jesus' hand," she answers sheepishly.

I take her hand. "Truth be told, Jesus—only I call him Yeshua, as I've mentioned—is always with me, and I ask him to hold my hand from time to time, too." Alice doesn't respond. "So are Mary Magdalene, Mother Mary, Anna, Archangel Michael...well, the whole upper echelon, the whole gang, really."

Alice pulls her hand back. I stop while I'm ahead. For a few seconds. Just can't help myself: "Works for me, anyway. We're all just playing a game down here...on Earth, that is. Maybe we're even acting in one giant play. And we have the opportunity to play different roles as well as invite various other characters in to act with." Alice nods. Wow.

I love myself and Alice and Jaye. I genuinely like each of us, too, which can be harder to accomplish than love. We're very cool people. Sometimes, I've felt guilty that I haven't had it worse, like so many have, but growing up in an empty shell and having my brother die so the US could try to get more resources through a meaningless war isn't the best either. And I've been so broke, I've actually been hungry and had to sofa surf here and there over the years.

I could've made more of my life, I suppose. But traveling all over and sharing love and light is a high calling, too.

I don't claim to have all the facts down, but I do know one thing: life is so short. Really, I woke up and I'm sixty-eight. Whoooosh! Where'd all those years go?

Alice and I watch Jaye as she sleeps. She's such a striking woman. All that laughing and playing, all that wisdom and talent, all those hopes and dreams in there—almost extinguished.

She's had her own ACEs...averse childhood experiences, as I learned about in my shelter training. Child of divorce. A sometimes-unbearable conservative mother. Maybe a too-wackadoo grandmother.

I've had my ACEs. Child of ice. Okay, that's not an ACE so much, but, as I just brought up, dealing with a brother dying for a ridiculous war is. And Alice: no father. No stable homelife until we were in someone else's home. It must've been too much for her.

"Do you think it's drugs or alcohol?" Alice asks, motioning her head toward Jaye.

"I don't think so. I can usually tell when the kids at the shelter are involved with those, and I haven't really seen the same thing in Jaye."

"How do we know it isn't mental illness?"

"Alice! After all this? I'm shocked at you. They thought homosexuality was a mental illness. Now, we know better."

"I don't mean regarding being transgender. I mean overall, but specifically leading to the suicide attempt."

"Oh." I didn't mean to jump all over her like that, but I really was shocked for a moment there. "I don't think so. You're a nurse and I'm a shelter volunteer; we would've noticed that before this."

Well, come to think of it, now I'm shocked even more in this moment here, thanks to a very surprising thought that suddenly occurs to me. As Alice takes her sleeping daughter's hand in hers, I think about how tragedy can wake us up. My thoughts turn to my mother and the tragedies she faced.

"Mother, you have safe passage in my mind from now on," are the words that go through my head. "I'm done with anything but love for you."

Chapter 28

Jaye

WTF? I wake up to find Mom holding my hand, which is in a restraint. Oh, right. I vaguely remember waking up and screaming and pulling tubes out of my body. Yeah, that was me, in this lifetime. Oh, and maybe there was another time, or forty, I woke up. Shit! The last thing I ever expected was to see myself back in this God-forsaken world. Fucking hell. When someone doesn't want to live, people should just leave them alone and let them go. As Gram always says, we'll all still be around—it's not like there's anywhere else, other than someplace still in the universe, we can go.

But she's not talking along that vein this time. "Honey, just where did you think you were going to go? Whatever you leave behind here is going to follow you there. It's not going to be left undone. And you'll have to get it done and taken care of, wherever you end up."

"I'd rather get it taken care of in a woman's body."

"But you've been telling us you're going to get a woman's body. And what if the struggle you have to work out is to be in exactly the situation you have? To be in the—quote—wrong body—unquote—and to work it out from there?"

"Just leave." I turn my back on them.

Gram puts her hand on my shoulder. "Jaye, we all have tough times, dark nights of the soul. Those are what bring us to the light once again."

Facing the wall, I utter the words that need to escape.

"What was that, sweetheart?" Mom asks.

"I was raped!"

They're so quiet I thought they'd been beamed up to a distant planet. Rapture occurred, right behind me. But when I finally turn around to face them, their faces are gray and their eyes full of tears.

Gram speaks from behind the hand she's pressed to her mouth. "Oh, Jaye. I'm so sorry."

Mom's mouth moves, as though she wants to say something, but words have become an impossible feat. Finally, she can talk. "Darling, I'm so sorry. Oh, my baby!"

"Not only was I raped, but when I called my friend Erin to come help me, she laughed at me!"

More silence until Gram starts sputtering. "Your friend…laughed…at you?"

"Yes, my friend laughed at me. She said, 'How would that even be possible?' How could she ask that? Let alone laugh. There must've been drugs involved. Slipped into my drink."

"Jaye," Gram says through her tears. "Oh, Jaye. I'm so sorry."

"And, Mom, if you ask me what I was wearing, I swear to God…"

"Of course I'm not going to ask that."

Gram puts her hand on my shoulder again. "Jaye, when did this happen?"

"Does it matter? It happened!"

"Did you go to the police?" Mom asks.

"You think they'd believe someone like me?" I roll away from them again, which is hard to do in hand restraints, but I manage it somewhat.

A while later, I turn back toward them, and they each take one of my hands. All those drugs I'm on wipe out the pain but they also wipe out me, and sleep seems to wash over me in waves.

At one point, I drifted back, but Mom must've thought I was still dropped off. "Just kill me now," she says to Gram. Then, she starts babbling: "I can't handle all of this. I just can't. You're expecting me to just shoulder burden after burden. I'm not strong enough."

"Are you talking to me or to God?" Gram asks. "Either way, we both know you're plenty strong enough."

"My heart can't take all this. I couldn't even feel my body when those words came out. As a nurse for almost thirty years, I've seen so many rape victims come through the ER. I've seen so many of rape's effects still haunting mothers in the maternity ward. My heart cries every time, for every one of them. And yet nothing was ever anywhere near as bad as this. I'd rather live through a rape than have my child live through one."

She's finally quiet, and I picture Gram patting her head. But then, the babbling starts again. "'Someone like me.' I've seen this so many times in the ER, too. My heart ached for the person—man or woman—who'd been assaulted as well as his or her family members who were at a loss over what to do or say. It's such a protracted procedure—a tough road for those brave enough to come in…although those who don't come in are brave in a different way. Anyone who encounters this situation is a hero, in my opinion. Or other awful situations…we're surrounded by heroes.”

Now, it’s Gram’s turn to babble. “‘Someone like me. Someone like me.’ Ah, dear Life. There’s always been ‘someone like me,’ someone who’s misunderstood, maligned, ill-treated. We humans are not advanced enough to just take people as they are, in all our myriad shapes, colors, appearances, designs, statuses, whatevers. All beautiful in our own way.”

She pauses, then. “You’re the expert—relatively—in this regard. In all the experiences I’ve encountered, I’ve actually never come face to face with one like this, at least, not in the immediate aftermath. What do we say?”

“We don’t say as much as we listen. That’s the main thing to do.”

Gram’s quiet for a minute as she lets what Mom said soak in.

I could hear Mom’s smile through her next words. “In nursing school, we do learn some airy-fairy stuff that’s really not so airy-fairy after all.”

The hospital transfers me to the psych ward so they can keep an eye on me a while longer. Mom, Gram, and I have quite the cozy Thanksgiving in my hospital room. But we still have that oh-so-wonderful at-the-Thanksgiving-table family squabble that I know is happening all over the country at this particular moment in time. Ours might’ve been, oh, just a little more intense than the usual political fare, though. So much for them walking on tenterhooks since my suicide attempt. They seem to be over that, and my rape, too. At least, for dinnertime.

“Go ahead, make me wish I had killed myself,” I mutter when Mom jumps on her Jesus thing.

“Don’t even say that, darling!”

“But I’d be with Jesus, Mom. I’d be safe. I’d be with your best friend, your Lord and Savior. Isn’t that what you’ve always wanted for me?”

“Well, it doesn’t help much to turn to Him after you die. You need to turn to Him beforehand.”

“Ahhhhh, tricky.”

She does her lip-pursing thing she’s always done so well.

“I am done being a walking apology,” I say. “Nothing I’ve ever done has been enough for you. I get a B, you ask where's the A?"

"That's not true! You were the one pushing yourself so hard for A's. And I'm done being a walking apology to you, too. Nothing I say is ever enough. Nothing I do is ever enough. I'm just so lame, so unknowledgeable. I've had life in my womb and helped it come into the world. I hold newborn babies every day. I ease the concern of new parents. I've held people as they took their dying breath, and I've brought peace to their loved ones. But excuse me if I can't jump up and say "hooray" when you tell me that you feel your entire life has been a mistake."

"It's your high-and-mighty trip that I object to."

"But you're always so high and mighty about your veganism thing and your transgender thing and even your goth thing."

"And you're always so high and mighty about your Catholicism and having to believe in order to go to Heaven."

Mom turns to Gram. "And you're always so high and mighty about the whole One Love thing, and peace, love, and apricots."

"Apricots?"

"Whatever." She turns back to me. "It's as if those of us, who are happy with—or at least accepting of—whatever gender we came in, aren't quite with the program and never will be."

"We're already in Heaven," Gram says. "If we'd just let it be so."

"We are not in Heaven!" Mom practically shouts. "Heaven comes after this. That's the whole point of Heaven."

I do the head-shaking, jowl-blubbering, noisy thing. "Great way to keep the mischievous population in check, huh? Promise them something that comes later after being good, at least as those in power define good. Don't get me wrong. Imagine how worse the world would be if so many people didn't believe in the promise of a better life in the hereafter. But it might keep them from making the present all it can be."

Mom then turns to me and says something that would've made me fall over if I hadn't already been sitting down. "I'll stop talking about church if you stop talking against it."

"Wow! Did you really just say that? Deal!" We fist-bump. But then, as we finish picking at the turkey—and faux-turkey—dinner Mom and Gram had snuck in, I mumble something that starts Mom's waterworks again.

"How's that, Jaye?" Gram asks.

"I wish it had worked," I say. "I'd rather be wherever and in whatever comes after this than to be here now. I mean, as you say, Gram, there's nowhere else to go. We're still here, wherever here happens to be in the moment. We'll still be in the universe."

"Lord, give me strength," Mom cries. Oh, she just has to do her thing.

And Gram has to do her Gram thing. "But as I've said, you can't leave anything undone. It has to get done—and here and now is better than there and then."

"But, like I said, I'd choose to come back in a woman's body."

Gram's not having it, at all. "But what if that's not what the lesson is to be about? You might be here to learn how to transition a body as well as overcome being a—scary air quote—social outcast—end quote—while moving a whole section of humanity forward. That's what you're doing, and you're doing it very well. Or, maybe, you might be here to learn it doesn't matter what body you're in. The evolution of you involves accepting wherever you are and whatever you're in."

"I wish I could cast a spell on all you cis people, so you'd know what it's like to be in the wrong body."

"'Do unto others as you would have done unto you.'" Oh, Mom.

"That sounds fine in theory." Oh, Gram. "But we are a planet full of people who hate ourselves! So, what we're doing unto others *is* what we're doing unto ourselves. The hate people inflict on others is the hate they feel for themselves."

Okay, Gram was getting on a roll. "Take, for example, a warlord keeping food from the starving people. How much must he hate himself to do that to others? Take Trump…"

"Oh, here we go. Dump-on-Trump time. I need to be fortified for this." Mom opens the pumpkin pie and helps herself to a large slice with a generous serving of whipped cream. "Egads, what am I doing?" She reaches into a shopping bag. "Sorry, sweetheart, I forgot for a minute. Here's the vegan version." She hands a darling little pie to me.

Gram carries on, unabated. "He obviously hates himself, and he's lashing out like a hurt bear, hurling that pain everywhere he can because he can't stand himself and he can't stand feeling all that hate."

The nurse walks in again then, just as he has been all afternoon, doing this or that.

Mom's mouth is fairly full, but her words are still clear. "He is not! You know I'm not the biggest fan of the man, but he's not doing what he's doing because he hates himself."

I shake my jowls again. Not my most feminine feature, but anyway. "He—and many like him—would not be denigrating people or considering them second-class citizens if they didn't hate themselves. And how can they profess to love God when they treat people so badly?"

My very-loud-yet-unspoken message to her hangs in the air. She doesn't bite, so I continue. "If we loved ourselves, then we wouldn't need to be told to treat people the way we'd like to be treated—we already would be treating them that way."

The nurse smiles. "This is not the same Thanksgiving-dinner conversation I'm hearing in the other rooms. Even your political discussions are at a whole different level."

"That's us," I grin. "A whole different level, three times over." The nurse smiles again and leaves. I take Mom's hand and then Gram's. "I'm so grateful for you both."

"Same here," they say through their tears, petting my hands, which would've been annoying if it weren't so adorable.

"If there's one thing I could change about the world," I sigh, "it'd be for everyone to accept people as they are. Now." I think for a minute. Maybe it's the drugs—are they a truth serum? "Even me, too, I guess. That's where it starts."

I don't glance up, so I can't see them looking at me, but I can sure feel it.

Chapter 29

Alice

It's way too late to do a rape kit—that timeframe is just seventy-two hours. James is pretty sure he'd recognize the person who hurt him, though, and is considering his options. There's absolutely no sense in leaving a crime like this unreported. Who knows who else this man would hurt? But there's no pushing James.

"Lemme think about it more," he says.

"Whatever happened to your boyfriend?" I gently ask.

"He's around. He just wasn't around that night."

"I take it you're not monogamous."

"Oh, hell no! Are you kidding me? He was probably off with his other girlfriend."

Oh, right. Silly me. How could I forget? I don't say anything more. But, ugh! Gag me. It all sounds so complicated. I had trouble keeping track of one person. Doesn't having so many partners mean you can't go as deep? Not wanting that question to be misconstrued, I just keep it to myself.

We bring him home on the Monday after Thanksgiving. His friends come by to sit with him in turns, with Charles and Vision taking most of the time.

Feeling like an intruder whenever I try to be helpful, I decide I have to get out of the house. So, here I am at church again, where a small group of us has assembled to put together a holiday mailing. I could stick Christmas stamps on envelopes, I think to myself, but that's about it right now.

The church folks seem surprised to find me so quiet. No one in this particular gathering is among my closer friends, so they don't know much about my personal life. In fact, I still haven't told anyone about James, not counting the few people I run into when I'm out with him in public, who certainly know then. But, so far, the run-ins haven't included anyone from church.

I tried a couple of support groups (online, in order to be somewhat anonymous), but they weren't really my people. They were all cheerleady and rah rah for trans. You hear about the trans kids with their crazy parents. Okay, here I am, that crazy parent. Where are the other crazies like me?

The public at large still doesn't hear all that much about this because we're not allowed to say anything. No one was wailing the way I wanted—and still want, sometimes—to. I haven't even told Father Moore, who's probably heard it all. Maybe, I should talk to him.

The best sermon he ever gave was about the ark. No, not the way you probably think he talked about it. He said, "It wasn't the animals that were the danger for the ark...it was the termites." Meaning...it's our own thoughts that can bring us down. Or our own people.

"I saw a sign on a bathroom the other day," an older gent states. "It said, 'For people who stand.' On the other door it said, 'For people who sit.' Can't they just use the bathroom they're anatomically designed for and avoid all this unnecessary brouhaha?"

Unnecessary brouhaha. Is that all this is to you, you old fart? Just an inconvenient much ado about nothing to your view on how life should be? Imagine living with this day after day after day!

"They just need a good kick in the rear," the man adds.

Maybe you do, I want to shout.

Sticking stamps on envelopes suddenly becomes too much for me and I head home. I pull into the driveway, turn the car off, and sit...for an hour...maybe two. That older gent doesn't get the new generations, not that I'm much ahead of him. I look up at the lights shining in the windows of my mother and child's bedrooms. I don't really get them, *really*. And they don't really get me, *really*.

Yes, James—me, too. If there's one thing I could change about the world, it'd be to accept people as they are. Now.

Hmmmmmm. That includes that old man at church. That mother and child in my house. And I guess it starts with me, as well.

But back to church I go, at least to sit by myself. Once again, the sun shines through the stained glass, casting most of me in a purple glow with some red on my hands. I look at them and think of all the babies they've held, all the IVs they've put in. How much caring they've done.

How many years and comings and goings they've handled—literally, haha
.

My midday musings in church have taken a turn, I must say. As I sit under Mary's gaze, I think about how she stands for love.

I stand for love, too—love of country, love of church and state, love of children both born and unborn. Maybe the Christian Right thinks that marriage can only be between a man and a woman because, and this would be what's underneath calling it the word of God, ultimately that's the marriage that will further humanity. Many things start out for that purpose, such as being kosher. Staying alive to procreate is a good purpose!

But, even now, part of me is still horrified over my child and those signs on bathroom doors. Can you imagine how I'd feel if this wasn't already somewhat ensconced in today's society? How about those parents ten or twenty years ago? But even they probably would've had some indication that their child was somewhat alternative. Wouldn't some kind of warning signal have lit up on their parental dashboard? Okay, maybe it wouldn't be a warning signal. Let's make it a "heed this" signal instead. Shouldn't it have lit up on mine?

"Would you like to give a confession?"

"Huh?" I hadn't seen the new, young priest approaching me. I still don't see him, as he's backlit by the sun on the stained glass. I guess I am sitting kind of close to the confessionals. Oh, and I guess it is Friday afternoon. Time to unload all those heavy sins from the week.

I follow him over to the confessional. He sits in the center booth and I kneel in the booth next to it. He slides open the little window between us.

And then…nothing. My mind is blank.

"Bless me, Father," he prompts.

Ah. "Bless me, Father, for I have sinned. It has been about six weeks since my last confession. In that time, I…" I what?

"Go on."

What is my sin? Is being horrified a sin? Is mortification a sin? What's behind that? It's getting to be that I'm mortified to be mortified. And…am I still so mortified?

"I…I…I don't love my family as much as I should. Or I love them, but I don't love things about them."

"Our Lord said to love the sinner."

"Yes, I do that. But…"

"But what? Love the sinner. That's your entire job." He pauses for a few seconds. "Are they truly sinning?"

What an interesting thing for him to ask, as if he knows the sins could be up to interpretation. I call to mind this ongoing obsession with the goth/dark side of life. "In one way, yes. Maybe." Then, I think of this ongoing new expression of self and of loving. "And, as for the other way, I'm not so sure anymore."

Mother sniffs. "You smell like church. Again."

"It's not like I try to hide going there from you."

"You couldn't if you wanted to, what with that incense and candle smell. And it's not like you do a lot of shopping or other things like that."

My mind wanders back to the last time I went shopping, at least formally—not the bopping about in Pt. Reyes. Was that awful day really the last time and was it really that long ago?

"Did I ever tell you who I happened to run into in the dressing room at The Rack?"

Mother doesn't even have to guess who. "No! When was that?"

"Last spring. We came out to the three-way mirror wearing the exact same dress."

Mother laughs. And laughs. And laughs. She practically falls over onto the floor, she's laughing so hard. Against every ounce of my will, a smile crosses my face.

The next evening, after work, I walk into the kitchen. While my beautiful child (no, still can't say or even think the preferred name, but isn't "my beautiful child" progress?) is glued to his computer, Mother stares into space in a very odd way. Something seems off.

"You okay, Mother?" No answer.

My child looks up from his laptop in alarm. "Gram?"

"Mother?" I shake her arm. "Mother!"

She seems to journey back from wherever she'd been traveling.

"Oh!" she smiles. "I think I was having a dream. More than a daydream, I mean."

"Scared me to death!" I shiver.

I'm not the only one shivering. "Gram! Don't do that!"

"Did you have a flashback to Woodstock or something?" Okay, maybe some levity isn't exactly what's called for right now.

"No. Well, no to Woodstock and yes to something. This was more like a flashforward to the future. It was something, alright."

"Oh! You're giving me a headache."

"Sniff some peppermint oil for that."

"Didn't you just tell me to take some for a stomachache the other week?"

"Yes. It's great for that, but also headaches."

"Oh, gag me. And, anyway, so much for all those crazy powders and supplements and oils you've been taking all these years. You still had a stroke."

"Those crazy powders and stuff probably saved my life. My mother had a stroke, too, and never came out of it. At least, I'm out of it—the stroke, that is."

"I was going to say…yeah, you're out of it, alright." I instantly regret saying that.

Chapter 30

Starr

For the first time ever, as far as I can recall, Alice says, "I'm sorry. You do whatever you want." Knock me over with a…what's lighter than a feather? Knock me over with that. Wow.

I haven't felt anything too dark emanating from Jaye's room since she came home from the hospital. I also haven't felt a whole stinking fish-fry of judgment flying from Alice toward Jaye's visitors, either.

Well, except once. She was walking by Jaye's room, while I was sitting in mine, and we both overheard Vision say, "How'd your mom take all this?"

"She was a rock star, believe it or not. Well, for her, anyway. Soft rock, that is."

I think Jaye saw Alice walk by her doorway just then.

"She's coming around," Jaye said quietly after her mom slipped into her bedroom and shut the door. "She still has a way to go, a long flight ahead, but, at least, she's at the airport."

Later, I heard Alice's door open and her footsteps on the stairs. I figured she was headed to a graveyard shift, which she sometimes takes when a coworker gets sick or goes on vacation. When I went down to the kitchen for a minute, though, I noticed Alice's car sitting in the driveway. Maybe she went for a walk? Not likely. And no Alice appeared in the house as the hours ticked by.

I turned the light off in my room and looked outside. With the help of the streetlight, I saw an Alicey shadow in her car. I could practically feel her thoughts spinning. As I tuned into her, I could feel resignation, then some acceptance. Oh, there went a slight battle. Surrender. And there went that battle again. Fatigue. There went the shoulders tightening. Then, dropping from exhaustion. Those shoulders can get so tired from carrying the weight of the world.

Maybe, I really could feel what she was feeling. Or, maybe, that was all me, about her…and in regard to what I know she feels about the situations of her life. My shoulders dropped, as well.

Yes, Jaye—me, too. If there's one thing I could change about the world, it'd be to accept people as they are. Now. And, yes, I suppose it starts with me.

Me. Getting older, I ponder as I look in the mirror. Not too bad, I must say, but I honestly didn't think this'd ever happen. Weren't we going to stay forever young?

○

"If I had one thing to tell the world," Jaye says a few nights later, "it'd be to let people be who they are...as long as they're not hurting anyone else."

Alice joins in. "If I had one thing to tell the world, it'd be to let the love of Christ into your heart—let yourself be saved by Jesus—and let people be who they are, as long as they're not hurting anyone else."

I add my two cents, or, better yet, my profound wisdom of the ages. "If I had one thing to tell the world, it'd be to remember that you're Love in form, and let people be who they are, as long as they're not hurting anyone else.

"Maybe, we *are* all saying the same thing," Jaye smiles, "from dramatically different places, to get to the same place."

"Maybe," Alice and I say together.

○

Alice's brow furrows at her computer screen. "I'm filling out an application for a continuing-education class, and they're asking me what my preferred gender pronouns are."

"Cool! Way to disappear, patriarchal, big-medicine conglomerations." Alice doesn't respond, but that doesn't slow Jaye down any. "Did you know there are more men named John than there are women CEOs? A hundred years ago the suffragettes were beaten and imprisoned for wanting to vote."

"You're quite a woman, Jaye," I smile, looking up from my laptop.

"Thanks, Gram. Mom, I shouldn't have to be telling you all this. But you're still stuck in your subservient thang."

"Submissive. Not subservient." Alice seems to have concocted her own brand of Catholicism crossed with Evangelism crossed with...I don't know what.

Jaye crosses her arms in front of her face.

"Whatever are you doing?" Alice asks.

"Pulling a Wonder Woman move to ward off what you just said. Besides, it takes a strong man to give the space for a woman to fully be a woman."

Alice isn't falling into defensive/reaction mode either, although her brows furrow again. "We were made from Adam's rib, not his feet."

"Mom! Adam and Eve were not the first people here. The Bible goes on to talk about their sons killing other armies, some other people. That's *other people*. Emphasis on other and people."

"That's not what they meant."

"How do you know what they meant but didn't say? You who take the Bible literally?"

"They wrote it that way, but it's not what they meant."

"Mom, you either take it as it is—or not."

I aim for diffusion. "Alice, that's the equivalent of guys who leave their socks on in bed."

"Whaaaaaaaaaaat?"

"OMG," I giggle, "that used to drive me crazy. If they're already taking everything else off, why in the world would they leave their socks on?"

Alice puts her hands over her ears. "Na na na na na na na—I can't hear a word you're saying!"

"They were just in a hurry to get to you, Gram." Jaye then sings, to the tune of "You Can Leave Your Hat On," "You can leave your socks on."

"Joe Cocker was at Woodstock. He was the shit."

Alice's brows do a times-three furrow. "Is that a good thing?"

"Yes."

Jaye's impressed. "Look at you speaking Gen Z and sounding legit this time!"

I turn off my computer. "I'm off to the shelter so I can wrap my arms around those kids."

In the car, I download a song from Joe. Cocker, that is.

If one weekend changed my entire life, that was it. Over the years, the romance, intrigue, and notoriety of being part of the movement that became Woodstock—Woodstock!—has probably added even more layers to my life that might not have been there otherwise.

"You were at Woodstock?" The older folks asking that question look moonstruck that I was actually at this singular event of the ages. The younger folks asking that question look at me like I invented the computer or something.

A promise was made there. I'm still working to fulfill that promise and will until I die.

Chapter 31

Jaye

Mom, Gram, and I sit—where else? I scroll through Instagram on my laptop, looking over friends of my friends to see if I can recognize that guy. Yes, *that* guy.

"Seared into my memory," as Christine Blasey Ford phrased it, along with "indelible in the hippocampus," was this grotesque grin and this syrupy-sweet-but-not-real "Are you feeling okay, darlin'?" What is he, anyway? Gay? Bi? Undecided? Surprised to find me with male parts under all that fishnet and got pissed off? So much for me being against labels. I wanted to know all about his. And, no, he wasn't surprised about my parts. He knew.

Vision and their latest squeeze and a few others of our crew went to McRay's, a bar near the highway often frequented by rednecks. But they generally left us alone after I decked one of 'em one night.

That guy had tagged along with one of us and started flirting with me. "You're a long cool woman in a black bustier," he said, riffing on that old song and totally mispronouncing that word.

I wasn't interested. At all. "Yeah…well, sometimes I'm a hot mess in a dumpster fire at a train wreck."

He laughed—too much for something that unclever.

Vision was holding court at the end of the bar. They do that from time to time. I tried to home in on that conversation and shrug this dude off.

And, yes, unfortunately, I took my eyes off my drink, and then, I took a sip of it. As if from a million miles away I heard his voice. "Are you feelin' okay, darlin'?" He laughed. "Oh man, you're really out of it, huh? And you are a man. You're all man, even if you're trying to hide it."

The bar started spinning. The next thing I knew, I was in a dark room, and he was pounding himself into me. I moved to push him away, then CRACK! His fist practically broke my jaw. All was black.

The next morning, I awoke and then froze as the images and sensations of the night before came flooding in, although slowly, given my groggy state. Different parts of me throbbed with pain, from my head to my butt. I froze again as a snore erupted near my ear. That monstrosity was lying right behind me! How could I get out of there without waking him? I could barely even open my eyes—one was swollen shut. The room was in semi-gloom from the closed curtains. I started to move, hoping beyond hope to simply slide out of the bed and make a run for it.

He awakened with a snort and a start. "Oh, hi there, darlin'," he drawled. "Good morning."

A tear slipped down my cheek, which was turned away from him. How big was he? Could I take him on, now that his fucking drugs hadn't disabled me?

"You sure seemed to enjoy yourself last night," this fucker had the nerve to say to me.

Right. In what alternate reality were you? Into necrophilia much?

"Here," he said, "you just stay here. I'll get us some breakfast."

Breakfast? He slipped out of bed, and I must've passed out again, because the next thing I knew, there was a plate of eggs and toast being held under my nose.

"Sorry, the toast is a little burnt."

I rolled away from the food and its offending smell, about to be sick to my stomach. He pushed the plate toward me again.

"Eat it, you little bitch. I went to all the trouble to make it."

Little bitch? Does that mean he's bigger than I am? A lot bigger? Turns out it didn't matter.

Until that very moment, I thought projectile vomiting only ever happened in *The Exorcist*. Uh, that'd be no. I threw up all over him. It was even a pretty shade of green, worthy of Linda Blair, if I say so myself. And it seriously landed allllllll over him! I would've laughed at the stupid and stupefied expression on his face if I hadn't been so scared. After he made a beeline into the bathroom, I grabbed my clothes and dashed to the door.

Turned out I probably couldn't have taken him as the bastard's quite large, but even if I could have, I prefer the poetic justice of the way he was taken.

Well, after the fact, I found out that as he was leading me out of the bar, I apparently winked at Vision and a few of the others. They took that to mean I was good with going with this guy. I have no idea why I would've done that. Note to self and everyone: double check on friends…make sure they're really solid with whatever's going on.

When I finished relaying that whole scenario to Mom and Gram, I shook my head. "For half a second, I was going to eat those nasty eggs and burnt toast with him. If I hadn't been so sick to my stomach, I might have. How could I be so crazy to even think that?"

Mom sighed. "Oftentimes, rape victims do stay with their assaulters, sometimes for an hour, sometimes for much longer. They're trying to make sense of it all, to see if it was perhaps something they did to mislead them—in their minds, that is. There is no misleading an assaulter. But they want to spend some time to try to get inside the person's head. They might even stay around for years, trying to make sense of it. Look at Harvey Weinstein's accusers."

As I've said, Mom's being a nurse does come in handy sometimes.

In addition to dealing with the worst experience of my life, I'm getting more and more pissed off. Fuck the fishnets and the bustier—which would be the police's justification for him raping me—I decided I'm going to find this guy and not let this happen to anyone else.

And as far as Erin (that pitiful ex-friend who laughed) goes, she's been banned from my circle. She tried to apologize a few times, but it was way too little, way too late. Plus, she still didn't grok it. Get an afterlife.

Found him! Thank you, Instagram. He's a friend of Vision's housemate. I knew he knew somebody. I pick up the phone and call the police. Mom and Gram dab at their eyes as I inform the woman at the other end of the line what happened.

"I'm going down there to give the rest of the report," I tell them after I hang up. Mom puts her hand on mine.

"Sometimes, I think a disease infects humanity and it shows up in acts like rape, hate crimes, and the like." That's Gram talking.

Neither Mom nor I respond at first. She's right, in a way.

"How could anyone even think of hurting another person like this?" Mom asks. "What goes on in their heads?"

"I sure don't know," I murmur.

"It's a young planet." That's Gram again, of course.

The policewoman at the station leads me into a private room. The only feelings she shows about talking to a trans woman who's just been raped are sympathy and compassion, along with assurances regarding my nervousness. The other policemen in the station? They're not quite on the same wavelength. Is that a laugh? Up yours, assholes. I have to do this. Ain't nobody going to stop me, even you.

"I've talked to so many women about this," the cop says once it's just the two of us. "You're not alone. I'll try to make this as easy as possible on you."

I told her everything I told Mom and Gram and tried to remember any other details.

"Does he have any scars or birthmarks, especially in a place you wouldn't see in public?"

I smile, but it's a grimace-y one. "As a matter of fact, he does." The dude has a birthmark in a place that might not see the sun very often. I really did not want to know that about him.

Then, as I start to cry, she puts her hand on mine.

Through the hospital network, Mom found a rape counselor for me. Sometimes, it seems like Darla's not quite sure what to make of me either, even though she's a hip-ish millennial and bisexual. But she knows about rape herself, unfortunately. I hate talking about it. But I hate not talking about it even more.

"Do you know that about half of transgender people and bisexual women are sexually assaulted sometime in their lives?" Darla asks me in her way-too-neutral-tone office. "We experience rape at a much higher rate than heteros, which is still too high—thirty-five percent for straight women, ten percent for straight men. The LGBTQIA+ community also has a higher rate of stigma, poverty, and marginalization, any one of which (let alone all three) can put the risk of rape higher."

"Shit," is the only thing I could think to say. My mind goes kind of blank, as it does kind of a lot these days.

My whole world has changed. Nothing's safe. Darla assures me my hair-trigger emotions will chill—I just need to keep talking things out.

Here's another great thing she says to me: "For a long while, the rape is going to be the first thing you think about when you wake up. And then, one day, out of the blue, it will be the second thing. And then, one day, you might think about it around 10:30. And then, one faraway day, maybe you won't even think about it, at least not that day. But it's something you'll have for the rest of your life, spurring you on."

My friends have formed a posse around me, not leaving me alone much of my waking hours these first few weeks at home. Charles stays with me every night, these days—just him, though, no one else, at least for the time being. But I still jump and start when I accidentally roll into him or something, after the snuggle phase of the night. Some people can't be touched after such a trauma, but despite that initial jumpy reflex, I want him by me, his whole body touching mine from head to foot.

I can finally fall asleep again after dawn, so I'm sleeping even later than usual. Sometimes, as I wake up, I overhear Mom, Gram, and Charles chatting in the kitchen. Mom is really into him. I wonder what her trip is.

Often, before I'm even fully awake, though, my body goes into some kind of panic mode. Something's wrong! What is it? Oh, shit! And then the memories come flooding in again.

Darla recommends writing in my journal, screaming, reading, video games, doing art, anything along those lines. But that's what I generally do every single day, before this even happened. She also tells me that trauma can rewire the brain. Yeah, as if my brain needs anything else messing with it right now. She gives me the name of a massage therapist/bodyworker, too, but I need to wait on that. I'm not sure I can handle a stranger touching me right now.

How long does it take to recover from sexual assault? I want that moment now, please. Will I ever fully recover? I'm not looking forward to having these memories and PTSD for the rest of my life.

I can't even imagine how the women who were assaulted by Trump deal with seeing him in the news all day every day, or any boss on a job, or even a relative who they just have to see at Thanksgiving. I'd quit the job and family functions. At least, I don't have to see my assaulter on an ongoing basis.

And about the day of my suicide attempt? It's a blur, really. I hadn't told any of my friends after that one laughed at me, not even Charles. I was just too ashamed. I just wanted…out. Of life. I couldn't get the sounds out of my head, even more than I was unable to wash the sensations off my body. The crack when he hit my jaw. The syrupy "darlin'" replayed over and over and over. The sound of my wretching.

The smells hovered around me, making me want to hurl. The

morning-after lingering scents of a man and an AMAB, unsurgeryed female having sex. Normally, I love that smell, but not this time. The sour smell of alcohol on our breath. The burnt toast especially would not leave my nose.

All I could think was, "I am not going to live with these sounds and smells and sensations for another sixty, seventy, eighty years. Not gonna do it. Not gonna happen."

I love making carvings on my candles with a Swiss Army knife Dad gave me for some camping trip or another. I grabbed that knife and started making carvings, going deeper and deeper, on my wrists. It didn't even hurt—at least, not more than my heart did.

I watched the blood flow. *The* blood. It didn't even feel like mine. At least, the scent of this seemingly other person's blood was starting to take over the smell of the burnt toast. If I'd known slitting your wrists takes so long, I might've tried another way.

Around noon, I heard some pings from my phone as my friends were waking up and texting me. Then, that was it. The next thing I was aware of was waking up in the hospital.

○

I know 'tis the season and all, but I wasn't ready to go back to work until about a week before Christmas. The store's a good diversion, though. I should've come back sooner. I'm hitting the gym more, including taking a martial arts class. I'm a big, strong woman. But this guy was bigger and stronger. Even if I'd had all this strength training and everything else beforehand, though, I still wouldn't have been able to stand up to whatever he slipped into my drink. I will never, ever, again leave a drink unattended, anywhere, anytime.

I'm starting to lie awake more, too. Unlike Mom and Gram lying awake at midnight (yes, I could hear Mom's bed creaking too, and figured it was keeping Gram awake, since it's quite the screechy symphony), I'm staring out the window watching the coming of dawn. Actually, come to think of it, Mom's symphony seems to have been calming down…at least, it was before my event and hospital stay, that is.

Snuggled in Charles' arms, I watch the sunrise. As God-awful as this time has been, I'm grateful it's showing me what love really looks like.

○

Mom got a lush, lovely, fourteen-foot-tall live tree and put it in front of the bay window in the living room. Normally, I'd be really against getting a live tree, but the smell was so…well, alive. It filled the whole house. Being in the living room with the tree was like…well, it was like there was another living being in the room.

Plus, I've heard that supporting the Christmas tree farmers is a good thing to do—for them and for the planet. I don't know if that's entirely true, but, even if just for this year, I'll go with it.

I bought presents for Mom and Gram, wrapped them, and put them under the tree. I was never really all that into Christmas, but, this year, the Christmas spirit's really grabbed hold of me.

Christmas Eve has brought a chill. Shivering, I search out Mom. One guess as to where I find her. (Wouldn't be the kitchen, would it? Ha!) "Can we get a fire going? Does the fireplace even work anymore? My tits are turgid."

Mom starts to get that look—yes, the one that says, "Must you?" But it fades and she even laughs. "Well, we can't have any turgid tits around here. Sure, let's start a fire."

Who are you and what have you done with my mother? Whaaaaaat? This woman is…something. Less fiery. But it's not like I put out the fire in her (I hope). It's more like she's surrendered, and the fire has turned into a warm, comforting, maybe even magnanimous glow.

Chapter 32

Alice

I love Christmas. Love, love, love, love, loooooove it. The Christmases of my childhood were nothing to write home about, since "home" was such a dubious concept for me for so long. Maybe that's why I love Christmas so much now—I really get to deck the halls and all that jazz and maybe make up for what I felt I was missing out on.

I start listening to Christmas carols in, oh, November. I didn't know Mother had a thing about "I'll be Home for Christmas"—I mean a real thing. Every time it comes on, she requests I switch to the next song (thank you, Pandora).

"What is up with that?" I finally ask her, after giving the song a thumbs down so she wouldn't have to hear it again.

"Every time that song came on, my mother would run to her bedroom, crying."

"Oh."

"It was written from the point of view of a soldier in World War II, and it always reminded her of her fella who didn't come back to her. The one who was blinded and married his nurse."

"I'm so sorry that happened to her," I whisper.

"Well, we all have something or other. Or several somethings or others."

"That we certainly do."

Mother stares out the window some more. "Connecticut is so cold in December."

I was about to say something glib but backed away from that idea. It wasn't the time. Mother seemed to be lost in a memory from long ago.

Christmas shopping! I just love, love, love that, too. Oh, just give me anything about Christmas and I'm happy, but especially Christmas shopping. Give me Christmas and I'm happy. Give me shopping and I'm happy. Give me both of my happy loves, and I'm over the moon. Throw in getting my nails done plus treating myself to a massage, and I'm in Heaven. I'm sorry, Lord. Close to Heaven. Please indulge my babbling—I'm just so happy to be happy, over the moon, close to Heaven.

Oh my. Here she is again—Robin, that acquaintance who was exiting the nail salon as I was going in all those months ago, the one who gushed about her Harvard pre-med son. This time, though, she remembers there's someone else in the conversation. And, this time, I'm not cowering.

"And how is your James? What's he up to?"

"Oh, about six-two now," I say. Six-five with heels on.

"Where's he going to school?"

"He's taking a break right now, figuring out what's next. You know some kids…have to do life their own way."

"That's for sure. I have to dash." And dash she does.

"Toodle-oo!" I call after her.

Christmas Day is surprisingly chilly and cloudy. I don't mind. That just makes the lights on the tree seem brighter.

"I'll go grab some more logs from out back."

Not only does my beautiful bambino get more logs, but he also starts another lovely little blaze—two in two days now—in the fireplace. What? Who? But I'll take it.

After warming ourselves by the flames, the two of us look around the living room.

"Whatever happened to that book nook idea you had? Remember when we were pinning charming nooks on Pinterest?"

I shrug. "Oh, that's still on the agenda, I suppose. The maybe-someday agenda."

"I'll help you build it."

I'm suddenly overwhelmingly, overflowingly filled with love for this person. "That'd be lovely."

All three of us prepare our meals together—vegan for our youngest here, prime rib for me, and rabbit food (no, not pellets, a huge salad) for Mother.

"How about we move the table into the living room by the tree and the fire?" I suggest.

"That sounds as warm and delicious as dinner does," Mother says.

"You're having a salad! That's not exactly warm."

"The seafood on it is."

Once we settle in the living room, Mother says, "Shall we say a prayer?" She turns to me. "Would you like to say it?" She addresses the shock that must've appeared all over my face. "We're celebrating Jesus' birthday, after all. And you're the one most celebrating that. Although I believe he was actually born in October. Or March. Depends who you ask."

I ignore that and say a prayer, and then, we quickly dive into our food.

Mother turns to me. "You're celebrating the return of the son, and I'm celebrating the return of the sun—s-u-n."

I'm in too good a mood to get into it with her. Thankfully my child doesn't go off in his direction, too.

"Very good," I say, buttering a dinner roll. They probably think I don't notice, but I notice all right. They exchange glances. "How about we file that missing-person report after dinner?" they both seem to ask each other. Haha! Life—what a kick…in the butt sometimes, but another kind of kick sometimes, too.

After dinner, on the way to taking the dishes to the kitchen, Mother passes the big mirror in the hallway. She doesn't exactly sigh, but she does let some sound escape from her mouth. Then, she chuckles.

"I feel like that Keith Richards meme, where he's looking out from that super craggy face and saying he's outlived Michael Jackson, Whitney Houston, and, oh… was it Elvis? And he bets we didn't see that coming."

My beautiful child and I laugh. Oh, when's the last time we laughed like this? It was long ago, whenever it was. Okay, it wasn't all that long ago but, in the time since the assault, my mouth seems to have gone out of practice for the motion of smiling that big. That's sad.

"Look at you knowing what memes are," I say to Mother when she comes back with three little plates with three different desserts on them.

She shakes her head at me. "Children these days! Can't be alive in this place and time and not know what memes are."

"Look at *you* knowing what memes are," my beautiful child says to me.

I shake my head at him. "Children these days! Can't be alive in this place and time and not know what memes are."

"Besides," he says to Mother, "you look a whole lot better than Keith Richards. I want your skin when I'm your age."

"By the time you're my age, your peers will have invented all kinds of potions to keep skin young."

"Maybe I can do that."

"Find a way to infuse an organic potion with light. That'll do it."

This day has been infused with light, that's for sure.

○

But…I'm so sorry. I still can't do it—think *she* or Jaye, that is—in my head yet. I'm still not able to do the PC discourse. It does seem, however, like it's becoming a possibility for some… decade, perhaps. As my child has said and as I've read in my research, acknowledging a chosen name is one of the most important things in deterring suicide in the high-risk trans population. But I still can't call him "Jaye." I've tried. So, I double down on being loving in other ways. Besides, I've always called him "sweetheart," "honey," "darling," and other endearments.

Once, not too long ago, when Mother and I were discussing this issue about names, I said, "I'm sure you would've preferred being called "Mom" all these years."

"I decided to pick my battles," she replied. "At least, you were calling me."

I think of how much thought and reverence went into choosing his name. His father and I must've considered several hundred names, and I'm not even exaggerating. When we decided on James, a chill went through me. For more than twenty years, every time I'd say his name, my being would remember that thought and reverence as well as that chill.

James comes from the Hebrew root for Jacob, which means to supplant, which is another way of saying to supersede. Even back then, I thought, well, James would certainly supersede his ancestors and life as we knew it then and bring in a new way of living. Oh, dear Lord. What a prophetic idea that was!

And that chill? I thought it was the most marvelous thing at the time. But maybe it was more prophecy. Ooohhhhh! That gives me yet another chill.

Would a better mother handle all this…well…better? I'm doing…well…better than I was doing before. I'm still a long way from perfect. I think I've finally realized this is who he is now—this she that's he's become. She's become. *She*. There—I did it! Without taking it back!

I love him (oops—that sure didn't last long) beyond measure. I would lay my life down for his. I've tried to teach him a high road of living, with loving the Lord and being a good Catholic. Many people might scoff at that, but it's the highest highway in my book.

How can I be better? I'll try again: Jaye...mms. Oh, just can't keep off the mms, the end of James. What is wrong with me? My mother was okay when I changed my name from Ambrosia. I could tell she wasn't thrilled, but she went along with it from the get-go. Sometimes, I wish James had gotten a hipper, more with-it mother...not this dud (at least in the hip-and-with-it department) that he ended up with. But I'm so happy he's my child.

As he's said, "It's just another experience."

I'm getting there with that.

If my child told me he was going into the military, I'd be scared. Proud, but scared, too. If he came home with a woman of color, I wouldn't blink an eye. It would be such a non-issue. Now, if he'd done that a hundred years ago, I might've had a completely different reaction. Not that that would have been the right reaction, but it wasn't as typical a situation in that time the way it is now. And my reaction wouldn't have been because of her color, but because of the difficulties I knew they'd face in society at that time.

Back to present day, if he'd come home with a guy, I might've had a moment of pause because I didn't see it coming, but I would've welcomed the guy...even despite what my religion preaches. So, maybe a few years in the future, I might've reacted completely differently to him being trans. This was absolutely, completely new to me, and I'm still gobsmacked.

We're not all born perfect. Some of us take a bit to come around to something. I'm not defending myself—just saying where I'm at.

We have surprised and confused parents all over the world. But they can't be. Not on this. It's not allowed. They—at least, the ones who don't toss their kids out the front door—have to get right on the program, despite all their fear and confusion. And I don't necessarily mean just fear of this unknown, but also fear of that known high suicide rate of trans people and fear of how society will treat them.

Some moments, I'm just fine. Other moments, even now, I still want to howl with rage and dread and bewilderment and "what did I do wrong?"

Hmmmmm. Just because I'm going through this doesn't mean

there's anything necessarily wrong with my child. My child is fine. Just making a choice, just living an experience, I suppose. So, while I'm supposing, I also suppose the problem lies with me.

○

And speaking of highways, as I was just above… "I think I'll be moseying on down the highway in January," my child says at the breakfast/lunch table a few days later. "Charles and I are going to go do this life thing down south."

"That sounds wonderful," I say, ignoring the slight pang in my heart. I couldn't possibly be missing him already, could I?

"Want to ask me anything about it?"

"All I'll ask from now on is 'Are you safe? Are you happy?' That's all that matters." I seem to remember my father saying something about it was good for him to find me seemingly safe and happy. Safe and happy. That really is all that matters.

My child stares at me for a moment after doing a triple double take.

My mother wasn't much better. "You don't *seem* to be a starbeing sitting in my daughter's chair."

I smile at both of them. "All these things that make you both crazy people…"

"Says you," the two say in unison.

"Are the things that make you, you. I wouldn't have you any other way. Who'd want to read the same book or watch the same movie over and over? And the contrast of shadow and light in photographs and artwork are what make them pop. Our differences are what make us, us. And they make our similarities feel even more special. We can celebrate both."

"Mom, that's a little off your brand, isn't it?"

I bristle a bit but stop when he laughs.

"I'll take it, though," he adds, taking my hand. Mother takes my other hand.

I think to myself, I love you both so much. I can't tell you both those words just like that, but I hope you know. I hope this love comes through me in a way that it can touch you.

I look over at my mother. I truly love you. You're crazy. You do things like discuss the Age of Aquarius and sniff peppermint oil. You're more of a snowflake than the kids are. But you gave birth to me and, as a young, single mother, raised me. Single parents are the true unsung heroes of this world. Life wasn't easy, but you showed me what love is.

One time, I said to you, "I don't know what to do with you."

"Love me forever?" you suggested.

I can do that.

I look at my child. I truly love you, too. No matter what you do, no matter what you say, no matter what you believe, you are the being I held in my arms when you first came into this world, and I finally knew what love was. My heart was cracked wide open in a way I had no idea was possible, and it could never, ever go back to its previous size.

You have been the biggest gift of my life. You're my only child. I would crawl over broken glass and scorpions if it would help you any. I will love you for eternity.

Chapter 33

Starr

Jaye looks at her mother and starts, then stops, then starts a sentence again. "Do…?" She stops and starts several more times. Finally, she can't hold back from asking any more. "Do you still think I'm a failure?"

Alice is stunned silent for a few seconds. "I never thought you were a failure!"

"I overheard you asking yourself in the mirror once 'How could I have failed him?' It should've been *her*, but I knew who you were talking about."

"Wondering how I could've failed you does *not* mean I think you're a failure. There's a big jump from one thought to the other. For one thing, as I've told you, it should kind of take some pressure off you if I take some of the blame."

Jaye doesn't say anything as she thinks about that.

Alice turns to me. "Do you still think I'm a failure?"

"I never thought you were a failure!"

"You thought you failed me. I can tell. It felt like the same thing as thinking I'm the failure."

"So, you know how I felt," Jaye says.

"I do," Alice smiles.

I think about my longer answer for a minute, before opening my mouth. "Well, I wasn't quite sure what to make of you, of the whole back-to-the-religious-right thing. I wasn't born hardwired to know how to handle all this."

"As if any of us are?" Alice rises from the table and heads toward the sink, but trips on the rug under the table and hits her head on the corner of the counter. As if in the most ghastly slow-motion sequence in a horror movie, I see her crash to the floor, blood oozing from her head.

"Mom? Mom?" Jaye's yell turns into a shriek. "Mom!"

I kneel down and grab her hand. "Alice? Alice, honey, can you hear me? Jaye, call 911."

The phone flips around in Jaye's hand as she fumbles with it. She drops the phone a few times before she can punch in 911 and put it on speakerphone.

"911, what's your emergency?"

"Please help us," she says. *"Please send someone right away!"*

"Tell them your mom fell and hit her head on the counter," I say.

Jaye repeats that to the 911 operator, and then, "She's bleeding and she's not responding to us!"

While we wait for the ambulance, the moments are microseconds and elongated at the same time. Is my heart beating? Have I breathed during the last two minutes? Every movement is exaggerated in time and timelessness, in weight and weightlessness. My arm seems to weigh a thousand pounds, and then my hand flies over to caress Alice's face.

"Please, just wake me up from this horrible dream," Jaye cries.

We debate moving her to the couch. I finally shake my head. "They sometimes say not to move people. It could break their neck or something like that. Let's have the EMTs move her."

Alice opens her eyes and looks at Jaye. Then, she looks up at me.

"The ambulance is on its way," I tell her.

"Nagajussdoyerhocusssshpocussssh?"

I smile. "At least, you still have your contrariness going. No, I'm not going to do my hocus pocus. Well, I always do my hocus pocus, really. But there's a time and place for ambulances and hospitals, too."

Alice slips into unconsciousness again.

Finally, sirens wail in the distance, growing ever louder.

The EMTs shut the door to the ambulance and speed out of the driveway. I follow close behind, Jaye beside me. We don't talk, but the air sparks with communication.

Several doctors and nurses rush out to greet the EMTs, who shout medical stats at them.

"Please, oh please," Jaye whispers. "Take me. I'd rather die."

I grab her hand. "You stop that right now, young lady! It is far from your time to die." We rush into the hospital.

After the briefest of conversations with the medical staff, the paramedics wheel Alice into the ER. A doctor and a nurse wheel her down the hall.

"Please, please, please," Jaye whispers.

The triage nurse shoos us to the main waiting room, where Jaye and I set up camp. After a few moments of sitting in shock, I crochet, just to bring me back to Earth, just to keep me from losing my mind.

"So, yarn and a crochet hook happen to be just a couple of the items in that black-hole-of-a-purse of yours, too?" Jaye teases as tears slip down her face. Then, she turns to texting her friends.

Every time a nurse or doctor walks through the swinging double door, we jump up. After an eternity, a doctor comes out and sits down by us.

"It's an epidural hematoma. We need to do a craniotomy."

"Will she be alright?" we both ask her at the same time.

"We have to see. But let me go work on her, and I'll update you in a while."

Jaye researches those terms on her phone, and she reads the results to me.

"What's the fatality percent?" I ask through my own sudden stream of tears.

"It varies on the severity."

After what seems like a dog's age, the doctor returns to us again. "We're not really sure about her condition," she says. "We have to monitor her. She's still unconscious now, of course."

"When will she wake up?" I ask.

"We're not exactly sure of that, either. But you can go be with her."

Following the doctor's directions, we find Alice's room upstairs. We sit beside her for a bit—a day? two? three? Felt like it—basically just watching her sleep. Then, Jaye and I take turns going home to get a change of clothes and some food.

At one point, Jaye looks up from her endless texting to Charles and Vision and drops her phone. "She's awake!"

I pivot to Alice. "Hiiiiiii," I coo to her.

"How are you?" Jaye whispers.

She blinks her eyes a couple of times.

"Does that mean good? You're doing good?" She blinks a couple of times again. I start to speak once more, but she's slipped back to sleep or unconsciousness or whatever. I would've loved a shot of that whatever.

The machine to which Alice is hooked up starts making that infernal racket (I sound like Alice!) I only ever thought I'd hear on TV and in movies. Over the next day or so, it happens once, twice, then three times. And, each time, a crew of nurses and doctors rush in to revive her.

Finally, her doctor comes in again. "I'm so sorry," she says softly after giving us a very grim prognosis for Alice's recovery.

Jaye sputters for a second. "Can we get a second opinion?"

"Of course, you can," the doctor says. "It's just…I'm not sure you have time for that. By the time you move her in an ambulance to another hospital, she might be gone. You might want to leave her where she's at least comfortable. But you can do whatever you want."

Jaye slumps over. After the doctor leaves, we just sit with her words for a while.

The moments do their fluctuating thing again—microseconds and elongated, elongated even more, then back to microseconds. I feel dizzy and lean my head on my hand.

"You okay, Gram?" When I pause for a few seconds, Jaye adds, "I mean physically. I know you're not doing okay emotionally. Your daughter is dying." We both start crying.

We then alternate between staring at Alice and staring out the window at nothing in particular. How many days have we been here? Or has it been just one very long day? Must be at least a few days. Another one is coming to a close, I notice, as I see the clouds lit up from the setting sun. They're orange and pink and…butterscotch-colored. Okay, maybe that's my imagination.

Jaye and I sit and sit—no phones, nothing. Just…Alice. I notice the clouds are lit up again, this time from the rising sun. And they're…butterscotch. That's not even possible, I chide myself. Yet, there they are.

I turn to Jaye. "If that machine-from-hell goes off and they run in here again, perhaps we should tell them to just let her go. What do you think?"

Jaye shrugs, then nods.

"I'm going to call her father." I leave the room.

"Should I fly out there?" Michael asks.

"I'm not sure," comes my slow answer. "I'm not sure how much longer we have."

"Well, I'll book a flight for first thing tomorrow morning. How's that?"

"Sounds good."

When I get back to Alice's room, Jaye leaves to phone Dan. She returns within just a few minutes.

"That didn't take long," I say.

"I didn't feel like hanging out with him much."

"Ah."

"Just told him I'd let him know when and where the memorial will be."

I just let her be with no more commentary.

The doctor comes to check on Alice again, and Jaye grabs her arm. "I don't understand. It didn't seem like that big of a fall. How could that do this to her?"

"It all depends how exactly she hit her head," the doctor explains. "Some people might have just a bruise. Other people might not make it. I'm so sorry."

After the doc leaves, Jaye and I just sit, tears streaming. Why does Alice have to be one of the "other people" who might not make it?

Late that night, Alice wakes up again. "Still…here."

"You mean us or you?" I ask her.

"Yes," Jaye says, "we are and so are you."

"But…saw…Jesus."

"You did?" Jaye asks. "That must've been wonderful."

Alice's eyes start to roll back, but then she jerks back to…what, consciousness? Life itself?

"I want you to know something," Jaye says to her through her tears. "You are a phenomenal mom and person. Momperson."

Alice smiles, but then her eyes roll back again. And then, back to us again.

"Honey, do you want to stay?" I ask her. "Do you want the doctors and nurses to keep reviving you?"

She blinks once.

"I think that means 'No,'" Jaye tells me, "since two blinks meant, 'Yes' before." She turns to her mother. "Is that right? You're ready to go?"

She blinks twice. I wipe away tears, as does Jaye.

Alice seems to gather every last ounce of energy she has to speak again. Her voice is so quiet, it's like she's halfway out the door—of

Life—already. She looks at me. "Love…you…"

"I love you, Alice."

"Love…you…Jaye." She smiles as Jaye looks puzzled. "No…not fading out…yet…Did mean…no…mms."

"No what?"

"Mms. Of…James."

"Oh!" We can't see her for a moment, due to the onslaught of new tears welling in our eyes.

"I love you, Mom. Mean it."

"Love…you…Jaye. Me…it."

"Mom."

"Beautiful…wo…man…in 'n…out."

Jaye tries to say thank you again but is too choked up.

"Love…" That's all she said, and then, I notice her life line goes flat. That friggin' machine starts making a whole bunch of noise yet again. What a way to go out—with all that clamor. A couple of nurses run in.

"Can you please turn off that thing?" I ask. "Just let her go." When the nurses look more than a little surprised, I add, "We talked to her about it. She's okay with leaving."

Right after they turn down the machine—but not off—and leave, I feel Alice's presence fill the room.

"Do you feel that?" I whisper to Jaye. She nods. "It's kind of like witnessing an angel being born." Jaye nods again. She holds her palms out and slowly moves them back and forth as if the energy in the room is tangible, which it is.

Much to my surprise, the hospital staff leaves us completely alone. We sit with her body for hours. By later that night, the energy in the room has dissipated somewhat.

"There's so much more I wanted to tell her," Jaye says.

"Tell her now. She can still hear you. She'll always be able to hear you."

"But what if this is really it? Lay this body down and there's nothing else?"

"How could that possibly be? Where else could we go but here in these universes?"

Exactly like her mother recently said, she says, "Universes? Just the thought of that makes me dizzy."

"Like the multiverse any better?"

"A little."

We're quiet again for a while. I slip out of the room just before dawn Boston time to let Michael know.

"Please let me know when the memorial is," he says.

"Of course."

As I walk back into Alice's room, Jaye quickly wipes away her tears.

"Just let them flow, sweetheart. Just let them flow. That's what they're for."

After a few moments of quiet weeping, Jaye whispers, "I didn't expect her to be the one to go."

"No one would've thought that. She was so healthy, despite her ridiculous food choices, and as strong as a bull, what with all her physical work at her job. I sure expected to go long before she did."

"Me, too. And I really tried."

"I'm so glad you didn't succeed."

Jaye's quiet for a bit, deep in thought. She then moves as if about to say something.

A nurse walks in, though. "We're going to be moving her soon," she says.

We both nod, without saying anything. After the nurse leaves, I gently probe. "You were going to say something?"

Jaye shrugs.

"Did you hear the last word she said?" I ask. She shrugs again. "The last word on her lips was 'love.' I love that." Jaye doesn't say anything, so I continue. "I once heard that Mahatma Gandhi went out with his word for God on his lips. Well, your mom did that. She said 'love.' Love, God, it's all the same thing."

Jaye still doesn't say anything but squeezes my hand and puts her head on my shoulder.

Back home, Jaye's friends arrive like a flock of crows—dressed in black—with very yummy food. They stock the fridge and freezer with Tupperware containers full of veggie delights. A bunch of my friends arrive with more standard mourning fare: meat casseroles, lasagna, and the like.

I find myself staying up late laughing with friends, some new, young ones and my old, old ones. Cancel that—my old, gold ones.

Funny how we laugh so much when we're in mourning. I think it's the body's reflex to deflect the stress of so much trauma. Not long after 9/11, I read an article about how many people felt survival guilt and how they wished they'd been first responders—such a noble calling. Even comedians said that, and I thought, "Oh, no, not you. Please do what you're doing, what you do best. We need you, especially in times like this."

We need the first responders, too, of course. Oh, Alice. You were a first responder, in a way, in your way, for so many, for infants being born, for all those people who showed up in your emergency room, for your daughter, for…me.

The first time I held you in my arms, I knew what love was. Love. We treat the word and the emotion so cavalierly, with such disregard. But holding you, flesh of my flesh and blood of my blood, I knew what love was. It hit me like a bolt of lightning. It expanded my heart so much that it could never, ever return to its original shape.

Dearest Alice. I've had enough people die in my life to know that you'll always be with me. But to bury a child, oh! In those moments, when I don't have the gift of shock, the blessed numbness of dreamlike denial, in the moments where the excruciating wound of loss slips in, oh! This expanded heart of mine is looking for the original, physical reason for its expansion, and in its sagging emptiness the aching agony is unbearable. Nothing in my life has hurt so much—not even come close.

Chapter 34

Jaye

"What about the whole Jesus thing, though?" I ask Gram the next day. "How the hell—pardon that, given this context—did she see him?"

"Well, we apparently see whoever we want to see. And Jesus is as real as anyone. So, that's a legitimate experience she had."

"I guess."

"I had a near-death experience once. A friend and I were in a car accident."

I rapidly shake my head, as I try to wrap my mind around this one. "I thought I heard every one of your stories a thousand times. Somehow, I missed this one." But then, I remember Mom mentioning something about it, maybe.

It's another sunny, warmish winter day for Northern California, so we're lounging out on the patio. We don't like to hang out in the kitchen much these days, if we can avoid it. Too Mom. We keep expecting her to walk in the door at any minute, and when she doesn't and we re-remember why, the pain stings all over again.

Gram chuckles. "I remember mentioning my NDE to your mom. It didn't go well—lots of eye rolling. Sorry I didn't tell you. I floated out of my body and was hovering above the car. I felt love all around me, kind of swooshing me up, up, up. But then, I woke up in an ambulance, my friend beside me. I guess it wasn't my time. I sure wish I could remember if I talked to anyone out there, but I'll always remember that love. That amazing love." Neither of us say anything for a minute. "I haven't been scared of much since that time. Only love awaits us. In fact, only love is here. There. Anywhere."

I pick at my salad that night. "She wasn't supposed to die. I was supposed to die."

"You most certainly were not! Neither of you were supposed to die. I was supposed to die. My death would've been in the natural order of things."

I pick some more. "No one should ever have to see a child die, Gram."

"And she almost had to see that."

I don't say anything, but tears start streaming down my face. "It hurts here, on this Earth," I finally whisper. "So fucking much. And it just doesn't stop. When will it get better? What will become of me?"

Gram puts her arms around me. "There's an art piece by Agnes Denes called 'Teardrop—Monument to Being Earthbound.' That about sums it up. Not that it's all tears, but tears are a big part of what makes us human."

"I can't live through this after what I just went through. I can't lose my mom on top of... well, those are two of the worst experiences anyone can go through."

"Yes, you can live through those. They will turn you into a powerhouse. You'll fear very little after all this. Plus, you'll have the most compassionate heart and be able to listen to people share their tragedies because you've been there."

She holds me as I sob. After a few minutes, hunger wins over tears, and I start stabbing my salad again.

"And who the hell dies just after Christmastime? How rude is that?" I laugh through my tears. Then, I laugh and laugh, on a laughing jag. We do have to laugh in times of great sorrow, I'm discovering. "Don't mind me. I'm just having a moment."

"Take as many moments as you need." Gram puts her arms around me again. "Not to be trite and sound like I'm quoting pop songs," she says, "but—truly—whatever doesn't kill you really does make you stronger."

"Oh. Well, I'll be a superhero."

"You already are one. And the world could sure use more superheroes."

"But two life tragedies in two months? It's not fair."

"No, it's not." We eat in silence for a bit, then she says, "People who've been to hell have a greater ability to help other people find heaven. They have the authority, the expertise, the mastery to help others more than most."

I just stab at my salad some more.

"You'll be okay," Gram says to me. "Way more than okay. You're a fighter, a warrioress, a priestess. They go through the fire so they can high beam their light out to the world."

She takes my hand. Again.

Mom. I miss her so crazy much it's ridiculous. And she just left. I hear it only gets worse and worse for a long time. There was a presence in the world and her name was Mom. I don't know how to live in this world without the presence, without her.

"She and I were just starting to become friends again," I say to Gram the following day. "I think she was just starting to get me."

"How wonderful that you had that, as short as it was."

"Oh, Gram, I wish my life could be as rosy as the one you live in."

"It can be."

"Oh."

"But don't skip the mourning and recovery part, either. That'll help get it rosy again."

"Oh."

As Charles and I make the slideshow of Mom's pictures for the funeral, Gram asks, "Ever think of going into filmmaking? That's an impressive movie you're making."

"This really isn't that hard," I tell her. "Anyone with a computer can do this."

"I couldn't."

"Yeah, you could. Even you could."

We laugh.

Dead bodies look like they're breathing…but maybe that's because we're expecting the body to be breathing. I'd be looking at her face and think her chest was rising. Then, I'd look at her chest, and of course it was still.

I've had friends die before, but I've never been around an open casket, with someone actually lying in it…well, dead, that is.

Mom didn't want to be cremated. She wanted the full funeral with the open casket beforehand. In lieu of flowers, we asked people to make donations to an organization for teen mothers that we knew Mom supported. Gram and I were surprised to see that Mom had left a plan in a documents folder on her computer's desktop. It's almost like she knew.

There's nothing like death to make you think about life. I regret every snarky comment. Although I wasn't supposed to be a doormat, either, and she just didn't…well, she needed help getting it. She was getting there to getting it, toward the end. And she did get it, really, in the very end.

I find myself talking to her all the time. Mom, we were so different but that certainly made things interesting. I'm sorry I was so rough and tough on you; I might've been taking my anger at society out on you.

I couldn't yell at our culture, but I could yell at you. Actually, I've certainly yelled at representative bits of our culture from time to time, like those oldies in that parking lot that time. And maybe a thousand others.

But you…I mean, you didn't make things easy with your rules and judgments and all, but…maybe I took a lot more out on you than I needed to. I wish…I wish…oh, I don't know what I wish.

If you can, please come back and talk to me. Tell me what you see over there. I'm glad you saw Jesus as you were leaving. Honestly, I am.

I'm so sorry. Not for all of it, but definitely for some of it. Not for who I finally let myself be, but that it had to be so clunky here and there and even everywhere sometimes. You needed a whole lotta prodding. Oh, sorry. I shouldn't pick on you, being dead and all.

Dead! How is that even possible? You were so alive just a few days ago. How can all of life change in just one second? Oh, Mom. I'm sorry. I'm sorry for my part. I'm sorry we couldn't get to happy sooner.

I love you. I love you. I love you.

Hug your people, people. You just never know what conversation will be the last. You just never know….

Chapter 35

Starr

Who in the world are all these people? And they just keep coming! Even the aisles in the back of the church are filled to overflowing with folks standing.

One after another, Alice's church members, friends, fellow Republicans, and coworkers—including nurses, doctors, technicians, admin folks, and even people she didn't directly work with, like the security and maintenance crews—have made an appearance to rave about her.

"Alice always remembered my birthday."

"She always had a bright word for a dark day."

"This beautiful spirit cared more about people than anyone I ever met."

"Every baby who was lucky enough to have Alice welcome it into this world is probably blessed with a special, magical touch for the rest of its life."

I glance over at Jaye. She has, "Wow! This is about my mom?" printed all over her face. I smile as her expression shifts to, "Yep, this is about my mom. I knew that."

Yes, my darling girl, you did know that. I'm so happy you had the chance to know that before it was too late. And I'm so happy she had the chance to know you, too.

And as funerals go, this one is quite the remarkable, stunning scene. All of Alice's groups mesh with Jaye's goth gang and my power-to-the-people circle. Alice is probably laughing her head off, up there in the warm, happy place where she's found herself.

A bolt of understanding strikes me here and now, after years of wondering why these kids were searching in the dark with all their goth stuff. That's where the light can shine more brilliantly! We can't have light without darkness. The word and the light come from the dark, after all.

Dan and Brenda had skulked in just as the service was getting started, and Brenda sneaked out just as things were finishing up. Dan stays at the reception long enough to give Jaye a big hug along with somewhat sincere condolences. I'm sure he's wondering if I'd had a part in Jaye's outfit, which was quite subdued in honor of her mother, but still: a simple, black sheath dress, black stockings, black heels. She asked my opinion about the hat with the black veil, and she put it away when I inadvertently grimaced. Her long, blonde hair cascades down her back in waves of spiral curls. At least, the lipstick is red and not black.

"Today is for Mom," she'd said about that.

Charles wears simple slacks and a dress shirt. He looks out of place with their crowd, most of whom had their wild plumage going in full force—hats with veils, striped stockings, pentagrams, corsets. Whatever did the Republicans think?

"Oh, the optics!" Jaye giggles to me, pointing to Vision standing next to Alice's priest.

Michael flies in and out within twenty-four hours to be there. "I'd stay longer," he says. "But my son's court date is tomorrow." He takes my hand. "At least, Alice didn't have to suffer much."

"Yes."

"I'm so happy I got to meet her, as short as it was."

"Yes." I've gotten very monosyllabic for some reason. I hope my hand in his conveys more than my words seem to be able to.

"I'll be in touch," he whispers, and then he's gone.

"I want a green burial," I mention to Jaye on the way home. "I love the idea of feeding the food chain and having a big, beautiful tree spring from my heart."

"That's absolutely awesome, Gram."

"How about you?" When she doesn't respond, I chuckle. "Kids your age think you're immortal. Death feels so far away." But then I realize I'm talking to someone who just tried to die.

"Not really," Jaye murmurs, as if she can hear what I just remembered. "We just saw a sudden death and too many kids my age are dying. Suicide, overdoses, shootings, bad health from all this bad shit in the food, water, air, and soil. The life expectancy is suddenly going down."

"True." I decide against talking more because despite that outburst, talking suddenly seems to be the last thing my-usually-so-loquacious granddaughter wants to do right now. I was so angry at the toll Viet Nam and drugs took on my generation, but these younger generations have an even bigger toll they didn't ask for, either.

Jaye and I meet with Alice's attorney. Surprisingly enough, she left the house to Jaye. No, leaving the house to her wasn't the surprising part…the leaving it to Jaye—yes, that name—was the shocker. She must've changed that fairly recently. Did she have a premonition or something? She also left a large sum to Jaye—in a trust, with stipulations for gaining access to the money: college, good grades, entrepreneurship. In other words, Jaye was pretty set for life and could do almost anything, but not nothing…not that Jaye would do nothing. Go Alice!

She left a trust for my health care and quite a hefty chunk for living expenses for the rest of my life. I don't need much under normal circumstances, but I'm so grateful. A dear friend of mine lost everything when she found out the hard way that Medicare doesn't cover long-term care. I'm a very lucky woman, considering how flakey (yes, I completely admit it) I've been almost all of my life. I've only ever known what was next—or at least where—by the direction my feet were pointing. I liked it that way.

Alice left some money to the homeless shelter I volunteer at! And some more money went to a few scholarships. She also left a generous (to me, anyway) amount for an organization in Somalia that works to fight against Female Genital Mutilation. How interesting. That Alice Walker talk I took her to years ago must've left an impression. I didn't think she had any interest then, or ever. Ah, how wrong we can be. Of course, she held that one very close to her chest. Couldn't let me know anything I ever did impacted her in a positive way. Oh, no. Not until she was dead.

Sorry, Alice. I know that's not totally true.

Jaye hasn't been talking much for a few days. The energy in the house seems to be shifting upward—that's certainly a major feat, given the heaviness from Alice being gone.

Gone! Yes, we always hear that a parent losing a child is the worst—the worst possible pain there can be. How right that is. The worst of the worst. Sometimes, I can't breathe. Sometimes, my heart feels like it's going to explode. It's not meant to hold this much pain.

There's supposed to be a right timing to things, along with a sense of fairness. This doesn't belong to either of those notions. Perhaps, very few people leave this Earth untouched by seemingly wrong timing and the seeming unfairness of life, though.

"What do you have on?" I'm in shock, absolute shock, at Jaye's flowing green skirt, with a belly dancer's belt slung around her hips.

"Like the look? My boho friend in LA bought them for me. I just never wear them."

"Love it!"

"Just…oh…trying different things. Honestly, you like it? It's not really me, though, huh?"

I wrap my arms around her. "Beautiful Jaye, my darling granddaughter, you are so you, no matter what you do or wear. You can't do you wrong."

"I'd love to fly out and spend some time with you," Michael says on the phone that night.

I can't speak, so he does. "That okay with you?"

"Yes," I finally whisper.

"I've been dreaming about you for fifty years. Should've gotten your phone number."

"Or at least my name." We laugh.

Oh, life. What a wild, crazy, mixed-up, wonderful, horrible, hard, easy, delightful, ridiculous, delicious, nasty, all-over-the-place thing you are. Michael arrives in time to help me celebrate my sixty-ninth birthday.

As every decade has come to a close, I'd think of all the things I hadn't accomplished yet, and I'd feel some pressure to hurry up and do more, be more. The have-more thing seemed to skip me entirely, for which I'm thankful.

But then, every new decade arrived with its spaciousness of another ten years to accomplish more, do more, be more. As the decades passed, the emphasis switched to mostly merely being more.

I spent my youth learning how to operate this body and mind of mine and yearning to get away from those parents I borrowed just to get this body and mind of mine. I spent my twenties and thirties raising one and then two girls (the second in my nanny gig). I spent my forties and fifties cavorting about. Sixty is such a poignant time because we can really see that this living thing we've taken for granted won't last forever. Some people don't take to sixty well, but it made me appreciate life all the more. And seventy—wow! It'll be such a privilege.

Oh, all the things I've seen in seventy years. I remember seeing Dick Tracy's two-way watch radio in the comics section of the Sunday paper and thinking how cool that'd be. I'd dial a friend and wish I could see her, and I even said once, "I wonder if we'll ever have phones where we can see each other."

And even bigger are the advances Jaye will see. She has maybe eighty-plus years ahead of her...maybe even a hundred. Oh, just think of these young people and the children coming in now who will do so much better than we dreamed of doing, the societal improvements (cleaning the air, water, and food), the millions of inventions we can't even fathom yet, and so much more.

I think of all the children Alice helped to bring into the world. Oh, Alice. My darling daughter. So much strength. So much stableness. So much Alice. So much hidden Ambrosia. So much.

Michael and I drive out to Point Reyes. After spending the afternoon walking along Limantour beach, we eat dinner at a quaint, quiet bistro.

"What now?" His eyes tell me he's not just talking about dessert.

"What, what now?" I giggle. "What would you like now?"

"It's so strange to really see the end coming," he says. "But we don't know if that end is in ten years, twenty, thirty, even forty."

"We might only be at seven-elevenths of our lives," I giggle again. This much giggling is not in my normal repertoire, but he's turned me into a nervous schoolgirl.

He's been taking exceptional care of himself all these years, so he could certainly last quite a while longer. I let out a long sigh. "Boston and Petaluma are far apart." I love my penchant for stating the obvious. "You have a clan back there. A small one, but still a clan."

"You...sparkle. I want some of that. And maybe I want to try California. And perhaps life with you."

"Can I get you anything else?" Why do waitstaff always show up at the most inopportune moments? Oh, well. It wasn't her fault. She didn't know.

"I think I just got everything I wanted," I say to her. After she leaves, I turn back to Michael. I still see the beautiful young man from so long ago. Oh, my Goodness! So much...life...since then. I made the best possible life that I could. Maybe someone else could've taken my life and done better. But I had mine and that someone else had theirs to go make far more perfect than mine.

The rest of my years, whatever I have left, swim before my eyes, and they're with this man I'd been waiting for. I look over at Michael, and he smiles at me, but perhaps with a faraway look in his eyes. Is he seeing this, too? Is he looking down the pathway of the rest of his years and seeing me by his side?

I think so, because he takes my hand and presses it to his cheek, as if he can't believe he finally found me and is never, ever going to let me go again. I know the feeling.

On the way home, after talking about a few of the things we've done and a few of the things still on the proverbial bucket list, I turn to him. "Would you be willing to go on a trip to Phuket, Thailand?"

"Sure," comes his quick answer, without even asking me why.

But I tell him anyway. "My brother was killed in Viet Nam, and that's where he was when he sent his last postcard to us. I've always wanted to go there, to the last place I knew he was happy. Not sure why I've waited so long."

"I'd love to be the one to go with you."

I blink back tears.

Back at the ranch, after driving Michael to the airport, Jaye's elated that Michael is moving into…well, my life if not this particular house. A moment later, though, she's suddenly inconsolable.

"I don't know what's wrong with me!" she cries.

"Honey, your mother just died and right before that you faced another atrocious, harrowing, life-shaking event. No other explanation is needed."

"I was so hard on her. I told her not to momsplain things to me, among a million other witty, snitty comebacks."

"Yes. Sometimes, they were deserved, though."

"Why couldn't she…why couldn't I…why couldn't we have gotten closer sooner?"

I shrug. "Maybe you were expecting her to speak Japanese when she'd never been exposed to Japanese. Metaphorically speaking, of course."

"But you speak Japanese. Metaphorically."

"I try to speak the Universal language. So, you heard it as Japanese."

"Why didn't she?"

I shrug. "She didn't know it."

"Why didn't she learn it?"

"I don't know. Believe me, I tried to teach it to her. But I think she did get it by the end."

Jaye gasps and then burst into tears again.

"Honey, what?" She wails into my shoulder. When the sobs subside, I gently question her. "Beautiful one, what is it?"

"I think I once said to myself that maybe I need to hit her over the head or something like that. And that I'd make sure she'd—quote—get it. But I certainly didn't mean to kill her!"

"You did not kill her."

The tears stream again. "Gram, I can't even stand this. I—what am I going to do? This hurts so fucking much."

"Oh, baby girl, just let the sadness wash over you. Let the tears come. They're a cleansing and release process. I've lost so many people in my life, and one thing I've learned is to let grief have its way. It passes more quickly when you just let it come and go. And the more you let it come, the faster it goes. Believe me, I know."

"I hate it."

"Death is what makes life so precious. Can you imagine how truly awful it'd be without it?"

Her tears progress into sobs and then into near howls. Okay, maybe it wasn't the right time for that last thought. But the storm passes over.

Oh, Jaye. You have your whole life ahead of you. All the things you'll see and do and experience, all the new technologies that will come in during your lifetime—it makes my head spin.

Oh, Alice. My Alice. You were so…Alice. You were so…who you were. I'll always love you. And you'll always have safe passage through my heart. Too bad you had to die in order for me to truly give you that safe passage sooner than later.

Hug your people, people. You just never, ever, ever know.

One night, the quiet around the kitchen table is too loud. "Did you know the actual age of Aquarius started on December 31?" I ask Jaye. "Just for that alone, I bet 2020 is going to be a wild, kick-ass year, leading up to that."

"Huh." Jaye scrolls through the news on her phone. "Did you hear about some virus in China?"

"Yes. Isn't there a case in Seattle now?"

"Well, that might make things interesting for a while."

"What are you two going to do, Gram?" Jaye asks me a few weeks later, as I'm getting ready to pick up Michael at the airport.

"Well, he and I are going to scoot about the country in the RV for a bit. Then, we'll see where we are with each other and if we want to settle down for a time." I hesitate. "I want to go to college, too, since I never did that."

"How cool!"

"I won't get the record for oldest graduate, but it'll still be something major for a woman my age."

"I love it!" Jaye takes my hand. "You're such a badass babe, Gram."

"And you're not going to believe this. I've been thinking I might become a model."

"Say it isn't so? What a great idea! Whoever would think of such a thing?"

I smile. "Someone actually approached me at Whole Foods the other week and asked me if I'd ever thought of it. Said I'd be a great model, and not just as a pretty face on the page. A great role model, too...like someone very, very wise told me a while back."

"You're so lit up, Gram. You need to shine that light in as many places as you can."

Tears slip down my face, and Jaye takes both of my hands in hers.

"What will you do about your friends, your bees and worms?" she asks.

"A human friend will take them for a while, if not permanently."

"Cool."

"What about Charles?"

Jaye shrugs. "We'll see. Charles and I were talking about SoCal, but now I'm not so sure about things. I have a lotta living to do and I'm way too young to settle down with anyone yet."

"And what about the specifics of that lotta living?" I ask. "She left the house to you, so you could stay here. Or you could sell it. Or you could rent it out and go live on a beach in Thailand for a while. But the trust does stipulate college."

"I'm definitely going back to college, and not just because I have to, to get the money from Mom."

"Right. Do it for you, not her."

"I am, I am. I think I might eventually go for a Masters in Social Work, to be a counselor. That kind of thing. Although I do like that beach-in-Thailand idea."

"Wow, social work. That'd be great." I tell her the importance of Thailand to me and that Michael and I might go—once this virus thing calms down, of course.

"Wow." Jaye stares out the window. "Strange how the money just skipped right over you. Your parents left money to Mom, and she bought this house, which she left to me. Plus, she had millions. I had no idea your parents were so loaded. And she kept working and living her life like she didn't have all that."

"Skipping me wasn't a completely dumb decision on my parents' part," I laugh. "I might've bought a pot farm with it, back before that was okay...or lucrative."

"Or a retreat center. Or an organization that cleans up the oceans. Or something else good for the planet."

"Yes. I would've had lots of crazy ideas. Actually, they wouldn't have been so crazy."

"I'm going to give you the money for a few of those not-so-crazy ideas."

"Jaye!" I take her hand and gently kiss it. I then throw my arms around my amazing granddaughter. "Let's go change the world."

"I think we already are," Jaye smiles, throwing her arms around me, too.

"Let's hope so."

"Let's know so."

THE END

In Loving Memory of

Peter Tork

one of my Earth Angels
who championed my writing
many years ago.

Author's Note

A number of people in the inner circle of my life have or have had lives similar to Jaye, Alice, and Starr. I've been lucky enough to have had countless conversations with them about their experiences, world views, opinions, and outlooks. This book could not have been written without that close walk with them all.

Over the past several years, I've specifically talked at length with transgender kids and adults, as well as their parents. The trans and gender-fluid people in my life have taught me so much, and I am happy to call myself a LGBTQIA+ ally who is now fairly well educated in this world. I don't want to go into more detail about anyone's identity and how they show up in my life, in order to honor their privacy.

One of my main desires for *Bazoomerangs* is that it can serve as a primer for cis people who've had little or no interaction with the trans community. So, I didn't particularly write this for the Jayes of the world. I wrote it for the Alices and the other people in a trans person's life who might not understand, yet could, and might then be part of their support system.

Millions of people all over the world are acknowledging their inner calling and becoming transgender or genderqueer, transitioning, and the myriad other opportunities they have available. Around them are millions more people who make up their family, friends, and other members of the general community. They might have no knowledge of the LGBTQIA+ life/struggle/wants/needs, yet once they gain some knowledge and appreciation, they then have the potential to be an ally.

Jaye, Alice, and Starr are their own people. None of the three women in *Bazoomerangs* are based on anyone in particular. As with writing all of my books, even if one of my characters starts out from a seed of someone I know, eventually that character takes on a life of their own and becomes their own individual person. This might sound crazy, but I know many other authors can relate. My characters sometimes say things, share ideas, and travel roads I hadn't even thought of.

One time, I mentioned in a screenwriting class that my characters surprise me. The professor said, "You mean to say that you actually say, 'I can't believe I just wrote that'?" The class laughed and so did I. But, well… yes, that's exactly what I meant and still do mean!

I'm so grateful for these wild and wonderful characters. And especially for this book, I'm so grateful for the wild and wonderful people in my world who helped me breathe life into them.

I also want to mention that I was raised Catholic. In fact, my mother wanted to be a nun. My dad talked her out of it. Good thing. Otherwise, you wouldn't have just read this book.

An early reviewer of *Bazoomerangs* said she appreciated that no one is made to be a villain. That's more in relation to the spiritual and political differences between the characters, and specifically regarding Alice's beliefs and positions.

While this book is in part comedic (or at least I hope you think so), this is in no way to make light of anyone's journey. I honor my peeps' paths and am grateful to them for sharing their trials, tribulations, ordeals, achievements, victories, ecstasies, and a laugh here and there.

One of the main jobs of a writer is to get inside the heads of people the reader wouldn't otherwise meet, to explore worlds the reader might not otherwise visit, to tell of adventures the reader might not otherwise experience—albeit with enough research and conversations to give credibility to those people, worlds, and adventures. I have written about many experiences that I haven't personally lived through, such as giving birth, for one. But I've certainly talked to enough women who've had babies to be able to write it down with veracity.

In fact, one of my favorite things about writing is getting to gain knowledge about so many things: having a baby, being a starbeing and experiencing Earth for the very first time, trying to make it as a Hollywood actor. Being tortured and burned at the stake or living through a crucifixion, not so much.

I love all of my books, of course, but this one was especially wonderful, enriching, and an honor to write. In fact, when I finished, I howled to my husband, "I miss Jaye, Alice, and Starr already!" I'd never said anything like that before.

I truly hope you enjoy their stories and journeys, too.

Love, peace, and blessings,
Ann Crawford
Lakewood, Colorado
April 2024

Acknowledgements

It takes more than a village—it can take a whole world to create a book. So many bighearted people have graciously given a bit of themselves to me, to my life, and to this book. I'm so thankful to you all.

First and foremost, my beautiful, beloved Steve—my biggest fan, cheerleader, and ground-crew leader. You make me laugh out loud every single day, sometimes all day—one of the biggest gifts anyone can give. Your playful, quiet, gentle humor fills the rooms of our home as they fill the pages of this book and all the others I've written since I met you. I'm beyond grateful for you. I love you, I love you, I love you…

My two stepchildren, my three sisters, and my late brother and parents.

The awesome team at Stephanie Castle Publications, most especially the magnificent Margot Wilson; the fabulous Randy Peyser of Author One Stop, Inc.; Lana McAra, master teacher from Heaven; and Chris Sowers, editor extraordinaire.

Extra thanks to Betsey Crawford, Diane Bishop, and my special team: Athena McDowell, Barbara Cox, Dana Swift, Frances Mary Frame, Grace Sears, Jenni Ashanta Lipari, Kathleen McGarry, Sherry Robb, Veronica Entwistle, and my many amazing teachers past and present. My beloved Guy, Kim, Liz, Marion, Sue, and Suzanne.

Gifted sound healer Mei-Lan Maurits and composer/musician Jonathan Goldman who provided my personal *Bazoomerangs* soundtrack…plus Scott McKenzie ["San Francisco (Be Sure to Wear Flowers in Your Hair)"], Galt MacDermot (the soundtrack for *Hair*), The Band, John Lennon, the Beatles, Joe Cocker, Janis Joplin, Simon and Garfunkel, and Crosby, Stills, Nash and Young—all of whom helped me get in the sixties and seventies mode for Starr.

The innumerable people I've met along the way whose snippets of conversation have become character quirks in my books, such as the wonderful woman whose boyfriend had a motor on the kitchen table. Actually, I think it was not just some lawn mower or tractor motor—it was an entire car engine. A special shoutout to Ann Hyatt Poplin, Beth Fonfara, Dan Seidman, Deepak Chopra, Diane English, Elizabeth Holdmann, Esther Crawford, Harriet Witt, Rev. Karyl Huntley, Rev. Katherine Revoir, Dr. Kathleen Levdar, Mark Waldman, Rev. Michael

Beckwith, Rev. Noel McInnis, Randy Westmoreland, Sandee Endahl, Steve Daubney, Steve Wilder, TC McCracken, and Zaya Heap. Very special thanks to the doctor in my life who's been patiently answering all of my medical questions for all my books.

This book involves a number of very complicated subjects, and I spent a significant amount of time researching and talking to people who are living these kinds of events. I'm especially grateful to the many members of the LGBTQIA+ community, including trans and genderqueer folks, along with their parents, who so generously shared their life experiences with me. I want to give extra, extra thanks to all the beautiful people who helped me create the character of Jaye.

My loving thoughts go to Bobbi and Nick Ercoline, the couple in the famous Woodstock photo. Bobbi died in March 2023.

I'd also like to thank Mic Opinion, *The New York Times*, specifically Morning Briefing and the Modern Love column, The Daily Skimm, hrc.org (Human Rights Campaign), loveisrespect.org, wikipedia.org, nbcnews.com, healthline.com, transequality.org, and cracked.com

Other Sources that Inspired Me

forge-forward.org, *Let's Talk About It! A Transgender Survivor's Guide to Accessing Therapy*

God, Deepak Chopra. HarperOne, reprint 2013

The "How to Speak Gen Z" videos on YouTube, produced by Sunday Cool Tees. They're not only quite helpful but also very funny!

Rocco Errico, "Light on the Language of Jesus," featured monthly in *SOM/Guide for Spiritual Living*.

Books by Ann Crawford

Available on Amazon
in paperback, Kindle, and audiobook versions

Contemporary Fiction
Bazoomerangs
A tale about three generations of vastly different women
living under one roof. What could go right?

Life in the Hollywood Lane
Quirky-crazy, sometimes humorous jaunt through
an actor's recovery after her BFF's suicide.

Alternative & Visionary
Fresh off the Starship
A romantic comedy about a starbeing who ends
up in the wrong place, right time.

Spellweaver
Mystical journey with a healer
during the Burning Times.

Angels on Overtime
Playful romantic comedy about what happens in
the scenes behind the ones behind the scenes.

Mary's Message—
An Alternative History of Mary Magdalene and Jesus
That title pretty much explains it.

Non-fiction
Visioning—Creating the Life of Our Dreams
and a World that Works for Us All
That title pretty much explains this one, too.

About the Author

Ann Crawford is the bestselling and award-winning author of ten books as well as a screenwriter. She's also an award-winning filmmaker and humanitarian. An avid traveler, she has been to all fifty states and seventy-five countries and counting.

Ann has lived "Oh, all over," from one shining sea to the other shining sea to the prairie and then to the mountain. (Yes, we're definitely mixing up our patriotic songs here as well as rocking that line backward.) Right now, she and her family live with a view of Colorado's Rocky Mountains out the window.

You are always welcome to follow Ann's effervescent blog at anncrawford.net as well as visit her on Facebook, Twitter, Instagram, Pinterest, and Amazon.

To inquire about having Ann speak or do a book reading for your group or book club either in person or via Zoom, please email info@lightscapespublishing.com.

Other Publications by Stephanie Castle Publications
(A division of Perceptions Press)

Perceptions Press

CASTLE CARRINGTON

TRANSGENDER PUBLISHING

Trans Fiction Available from Stephanie Castle Publications
Publishing Transgender Fiction
https://stephaniecastle.ca/new-releases/

God Save the Queen (2023)
H.W. Coyle

Inspired by Anthony Hope's *The Prisoner of Zenda*, *God Save the Queen* retells the story, but with a twist. A tiny Alpine kingdom is plunged into crisis following the death of its King when Crown Princess Fredericka is abducted while returning from England where she had been a lady in waiting to Alexandra, Princess of Wales. The former King's spymaster, Colonel Ernst Hartmann, suspects Duke Michael, the Crown Princess' cousin is behind the abduction in a bid to seize the crown for himself. Desperate to play for time, he devises a royal deception, one involving a most unlikely hero, Lieutenant Rupert Woodson of Her Majesty's White Hussars, a soldier who is as brave and daring as he is unconventional. In the wake of a desperate rescue mission on the Northwest Frontier, Rupert, along with Sergeant William Bryce and Bugler Neil Hayes, find they have become heroes. Recalled home to be decorated, Rupert takes advantage of this opportunity to indulge his passion for mountaineering only to come face to face with Colonel Hartmann who is stunned by the young officer's resemblance to the Crown Princess. Hartmann manages to convince the British government to offer him Rupert's services to play a role for which he is uniquely qualified, taking on the guise of Crown Princess Fredericka von Hoehental. Unwilling to abandon their officer, both Bryce and Hayes also manage to work their way into von Hartmann's deception. Ably assisting Hartmann is his dutiful daughter Gabriela, a woman who is appalled by Rupert's capricious manner and irreverent humor. Only slowly does she come to appreciate his behavior is yet another disguise, one carefully crafted to hide a deeper secret that Rupert is desperately unwilling to face. The sudden appearance of Rupert, where all believe he is the true Crown Princess, forces Duke Michael to resort to increasingly desperate measures in an effort to undo von Hartmann's counterplot. This leads to him abducting Gabriela and results in yet another daring rescue by Lieutenant Woodson of the White Hussars. (https://stephaniecastle.ca/god-save-the-queen/)

No Greater Love (2023)
H.W. Coyle

In the late summer of 1939, as France once more drifted into war a mother, anxious to spare her youngest son, starts him on a journey that does everything but.

Sent to live with his aunt and uncle in Normandy, young John-Paul Tesseraud avoids both conscription and the French authorities by assuming the identity of his cousin, Pauline Valery. The same attributes that caused his mother to fear for his safety, even at the hands of his fellow soldiers allows John-Paul to assume his new role with shocking ease. By the time France is forced to sue for peace, any thoughts of returning home to his former life are forgotten as John-Paul settles into a new life as Pauline, one that he finds to be a better fit for him than the one he left behind.

This new life is not without complications when Pauline finds that she has caught the attention of Erich Gerhart, a German soldier who has found something in Pauline that he has not felt for a long time—hope, the hope that even with the specter of defeat looming over Germany, he just might be able to emerge from this war with more than simply his life. To this end, he pursues Pauline with the determination and single mindedness that had, until then, been reserved only for his duties as a section sergeant assigned to the signal battalion of a panzer division.

Erich's interest in Pauline does not go unnoticed by Henri Fabre, a member of the Resistance, who encourages Pauline to cultivate a relationship with Erich. Fearful of being branded as a collaborator and the discovery of her failure to answer her call to the colors in 1939 that would surely follow, Pauline gives in to Henri's demands. What starts as an effort to avoid those problems turns into something quite unexpected as Pauline finds herself becoming infatuated with someone who is not only the enemy of her country, but ignorant of her past.

As Pauline attempts to carefully tread her way between the competing demands placed upon her by her duty to her country, her affections for Erich and the need to keep her true nature a secret, the coming Allied invasion of France brings the war her mother hoped to spare her from to Pauline's very doorstep.
(https://stephaniecastle.ca/no-greater-love/)

The Gambit (2023)
H.W. Coyle

Set in Tudor England, and drawing on Mark Twain's tale, The Prince and the Pauper and Shakespeare's Twelfth Night, this historical fiction tells of a young Lady Elizabeth, eager to experience life beyond the palace walls and Henry, an orphan boy seeking to flee the brutal conditions that are his lot in life. Though born into very different worlds, they are so close in age and looks that they could be twins. What begins as a lark and a case of mistaken identity evolves into an adventure of a lifetime for the two youths, one that is as dangerous as it is exciting in ways neither could have ever imagined in their wildest dreams. The freedom the Lady Elizabeth enjoys while assuming the role of a boy is tempered by the cruel realities of battle. For Henry, what should have been nothing more than a brief respite from a life of deprivation becomes something more as he is drawn into court intrigues that can be just as vicious and unforgiving as the back alleys of 16th Century London. As the two youths carefully tread their way along uncharted paths, the English King arranges for the betrothal of the Lady Elizabeth. Though he is no longer at court, Sir Robert finds he has no other choice but to do all he can to keep that from occurring, least his ploy to pass Henry off as Elizabeth is discovered. When she learns of this, Lady Elizabeth, aided by Sir Thomas, races back to England in an effort to undo a comedy of errors that threatens to turn deadly. (https://stephaniecastle.ca/the-gambit/)

Memoirs of a Cold Warrior: A Novel (2022)
Veronica Zerrer

Andy Lane (she/her) is born into the binary world of Cold War America. Assigned male at birth, she struggles to come to terms with identifying as female, believing that a colossal mistake has been made. As life goes on, she realizes the gender expectations of her from family and the farming world of the community in which she lives. She learns, early on, to play the part her world has created for her, hoping that being a warrior and finding a forever-love will be a "cure" that will let her live in peace with her body. She chases manhood while moving through the Army as an Airborne Ranger. But a special assignment in Germany with Counter Intelligence leads to a deadly confrontation with a Russian spy operation. Not even the burning love of the beautiful Jordanian woman, Sohaila, is enough to quench Andy's gender dysphoria. Only one thing remains for Andy, to meet her destiny in the deserts of Saudi Arabia in a desperate battle for the liberation of Kuwait. (https://stephaniecastle.ca/memoirs-of-a-cold-warrior/).

Dance of the Bacchá (2022)
H.W. Coyle

Jordan Allen Wallace is anything but your typical NYU sophomore. A veteran, Jordan's obsessive focus on his academics, coupled with a physical appearance that often causes people to mistake him for a female, sets him apart from his fellow students. With the exception of his sister, Emma, he has no friends to speak of and little in the way of a social life. That changes when Jordan meets Emma's boyfriend, Conner, an FBI agent.

What starts out as a prank turns into something serious when Conner seizes upon Jordan's unique qualities to help him obtain information about a professor at NYU, who fought the Soviets with the Mujahideen before coming to America. Repeated failures to slip an informant into the professor's inner circle forces Conner's superiors at the FBI to resort to methods that are progressively more unusual.

In Jordan, Conner believes he has found a perfect, if somewhat novel, solution. That solution involves a practice popular among some of northern Afghanistan's ruling elite. Known as *bacchá*, adolescent Afghani males dress as females in order to entertain their masters.

Step by step, Jordan goes from participating in some innocent fun to becoming an informer. In the process of adopting a lifestyle that is as foreign as it is challenging, Jordan finds he must come to terms with his own sexuality and gender. Doing so is difficult as he discovers time and time again that he has entered a world of shadows and lies, a place where neither friend nor lover can be trusted. (https://stephaniecastle.ca/dance-of-the-baccha/)

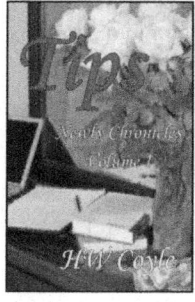

Tips (2021)
Newly Chronicles: Volume I
H.W. Coyle

College is a time of discovery, when students find out just what sort of people they are. This is especially true for Andy Newly, a freshman who embarks on a unique journey of self-discovery, one that defies convention and brings into question the most basic aspect of his being. It begins as a bet made between student waiters over who makes more tips, males or females. To determine this, they agree to a rather unorthodox experiment. Though feigning reluctance, Andy accepts the challenge of taking on the role of female waitress as part of the bet.

The original purpose is forgotten as Andy finds that his female persona is more than an act, causing him to question his gender identity. His behavior while Amanda—the name he has given his female persona—does not escape the notice of his friends. Along with Andy, they conclude that their experiment is having unintended consequences. Rather than stopping, Andy uses the opportunity to determine who he really is and where he belongs on the gender continuum. In the process he discovers that there is a vast difference between sex and gender. This already bewildering situation becomes even more complicated when a male college student becomes smitten with Amanda.
(https://stephaniecastle.ca/tips/)

A Different Kind of Courage (2022)
Newly Chronicles: Volume II
H. W. Coyle

How does a person go about rebuilding a life that they willingly tried to throw away? For Andrew Newly, this journey begins by realizing it will take a different kind of courage. His efforts begin by returning to where he and a group of friends bought into a crazy bet that changed his life forever. Together with those friends, he struggles to gather up the frayed threads of his life and begin the daunting task of building a new one for himself, this time as a girl named Amanda. Amanda finds that she must not only find a way of dealing with problems that are as confusing to her as they are complex, she must also come to terms with a past that seems to have no place in her new life. This difficult journey is complicated by Amanda's friendship with Tina Anderson, the daughter of an entrepreneur who has accumulated a fair number of enemies who prove to be as much of a threat to Amanda as they are to the Andersons, causing her to draw upon a past that she is trying to put behind her. (https://stephaniecastle.ca/a-different-kind-of-courage/)

Inconvenient Truths (2022)
Newly Chronicles: volume III
H.W. Coyle

Living on the edge with nothing but a safety net woven from lies to keep you from tumbling headlong into disaster and disgrace is as dangerous as it is demanding. For Amanda Newly, it is an inconvenient fact of life, one she must deal with every day.

Amanda is a unique college student. Bright and intelligent, she manages to maintain a GPA of 4.0 in a discipline where most of her fellow students are simply happy to survive. To the casual observer, Amanda presents the very image of a young woman who is on the verge of making all her dreams come true. The only thing holding Amanda back from achieving this elusive goal is a past that is totally out of sync with her image as a vibrant young coed, for the girl everyone knows as Amanda started life as Andrew Justin Newly.

In many ways Amanda is still very male, an inconvenient truth she must hide behind a veil of lies from all but a select circle of friends as she struggles to reconcile her past with her future. One aspect of Amanda's past that threatens to destroy her chances is not of her own making. Tina Anderson, the daughter of a wealthy entrepreneur and one of Amanda's dearest friends lives under a constant threat of kidnapping, a danger that Amanda once foiled and, as a result, leaves her vulnerable to retribution from those seeking to bring harm to the Andersons.

The journey Amanda Newly makes toward a new beginning is one that is as difficult as it is contentious. For Amanda must step outside the accepted norms, which define who and what we are, in order to discover not only what is right for her, but to build a new life for herself.
(https://stephaniecastle.ca/inconvenient-truths/)

A Lion in Waiting (2021)
H.W. Coyle

While serving as an observer with the British Expeditionary Force in 1940, Ian Wylie survives a massacre of prisoners. In its aftermath, he resolves to find a way of sitting out the rest of the war, safe from both the Germans and his responsibilities. At first, he finds sanctuary on a small farm owned by a teacher, Andrea Morel, who harbours him until an incident leaves her no choice but to send Ian away. With no wish to return to England and the war, Ian assumes the identity of Andrea's sister, Diane

Lambert, and accepts an offer to teach at a Catholic girls' school in Normandy. His efforts to turn his back on the war are frustrated by a local businessman who enlists Ian's aid in passing intelligence on German activities in Normandy to the Allies as well as by a group of schoolgirls who take it upon themselves to fight for the liberation of France. (https://stephaniecastle.ca/a-lion-in-waiting/)

The Legend of Alfhildr (2020)
HW. Coyle and Jennifer Ellis

For generations, a legend spoke of a young Viking girl who led a Saxon-Dane Army against a usurper. The story was passed from storyteller to storyteller, who freely embellished the feats of Alfhildr as they sought to entertain and enthrall their audiences in the great halls of their lords and masters. Some claimed she had been raised by a wolf, others that she was a witch. The truth was vastly different.

But before she became a legend, Alfhildr was a flesh and blood person with a family, a past, and a secret. With the passing of time, all but the legend was lost from living memory until an archeologist stumble upon something he has not been expecting. Bit by bit, Professor Bannon and his students come to realize that the legend once thought to be little more than a myth could be grounded in history. He also begins to suspect one of the students participating in the dig has a secret that links her to both the discoveries they are making and the legend. (https://stephaniecastle.ca/legend-of-alfhildr/)

Flipping (2020)
It cost him nothing, but it cost her everything.
Forest J. Handford

Born on a space station, Samir Zeka was raised Muslim, observes a Halal diet, fasts during Ramadan, and prays 5 times every day. An introvert, he mostly stuck to his work, his home, his family, and his church community, until the day he decided to push beyond his comfort zone and attend a party that would forever change his life. Intending to look his best for the party, Samir searched his neural link "mesh" for random looks until he came across one that suited him. After some fine-tuning, he "flipped" to the persona of Samantha, a late 30s East Asian, cat-eared woman with shoulder-length purple hair. At the party, Samantha meets Anna, someone who will change Samantha's perceptions of herself and transform both of their lives.
(https://stephaniecastle.ca/flipping/)

The Elysian Project: A Story of Betrayal and Payback (2019)
D. Axt

The Elysian Project is an expertly written, fast paced action thriller with a twist. It follows US marine scout sniper, Brent Chandler, his surviving teammate, Lyle, and his adopted father (the Gunny), as they go after those responsible for betraying Brent's sniper team during a military operation in Haditha, Iraq. Chandler's betrayal didn't just change the lives of his U.S. Marine sniper team forever. It set him on a path of unimaginable discovery. His quest for the truth and revenge quickly goes awry, drawing the attention of billionaire Stanley Tivador and the DOJ-FBI cabal he controls. The chase is on, from northern Minnesota's Superior National Forest to the Canary Islands. With help from the Gunny, his crotchety, retired Marine father, and Staiski, his friend and former sniper teammate, Chandler uncovers a terrorist plot of carnage inconceivable in magnitude and in lives lost. With seconds remaining, they risk everything to stop The Elysian Project. (https://stephaniecastle.ca/the-elysian-project/)

Partnership: A Novel about Friendship, Love, Family and Gender Transition (2019)
Stephanie Castle
Edited and preface by Margot Wilson

What happens when a lawyer, the son of a prominent Vancouver family, and a baker, the son of a devoted Catholic family who moved from Italy to Montreal following WWII, team up while going through gender reassignment? This humorous, yet serious, depiction of two families coping with gender dysphoria and the challenges of keeping family relationships intact addresses both legal and religious issues. The depiction and commentary on a range of human personalities in the hands of the author are both perceptive and entertaining. The underlying accuracy of this fictional story depends on the author's personal experience as a transgender woman and as a counselor in the transgender community in Vancouver. (https://stephaniecastle.ca/partnership/)

Far Side of the Moon: A Novel about the Life of a Trans Child (2019)
Stephanie Castle
Edited and preface by Margot Wilson

In Far Side of the Moon, Marjorie Burton and her husband, Jack, demonstrate all the attributes needed to help their child, Jenna, through a successful male to female gender transition. For children raised in an era when the condition of gender dysphoria was unknown, when anything unusual or unexplained was written off as a sexual aberration, it is small wonder that children, like the author, kept their feelings hidden out of shame and fear. Fortunately, that is not what happens with Jenna. (https://stephaniecastle.ca/far-side-of-the-moon-a-novel-about-the-life-of-a-trans-child/)

Coming in 2023/2024 from Stephanie Castle Publications
Publishing Transgender Fiction
https://stephaniecastle.ca

PUBLICATION COMING IN 2024
The World Turned Upside Down
H.W. Coyle

Condemned by a childhood illness that deprives him of the ability to ever assume his place in the world as a man, Richard Trent, the only son of the late Lord Dempsey, grows up in the shadow of his lively younger sister Katherine known to everyone as Kat.

An attack at sea and the death of his sister leads Richard to engage in a desperate venture, one he hopes will save a ship and its crew. By assuming the guise of his sister, he convinces the brigands to take him hostage in exchange for the safe passage of the ship to New York where the ship's captain will arrange for the payment of a ransom. While the gamble succeeds, it also sets in motion a series of events that presents a boy, whose pitiful lot in life once made him a recluse, with a choice that becomes more difficult to make the longer he defers his final decision. Upon arriving in New York, rather than admitting to the deception he used to save the ship and its crew, he allows his uncle and all with whom he comes into contact to believe he is in fact his sister.

Bit by bit Richard, who now is living as Lady Katherine Trent, or 'Kat' as *she* prefers to be called, blossoms in colonial New York. With the assistance of her cousin, James Keating, a British Army officer and his fiancée, Miss Sarah Gray, Kat begins to fashion a new life for herself, one that is as unconventional and out of step with colonial society as is the manner in which she is living her life.

With the same adroitness that once saved a ship and its crew from certain doom, Kat is able to establish herself as an independent and successful businesswoman while maintaining the appearance of adhering to the social strictures and demands of New York society. This delicate balancing act is made even more precarious when war comes to New York and Kat finds, though she is the child of an English peer, her sympathies lie with the Americans yearning for freedom and independence, goals she, herself, strives to secure in a world that events have turned upside down.

https://stephaniecastle.ca/the-world-turned-upside-down/

PUBLICATION COMING IN 2024
Grace
H.W. Coyle

A chance meeting between Lady Faith Rawlings, the spirited twelve-year-old daughter of an English earl off to visit her American grandmother, and George Lowe, the shy motherless son of a gentleman's gentleman, turns into an adventure of a lifetime when Faith convinces George to join her in first class dressed as her friend "Grace."

Their whimsical escapade becomes an unending nightmare when the maiden voyage of the *RMS Titanic* ends in tragedy. George, quick to appreciate their plight, manages to make his way up into first class by assuming the guise Faith had fashioned for him and seeing to it she makes it to a lifeboat. George is saved only when a young gentleman who believes George is a girl, who has been overlooked in the ensuing panic, offers up his seat in one of the last lifeboats.

When they are reunited aboard the *Carpathian* and George learns that his father did not survive. Faith makes it clear that she has no intention of abandoning him. Alone and at a loss as to how to deal with the tragedy, George allows himself to be taken in hand by Faith as the two embark upon a new adventure, one that proves to be as precarious as it is exciting, for he does so as Grace.

Bit by bit, Grace is drawn into Faith's world and is accepted, first by Faith's American grandmother, Charlotte Gilford, and then by Faith's mother, Lady Victoria Rawlings. This is no easy feat. Not only does Grace need to pass herself off as something she is not, but she must also overcome the barriers imposed upon her by society, one that determines the value of a person based on their lineage and birth. These are challenges that become all the more difficult when Grace is introduced to the charming Honorable Christopher Rawlings, the younger of Faith's two brothers.

https://stephaniecastle.ca/grace/

PUBLICATION COMING IN 2024
The English Courtesan
H.W. Coyle

The lives of two people, separated by centuries, are drawn together as the mystery surrounding a portrait believed to be an undiscovered work by a Renaissance master is unravelled.

Megan Ellsworth, an art historian with a past she'd rather forget, is offered the opportunity to research the origins of a portrait purchased by an entrepreneur. With the help of an army reserve officer who handles odd jobs for the entrepreneur, a man so different than any she'd ever worked with before, Megan finds herself drawn into a story that winds its way through the Byzantine world of late Renaissance politics, a time of great beauty set against a backdrop of unimaginable brutality. Along the way, the subject of the portrait takes on a life that mesmerizes her, for she slowly comes to appreciate she and a young woman dubbed "The English Courtesan" are, in so many ways, alike. https://stephaniecastle.ca/the-english-courtesan/.

Publications from other divisions of Perceptions Press:

Perceptions Press www.perceptionspress.ca
Castle Carrington Publishing www.castlecarringtonpublishing.ca
TransGender Publishing www.transgenderpublishing.ca
All Genders Press www.allgenderspress.ca

Made in the USA
Coppell, TX
15 December 2024

42719794R00134